Stand-In
SATURDAY

KIRSTY MOSELEY

Copyright © 2020 by Kirsty Moseley
All rights reserved.

Visit my website at www.kirstymoseley.com
Cover Designer: Outlined With Love Designs
Editor and Interior Designer: Jovana Shirley,
Unforeseen Editing, www.unforeseenediting.com

No part of this book may be reproduced or transmitted in any form or by any means, electronic or mechanical, including photocopying, recording, or by any information storage and retrieval system without the written permission of the author, except for the use of brief quotations in a book review.

This book is a work of fiction. Names, characters, places, and incidents either are products of the author's imagination or are used fictitiously. Any resemblance to actual persons, living or dead, events, or locales is entirely coincidental.

ISBN-13: 979 8681208334

For Dad. I miss you.

one

THEO

You know that super-awkward bit in *Love Actually* where you find out Rick Grimes is in love with his best mate's girl? Well, this is kind of like that, but worse because it's not my best mate's girl; it's my twin brother's fiancée.

Amy Clarke—object of my affection, girl of my dreams, and unfortunately for me, my brother's fiancée—plops down beside me on the sofa and steals the TV remote from my hand, instantly starting to channel surf through the Saturday night so-called prime-time TV.

"So, what have you been bingeing lately? Anything I need to add to my watch list?" she asks, eyeing me quizzically.

I shrug and take a swig of my beer. "Nothing noteworthy. I've been working a lot the last couple of days. I'm behind on my deadline."

"Oh, Theo, again? Do you just like to leave it to the last minute or what?"

"I do my best work at the eleventh hour."

As she's sitting so close, the sweet smell of her perfume wafts over me and the heat of her body presses into my side. I swallow and scowl at the TV, trying not to admit to myself that I love being this close to her. I know feeling like this about my brother's fiancée makes me a scumbag, but I can't help myself. You see, she *should've* been mine. I bloody well saw her first. Admittedly, I should have called dibs … but I was too chicken to ask her out. Now, look, two years later, she's marrying my twin brother, and I'm left sitting on their plush sofa in their classy and elegant apartment, wishing things were different and pretending like I'm not cut up about it and jealous as hell. Tragic really.

Amy shifts and tucks her legs up under her bum, and I turn my head slightly, so I can see her properly. Pale candyfloss-pink hair falls in loose waves around her cute face, her full lips are slick with nude gloss, and her sea-in-paradise-blue eyes are lined with a perfect cat-like flick of black eyeliner at each corner. Amy is that adorable, eccentric type of quirky girl that doesn't know how amazing she is. She also has no idea I'm crazy about her.

Sighing dramatically, she tosses the remote back into my lap after not finding anything decent to watch while we wait for everyone else to arrive for our big night out.

"Jared and I have been watching *The Witcher* this week. Trouble is, he keeps working late, so we only get time to watch one per night. Not skipping ahead without him is torture!"

I silently wonder if I'll ever meet a girl I like enough that I'd be willing to wait patiently to watch Netflix episodes with. My guess, no.

Maybe if I'd been brave enough to just ask Amy out at the start …

I frown down at my beer bottle, absentmindedly picking the corner of the label with my thumbnail. "What do you think would have happened if I'd got my shit together and asked you out at the start when we first met on that train?" The question bursts from my lips before I can stop it. Probably due to the fact that this is already my third alcoholic beverage, and it's barely seven o'clock. My brain-to-mouth filter is a little more lenient than it should be. The question is something that keeps me awake at nights.

Amy purses her lips and cocks her head to the side. I turn my head towards her and watch her think about what it would have been like to date me. I like her thinking about it. I truly am demented.

Her eyes meet mine, and a playful smile tugs at the corners of her lips. "My guess is, we would have got on brilliantly. We're so similar; we would have been laughing all night, and we'd have had a great time together. Things would have ticked along nicely, and we'd have had a blast. Then, at some point in our relationship, you'd have taken me home to meet your family, and there, I'd have clapped eyes on your brother and swooned over his broody face and inquisitive eyes. Maybe we'd have got drunk at a party or something, where Jared would have told me some nerdy math thing about his job, and I'd have been a goner while he talked about equations and algorithms. Of course, I'd have felt absolutely awful about it as I broke your heart after realising that Jared was meant to be mine, not you." She reaches out and pats my arm, offering mock support for the metaphorical heartbreak she would have caused. "You would have just been a path to me meeting your brother. Sorry, Theo."

Ouch.

But I knew her answer before she said it. I've always known the answer. Amy and Jared are perfect for each other. Me, on the other hand, maybe I'm destined to be alone because there can't be two girls out there as great as Amy, surely.

I nod along sadly. "Guess it's lucky I didn't then. Imagine if you'd shagged us both and had to live with the knowledge you'd let the brother go who was better in bed. You'd have been devastated and lusting after me at every opportunity. Talk about awkward," I joke, trying to pretend like her hypothetical rejection didn't feel like a punch to the solar plexus.

She laughs and slaps my arm as she rolls her eyes. "You wish."

Correct.

I'm saved from answering as the front door opens, and in walks Heather and her husband, Tim. They're Amy's best friends. I grin and offer a salute with my bottle by way of greeting as they let themselves into Amy's apartment like they own the place. To be fair, we all do it. We're round here a lot, hanging out, so things like the common courtesy of a call or knock before letting yourself in are a non-existent thought.

Amy pushes herself off the sofa and whistles appreciatively as she looks at Heather. "Damn. You look fit!"

Heather grins, running her hands down her figure-hugging black dress, smoothing the skirt against her thighs. And I have to admit, she does. Tim watches his wife with the self-satisfied, confident air of a guy who knows he's punching way above his weight. But they're honestly a great couple, and since they tied the knot just over a year ago, they've been walking around in a blissed-out bubble that makes us single folk nauseous.

Glancing over at Tim, who's wearing smart suit trousers and a baby-blue button-down shirt, I realise I've made a glaring error with my choice of attire for tonight's drinking session.

"Damn it. Were we supposed to dress up? I thought we were just going to the pub for a few cheeky drinks and then a drunken pizza on the way home," I groan, grimacing down at my worn jeans and faded *Jurassic Park* T-shirt.

Tim shrugs.

Resigned, I push myself up from the sofa. "I'm going to the bathroom," I lie.

Without asking permission, I bypass the bathroom and instead head to Jared and Amy's bedroom. Jared and I are twins. We shared a womb, so borrowing his clothes is my God-given birthright.

As I stalk to the wardrobe, I toe off my trainers and rip open the buttons of my Levi's. My gaze wanders over Jared's rows of expensive designer suits, all in their separate garment bags. There's a clear window at the front of each, so you can see what's inside without opening them—all the fancy stuff for my brother. I select a dark grey Tom Ford and unzip the bag, shimmying my jeans off before yanking the new outfit on. I ignore his shirts; a T-shirt with a suit is much more my style.

A quick glance in the mirror as I shove my shoes on, and what I see makes me give an appreciative nod. I look good. My light-brown hair is styled, though it is slightly longer than normal, so it flops a little. It looks deliberate though, so I'll allow it. Jared pays a fortune to get his suits tailored to fit his athletic, lithe, six-foot-two frame, so since we're pretty much identical (at least physically), they look perfect on me too. It fits in all the right places to show off what's underneath without actually showing anything at all. Smart and professional, but with the T-shirt and trainers, a little bit of fun and me peeking through.

Just as I'm fussing with my hair again and reaching for Jared's aftershave, Amy walks in.

"Um, ever heard of knocking?" I joke, chuckling.

"This is *my* bedroom!" she scoffs before raising one eyebrow. "Does he know you're borrowing that?"

I shrug one shoulder, uncaring. "He always knows. He just has the sense not to bother trying to stop me anymore."

Amy playfully tsks her tongue. "You'll be thirty next month, Theo. You really should buy your own." She crosses the room, walking over to her dressing table. She picks up her bangles, sliding them on as we make eye contact in the mirror.

"Nah. Why buy my own tailored suits when I can wear my body double's?" I reply. "Plus, I only need them for one day every two weeks when I meet my publisher. It's not like

I need them every day like he does. He has so damn many; he doesn't even miss them anyway." I gesture at the rack of my twin brother's expensive designer suits in example. "Means I'll be able to borrow this for my meeting Monday, too, and then he can have it back." I throw her a disarming, hopefully charming smile.

She chuckles and shrugs in response, reaching for a pair of diamond stud earrings, carefully putting them in. She knows what I'm like. I don't know why we're bothering to have this conversation.

"If you wear it tonight to go out in, won't it smell of stale beer, doner kebab, and shame come Monday?"

I turn to her and offer a winning grin. "I'll Febreze it."

She rolls her eyes and picks up her handbag, shoving a tube of lip gloss and some mints inside. Without my permission, my eyes glide over her as she bends to tie up her ankle-high silver Converse. She's wearing black shorts that come to the top of her thighs with a pair of black tights underneath, which have some sort of shimmery silver thread in them, and a fitted pink T-shirt with a V-neck that makes my upper lip sweaty. I force my hands into my pockets and blink, trying to control my attraction to her before tearing my eyes from her arse.

Bad, Theo. Bad.

"What time is Jared due back from his conference?" I ask.

She straightens and pushes her curls behind one ear. "Any minute now."

As if on cue, the front door opens and closes, and a grin stretches across Amy's face as we hear Jared's voice float in from the living room. The squeal of delight that leaves Amy's mouth feels like a punch in the dick.

She darts from the room, and I follow slowly behind, watching as my mirror image drops his overnight bag and turns towards her; his grin matches hers as she leaps into his arms without giving him time to compose himself.

Jared staggers back half a step as he catches her and laughs, his lips immediately crashing against hers. Her legs are around his waist, arms tight around his neck; one of his hands is on her arse, and the other is fisted in her hair while they practically devour each other as if they hadn't seen each other in months instead of just the one damn day Jared had to go on a course for.

There are figurative sparks. Their lust hangs in the air like a silent fart that everybody smells and finds distasteful but is too polite to acknowledge.

Lucky bastard.

I lean against the doorframe and watch them, my mind whirring. The thing is, as much as I'm crazy about Amy, deep down, I *know* she's better off with him. She and I never would have lasted. If we'd got together at the start, she's right; she would have fallen for Jared regardless. They're inevitable.

They're perfect for each other. He completes her, and I've never seen my twin happier than when he's with her. When he smiles down at her and his eyes twinkle with joy, I can't even begrudge him having her. Jared is great, an amazing brother and my best friend. He's a thoroughly decent bloke, and I would do anything for him. He deserves her and to be as happy as she makes him.

But knowing all that doesn't douse my jealousy in the slightest. All my life, I've never been envious of Jared for anything, not the high-paying job he has or the flashy car, not the expensive suits or the nice apartment, or the fact that it seems he was born with his shit together. Nope. I've never coveted anything my brother has … until her.

Tim rolls his eyes before pretending to stick his finger down his throat and gag. "You know, people pay good money to watch this kind of stuff online."

"If you're paying for it, you're looking in the wrong places. Plenty of freebies out there if you know where to look. I can hook you up with some links if you need it," I reply, winking at him as I head to the kitchen and help myself to another beer.

Tim laughs, his hand sliding across Heather's back as he sends me a knowing grin. "We don't need it. Thanks though."

"Smug git." I roll my eyes.

Jared and Amy are having a quiet conversation with their foreheads pressed together, staring into each other's eyes. She's still attached to his front like a new appendage.

I flop down on the sofa and pretend to watch TV. "How's work going?" I ask Tim as Amy finally detaches herself from my brother.

Jared slaps me on the shoulder in greeting. "I'll be five minutes; I just need to change, and then we can go meet everyone else."

I nod in acknowledgement.

Tim blows out a big breath. "Man, work's busy. I can't wait for next weekend, so I can have a whole weekend off! It's gonna be lit!"

Heather laughs. "Lit? Are you trying to pretend to be younger than you are again?"

I grin. "Is there something happening next weekend?"

A sharp slap to the back of my head makes me wince and chuckle at the same time.

"Only the wedding of the century," Amy chirps excitedly, grinning at the thought of her impending nuptials.

"Oh, is that all?" *As if I could really forget!*

Secretly, I'm dreading it. My grand master plan is to get drunk—so drunk that I can look back in years to come and not remember a bloody second of it.

"You have a plus-one, by the way. You said you'd be bringing someone," Amy continues, sternly looking at me.

I roll my eyes. "I will. I'm not a savage."

"Well, do we get to know her name yet or what? We need it for table plans and name cards." She leans over and grabs the bowl of peanuts from the coffee table, taking a handful and stuffing them in her mouth before offering the dish to me.

I shrug and reach out, taking a handful too. "Not likely. I don't know her name yet. I'll let you know when I do." I shoot her a grin.

"You're such a dog!" Heather jokes, laughing, sticking her tongue out at me.

I laugh good-naturedly.

I'm not a dog though. I'm just not a monk either. Despite being trapped in my one-sided, unrequited, awkward crush scenario, I still date. Hell, I'm a guy. If I'm not thinking about work, football, or food, I'm thinking about sex. I still have needs, and sometimes, my right hand just doesn't cut it. I'll be honest; I'm always on the lookout for someone to blow my mind, someone to take my mind off Amy and make me feel less shitty inside. So far though … bupkis. I haven't found anyone who holds my attention for longer than a few dates.

"I can set you up with someone if you want," Tim offers, sipping at his beer. "There are a couple of cute nurses I work with I could introduce you to." He flinches as his wife reaches over and tweaks his nipple through his shirt. "Ouch, babe. What was that for?" he asks her, wincing as he rubs at his chest.

Her eyes narrow. "*Cute* nurses?"

Tim scoffs and waves at me. "For Theo! Why would I need to look at any other woman when I have you, waiting for me at home, all perfect and feisty?"

That seems to have been the right thing to say because she softens and snuggles at his side, reaching out to rub at his sore nipple too.

"Cheers, mate. I'll keep it in mind," I reply. "Maybe I'll meet someone tonight; you never know."

Amy smiles brightly. She likes the idea of me meeting someone; she's one of those girls who is happy when other people are happy, resulting in her playing matchmaker for me several disastrous times in the last few months.

Jared walks back into the room then—dressed in shiny black shoes, perfectly pressed trousers, and a white shirt—and he makes me glad I decided to change and steal one of his suits.

"What are we talking about?" He takes the beer bottle from my hand and drains the last half in one go while I frown at him in indignation.

"Theo's non-existent date to the wedding," Amy replies.

Jared points the bottle at me. "If you show up without a date, Amy's nanna is gonna be all over you like a rash. Be prepared. You might wish to try a little harder before it's too late," he teases, his eyes twinkling with amusement.

And I know he's not even a little bit joking. Amy's eighty-something-year-old eccentric nanna, Peggy, is hilarious … at a safe distance. But if I don't have a girl to act as a shield, she'll make me her personal bitch all night.

My mind flicks to my predicament. I know I'm running out of time. I thought it would be easy to find a date for their wedding. I'll be honest; it's never usually hard for me to find female companionship. I simply flash my smile, temporarily suppress my dorky side that most girls don't like, and—Bob's your uncle—I'm balls deep in dates. But this time, it's slim pickings.

With time running out, I even resorted to going back through my little black book (also known as my WhatsApp conversations and text message threads) to see if there was a good option among my recent hump and dumps, but there's no one on there I'd be interested in taking with me and having the date immortalised with a family photo. Things got so dire after my mum threatened to get involved and find me someone that, last week, I decided to venture into my Facebook Messenger's Other folder, hoping to find an eligible bachelorette. Unfortunately, there was nothing in there either—well, apart from unsolicited dick pics and messages from long-lost Nigerian royal relatives who wanted to send me some money. At this rate, if I don't ask someone quickly, I'll be eating my plus-one's food, slow-dancing on my own, and crying myself into a gin coma by midnight.

Maybe I'll have one last look on Tinder later when I get home, see if anyone's worth a swipe. If there's no one, I'll likely admit defeat and go alone, let Peggy paw me all night and introduce me as her toy boy plaything, like she did at the last family party we went to. I shudder at the thought.

"Look, I'll sort it, all right? I'll have a date for the wedding next weekend. Stop stressing about it. Everything will be fine, I promise." I reach up and use one finger to draw a cross across my heart.

Maybe I'll have to resort to paying someone. *What sort of money would a high-class escort charge for a long weekend? Probably more than I can afford.*

Jared rolls his eyes and sighs in exasperation. He hates that I live on the edge and roll through life on a breeze. It makes him nervous and anxious. He's Mr Responsible and Organised. We're total opposites.

I slap my thighs to get everyone's attention. "Right. Anyway, come on. If you're ready now, let's leave the girls to it. You know I get awkward when I'm surrounded by couples. I hate being the third wheel. Let's go get this stag party started and get absolutely shitfaced!"

I stand and walk to the door, pulling out my phone and pretending to be engrossed in the screen while the guys spend an exorbitant amount of time saying goodbye to their significant others before they head off to meet the rest of their girl pack for their night out too.

I'm still wearing Jared's suit. He hasn't noticed, or if he has, he hasn't mentioned it. As always.

Two

LUCIE

What a sad day it is when you realise your whole life can fit into one suitcase and two boxes.

I smile awkwardly at my parents as they heft my belongings through my front door. "Oh, you guys didn't have to bring that over." Translation: I wish you'd burned all of this.

My mother smiles sympathetically and waves a hand before pulling me into a hug; it's a bone crusher, complete with a back pat and rhythmic rocking motion. "Luciella, it's been too long. Aww, my baby!" Her thick Italian accent feels like a warm blanket wrapping itself around my heart.

She cups my cheeks, smooshing my lips together uncomfortably, and then proceeds to tell me in fast-paced Italian how much she loves me and has missed me. You'd think it's been weeks since I saw her, but nope, four days—that's all. She's just a drama queen.

"Mamma, it's so lovely to see you. You should have called and let me know you were coming." I try for nonchalance, but really, a little bit of notice never hurt anyone. Plus, maybe then I'd have changed out of my pyjamas and put on a bra!

I force a smile and look over at my dad, who's wiping his forehead with a handkerchief after having lugged the boxes up three flights of stairs to the flat I now share with my best friend. Well, share or sublet a room Aubrey used to use as an office—same thing.

"*Ciao*, Papà."

He smiles, his dark eyes twinkling. "Hello, my *bambina*."

My mum cups my cheek and looks in my eyes. "Luciella, why is Lucas bringing your belongings to our house? Why didn't you arrange to meet up with him, see if things could be worked out? Huh?" She pouts at me.

Because he's a cheating scumbag. I suck on my teeth, so I don't say that out loud.

Things are ... difficult. Lucas's dad and my dad are business partners, and also, they're best friends. Lucas and I pretty much grew up together; it was probably a given we'd get together at some point. Our parents eagerly pushed for it. My mother has always adored him. Lucas is even vice president of sales at my father's company. As much as I wanted to, I couldn't heap a pile of crap on them and drop the bomb that Lucas, my loving fiancé, had cheated on me. This is our problem, not theirs. So, instead, we've told everyone it was an amicable split. Therefore, much to my chagrin, our parents still advocate for us to get back together at every given opportunity.

"Mamma, stop pushing. It's not going to happen. We're over." *He's moved on.* I shrug and raise my eyebrows.

She lets out a huge sigh, brushing her long, glossy brown locks away from her face. "I know what you always say. But a mother can have a little hope." She smiles weakly before turning back to glance down at the boxes. "Tomas, where is the food package? Did you leave it in the car? Don't just stand there. Go get it! *Oh mio Dio.*"

My mother is the only one who could get away with ordering Tomas Gordio around like that. He's an important man, known for having a sharp tongue and an even sharper eye for business, but he adores her too much to argue with her. Growing up, I always hoped I would find someone who loved me as much as my father loved my mother.

I grin, my ears perking up at the mention of food. My mother, being a traditional Italian woman, loves to cook. Her food packages are legendary, and it means Aubrey and I likely won't have to make dinners for a couple of weeks. My mouth waters at the thought.

My best friend wanders into the hall. "Did someone say food?" She grins at my mother before pulling her into an affectionate hug. "Hi, Stella."

As my dad makes his way back downstairs and Aubrey drags my mother into the living room, I look back at the boxes and frown. These are remnants of the past, a leftover casualty of my broken-down relationship. My ex-fiancé texted me last week and told me he was boxing up the things I'd left behind at *our* apartment. He was *having a clear-out*, apparently. Likely so he could move his new plaything into my home to enjoy my beautifully decorated apartment and newly fitted kitchen.

There's an envelope stuck on the top box, so I bend and tear it off, my heart clenching at the familiar, messy scrawl. Inside is a note.

> *Lucie, if I've forgotten anything or if there's anything else you want to come and get, do let me know.*
>
> *I hope you're okay.*
>
> *Lucas*

There's no kiss on it. Eight years together, and I don't even get a measly *X* tagged thoughtlessly on the end. My eyes trace over his name. Lucas and Lucie—even our names match. Everyone thought that was a sign we were meant to be. Spoiler alert: everyone was wrong.

I screw his note into a ball, carelessly tossing it into the top box, pushing the packages against the wall with my foot.

When I stormed out of our/his fancy apartment three months ago after coming home and catching my loving fiancé screwing his nineteen-year-old personal trainer on our/his couch, I packed up all my clothes, shoes, and a couple of my favourite handbags, and I left without looking back. Whatever is in these boxes is nothing I want, likely just junk and knickknacks accumulated over the span of our years together. Merely brainless and meaningless tat that defined our whole lives at one time, now demoted to being unwanted and dumped in a box to collect dust.

The boxes clutter the hallway and stop me from being able to close the front door properly, so I grab the handle of the suitcase and drag it down the hallway to my room. It's not exactly the nicest room in the world. Plain magnolia walls, accentuated with empty picture hooks and Blu-Tack grease marks, and cheap pine furniture the bestie and I sourced from the local charity shop. It's not the luxurious grandeur of the trendy, sparkly two-bed apartment Lucas and I renovated together. I can't complain though. I can't afford to live on my own and am super lucky Aubrey is so awesome that she is willing to give up her home office and instead work from her bed, so I can have a roof over my head without having to resort to moving back in with my parents at twenty-six. What a shameful disaster that would've been.

Unzipping the case, I pop the lid and let my eyes rake over what Lucas has deemed mine. There are framed photos of us, things we bought while on holiday, some key rings, my stuffed bears he bought me when we started dating, a couple of CDs and DVDs, and the Magic 8-Ball I've had since I was a teenager.

I flop down on my uncomfortable bed and pick up the 8-Ball, rolling it in my hands as I think about what a catastrophe my life is now. I have nothing to my name but clothes, this suitcase, and two more boxes full of crap.

I shake the 8-Ball and close my eyes. "Is Lucie a loser?"

Flipping it over, I eagerly watch the inky-coloured window as the little triangle floats to the top.

It is decidedly so.

"Oh, charming. I get more support from drunk strangers in the ladies' loo of a club," I scoff, tossing it onto my bed.

But to be honest, it's true. At the moment, I *am* a loser who has nothing going for her.

When Lucas and I were together, I naively tied my life around his so completely that I didn't even think about what would happen if we didn't make it. He was the one with the fantastic prospects and fast-track programme up the business ladder. He's five years older than me, so he was just starting his shiny job after graduating university with honours when I was about to head off to start the English degree I'd always dreamed of. I was eighteen, stupidly in love, and just plain stupid. I let him talk me out of it. Me going to university meant less time spent with him—and honestly, what did I need a degree for when he was the big earner anyway? So, instead, I pushed my ambitions aside and took a position at the family company as Lucas's personal assistant. I didn't even mind really. Well, not that I admitted anyway. And to be fair, I was an absolute boss at it. With my organisational skills and eye for detail, I practically ran the place—and him! He couldn't do without me … until he could.

Hindsight, what a bitch.

Blissfully unaware of any problematic future, we moved into a fixer-upper apartment he'd bought with his first year's commission. I was young and a lowly PA, so Lucas paid all the bills and put his name on the mortgage and car ownership agreement. His credit card bought the refurbishment and all the furniture while I paid for food and other essentials. It didn't matter that I'd picked everything out, that I supported him and enabled him to go get that life he had. It was all *his*.

Legally, I could probably fight him for some kind of severance, maybe under the law of civil partners or common-law spousal entitlement or something, but I couldn't do that without dragging our parents through the mud and into our drama. So, I walked away. Three months ago, I calmly walked out of his apartment with my clothes and announced I never wanted to see him again. Okay, so maybe it wasn't *that* calmly. Maybe I screamed a little in Italian and set a curse upon his children, cut up his designer jeans, and poured bleach into his houseplants—but I didn't kill him, so that's technically calm, right?

Unfortunately, our break-up left me not only heartbroken and homeless, but also jobless because I couldn't be expected to work for the man who had stomped on my heart. I'm not a masochist. I went from having everything and planning a wedding, picking out names for our future kids, to no roof over my head, no job, and no real prospects.

Thank the Lord for best friends; that's all I can say. My lifelong bestie, Aubrey, stepped in and bumped my life back onto the tracks again. She gave me somewhere to stay, listened to me cry, watched Meg Ryan movies with me until our eyes bled, and bought me chocolate and ice cream until we both gained almost ten pounds. Then—and best of all—when I couldn't find anyone to hire me as their personal assistant anywhere in the city, Aubrey found me a job where she works. Granted, it's a (very) low-paid internship, but it's for a publisher, and as I was a huge bookworm, growing up, working for a publisher is literally everything I've always dreamed of. It's everything I gave up in favour of being what Lucas wanted me to be.

I'm on the first rung of the ladder right now, paying my dues and earning my stripes, but with a little luck and a lot of hard work, at the end of my one-year contract, I'm hoping to earn the junior editor position, which is awarded to one intern who deserves it the most. All I have to do is beat the two other girls who started the same time as me six weeks ago and prove I want it and deserve it more than them. Shouldn't be too difficult. I'm not afraid of a little hard work or competition.

I hear my mother and Aubrey laugh in the kitchen, so I reluctantly push myself up to my feet and head out to them. My mother has taken over the kitchen. She's heating a lasagne while my dad and Aubrey tear and share some focaccia bread, dipping it in Mamma's homemade dressing. It smells like my childhood in here.

I smile and tear off some bread too.

Aubrey grins, her face flushed with pleasure. "Our freezer is full. It's official; I love your mother—as if she didn't already know." She playfully bumps my mother's shoulder and stuffs in another mouthful.

My mum looks up at me. "Lucie, I wanted to remind you about your father's retirement party at our house. I know you said you would come, but I wanted to check that you haven't changed your mind. It's important to your father. It will look so strange if you don't come. People will ask questions."

Oh, there it is …

My stomach clenches. I chew slowly and nod, my eyes fixed on a drip of oil I spilt on the kitchen counter. "When is it again?" I know when it is. I'm just stalling and praying an amazing excuse will fall from the sky and hit me like a meteor—even an actual meteor would be welcomed.

"Not next Saturday, but the one after. Lucie, you have to come and show your face." Her voice is half-pleading, half-instruction.

"Is Lucas going?" It's not the question I want to ask. I want to ask if Lucas's side piece is going, but I can't.

"Yes, of course. I can't very well uninvite the Maitlands because you two are having a blip. You never know; maybe you and he could talk some, dance, remember what you love about each other," she says softly, her hand covering mine.

A blip.

I smile weakly, avoiding Aubrey's hard glare; she hates that I've not told my parents what he did. "I'll be there." And I'll be looking so drop-dead gorgeous that Lucas will fall at my feet and beg for forgiveness. If I must go, I'm going in style, and I'll be looking a ten out of ten just to spite him.

I need a drink. I head to the fridge and pull out a bottle of wine, holding it up in offering. "Who wants one?"

"Me!" Aubrey chimes in, heading to the cupboard where we keep the glasses.

Mamma tsks her tongue. "Luciella, it's barely three p.m.!"

I nod and wink at her. "It's Sunday. All bets are off on Sunday. Three p.m. is wine o'clock by my count!"

Three

THEO

I groan as my alarm chimes annoyingly loud next to my head. Raising a hand, I blindly slap at my bedside unit, attempting to grab my phone, my brain still in a sleep-filled haze. Finally, my fingers find it; cracking open one eye, I eventually manage to swipe the screen and dismiss the alarm. The clock numbers glare back at me: 7 a.m.

I'm so tired, I can barely lift my head. I've had maybe three hours of sleep. I was working in bed, so I don't know what time I eventually drifted off, but I definitely remember seeing four a.m. and hearing the birds chirp. As I move and roll to the side, pencils and papers crunch under me, and my sketchbook falls to the floor with a thump.

I swing my legs over the side of the bed and sit on the edge, contemplating my life choices. *Do I really need my job? I can live off my savings for a while if I only eat supermarket brand noodles and bread …*

"Ugh," I moan, roughly scrubbing a hand over my face in a bid to wake myself up.

It's Monday—colloquially agreed upon as the worst day of the week. It's the only day I ever have to set an alarm. The rest of the week, I have a cushy work-from-home job that I usually start around mid-morning, maybe later, depending on what time I roll out of bed. Being my own boss is how I win at life.

Forcing myself up, I stomp to the kitchen and flick on the kettle, yawning widely. Spooning coffee granules and sugar into my cup, I can barely keep my eyes open, so I add another half-spoon of coffee. I'll need the caffeine today for sure.

Today, I'm meeting with my publisher. I'm a freelance book illustrator, but I work for the same firm around ninety percent of the time. Once a fortnight, I have to get dressed up in adult clothes and make the trek to London on the train to meet with them and show them what I've been working on for the last two weeks. I show off my mock-up design ideas for the book, they approve them or request changes, and then I spend the next two weeks turning them into reality while mocking up the next two weeks' worth of ideas. It's monotonous, especially because, right now, I'm working on a series about an anxious monkey turned detective. No, I'm not joking; it's an actual monkey detective with anxiety issues. At least it's better than the cat series I did a year or so ago. That book turned into a massive bestseller, so the author and publisher decided to turn it into a series. After illustrating its twelve books, I never want to draw another cat again. I couldn't argue with the money though.

After a too-long shower, I'm almost out of time. It's always like this. I think I'm fundamentally programmed to be late for things. My twin, Jared, got all the punctuality, leaving me always running to catch up.

Shoving on my brother's suit I wore to his stag do on Saturday night, I pick up a T-shirt from the chair in the corner of my room and give it a sniff. *Clean enough.* An extra squirt of aftershave will hide any traces that I wore it recently.

My coffee is now cold, but I chug it anyway and head out of my flat, stuffing all my papers and notebooks into my battered briefcase as I go.

As usual, I have to run for the train. I can see Amy on the platform, grinning and rolling her eyes as I jump on the first carriage and blow out a big breath. My stomach grumbles angrily at me, so instead of choosing a seat, I head straight for the refreshments carriage, buying more coffee and two small packets of biscuits. Everything always tastes terrible from the train, but with only two minutes to spare before it left without me, I'm glad I decided to forgo the café and came straight here instead. Sitting on the platform for an hour to wait for the next train does not sound like my idea of fun. Plus, this way, I get to see Amy too.

You see, this is where it all started. Around two years ago, I decided to get an earlier train than I needed, so I could visit the comic book shop in London before my meeting. It was merely a spur-of-the-moment decision. That was the day I saw the cute, petite conductor who worked the 8:09 a.m. Cambridge to London train. She dazzled me, and I remember that journey going past way too quickly. After that, every time I had to go to meet my publisher, I forced myself to get up earlier and board her train just so I could see her. It became my routine. For months, this went on. I'd flirt with her, but I never had the nerve to ask her out.

And then, one day, everything changed. I found out she was dating my brother, and I was instantly thrust into Inappropriate Crush on My Brother's Girl Land. There was a little drama, but it all worked out in the end. Well, worked out for *them* anyway. They're together, and here I am, still single, still fancying the shit out of her, still doing the five-knuckle shuffle on my own, night after night. Depressing.

Armed with my drink and snacks, I carefully head back through the train and flop down on a spare seat with a table, purposefully choosing one away from other people. Don't get me wrong; I *love* people, and normally, I use the journey to chat with random strangers, but today, I'm too damn tired. I have just under an hour on the train; I could either sleep or use the time constructively to put some finishing touches to my illustrations before my meeting. I decide that, as appealing as the first option sounds, I need to get more work done.

Settling back in my seat, I sip my coffee and stifle a huge yawn as I watch the scenery whizz past the window. My lack of sleep is my own damn fault. As usual, I'm behind with my deadline. Every fortnight, I vow not to let this happen again, and every weekend before my meeting, I'm left doing a whole week's worth of work in two days. I suck. It's my own fault though—always is.

Instead of working last week, I binge-watched a Netflix true-crime drama about innocents on death row. It wasn't even particularly good. I just got invested, and I'll admit, I'm also a lazy sod at times. Working from home is hard. Staying self-motivated when you're squirrelly is harder. I've often thought about hiring an office space with strict work hours, even considered getting some form of a boss and taking a proper job rather than freelancing (my publisher is always trying to put me on the in-house staff list), but it's all too … grown-up for me. Working from my bed is a perk of the job and one of the reasons why I decided all those years ago to become a book illustrator instead of going down the more generic and dependable income route of some sort of design field.

I sigh and run a hand through my hair as I pull my sketchbook from my briefcase and open both packets of biscuits, starting to draw.

I'm lost in my work, so I don't hear Amy until she stops at my side and reaches out, stealing my last biscuit. "Sharesies," she states, biting it in half, dropping crumbs down her train uniform.

"Rude," I mumble, looking up at her as I pull my pre-purchased ticket from my pocket.

She points an accusing finger at me. "You almost didn't make it again."

"I had two minutes. Don't be dramatic."

She rolls her eyes and takes my ticket, punching it.

"How was your hen party? Did you wear a veil covered in condoms and have to do shots from some oiled-up stripper's belly button?"

She taps the side of her nose and narrows her eyes. "The first rule of hen night is—"

"We don't talk about hen night!" we both say at the same time, laughing.

Hopefully, she had a stripper, so at least one of us got to see a professional strut their stuff in a G-string because Jared had strictly forbidden strippers from his stag night. Party pooper.

"How's Jared?" I ask.

She chuckles. "Still hungover. He barely got off the sofa all day yesterday."

"Excellent." I grin proudly.

He was absolutely wasted Saturday night; hell, we all were. I performed my best-man duties perfectly and made sure he didn't call it a night until he was singing karaoke and dropping pieces of his kebab down himself on the way home.

"I'd better get on; we'll be arriving soon." She glances over at my sketchbook and smiles. "Those are amazing, Theo." She affectionately pats my shoulder and moves on to the next passenger.

Ten minutes later, we pull into the station, and I pack all my belongings, heading out. It's mid-August, the height of summer, and today is a beautiful, sunny day. It's much hotter here in London than back home in Cambridge, almost stifling with the lack of breeze. I take a slow, leisurely walk to my publisher's office.

The receptionist beams up at me as I step in. "Theo! I was just thinking about you."

I grin. "All good things, I hope?"

"Of course." She chuckles and slides me a visitor's badge across the counter.

I clip it on my breast pocket. "How's your daughter? Did she get her A-level results back yet?"

I always chat with Donna, the receptionist, on my visits. She's a lovely lady, a mother of five girls ... yes, five. Her eldest sat her exams a couple of months ago, and Donna couldn't be prouder of her and loves to boast and brag about her achievements.

"Not yet. She picks them up this Thursday." She chews on her lip, her shoulders tightening.

"I'm sure she did great; don't worry."

We engage in casual, friendly chit-chat for a few minutes until some bike messenger guy comes in behind me and Donna has to stop to sign for some parcels.

I grin and tap on the marble counter as I send her a wink. "I'd better stop monopolising your time. I can't wait to hear all about results day next time I come in!" I say as I walk towards the back of the lobby where the lifts are.

When I press the button, the doors open almost immediately. I step in and pull out my phone, mindlessly checking Twitter for anything new or retweet-worthy. Just as the lift doors are beginning to close, sounds of heels clacking quickly on the marbled floor in the lobby catch my attention.

"Oh, wait!" a female voice calls. More clacking sounds, closer now. "Hold the lift, please!"

I act on instinct, absentmindedly shoving my hand out and catching the heavy doors before they close, forcing them back open, my eyes barely lifting from my phone screen for more than a second.

"Ah, thanks so much!" There's the faintest twang of an accent, but I don't give it too much thought. The woman huffs a breath and steps into the lift.

"No problem. What floor?" I ask, flicking my eyes up to the panel on the wall.

"Oh, eight, please."

I nod. That's the same floor as me. I smile and look over at her, expecting it to be someone I've seen before if she works on my publisher's floor; after all, I've been coming here regularly for the last five years, so I know almost everyone.

When my eyes land on her, I feel a jolt of surprise. I don't know her, have never seen her here before, but oh hell, do I want to!

The girl isn't looking at me. Instead, she's frowning down and rummaging through a ridiculously massive handbag that dangles from the crook of her elbow, obviously trying to find something.

I take a moment to study her before she catches me.

She's probably a little younger than me, mid-twenties maybe. Dark brown, almost-black hair falls in perfect, messy waves down to the centre of her back and frames her pretty face. Big, almond-shaped green eyes turn down slightly at the edges to give her an almost-exotic look; they're rimmed with impossibly long black lashes. Her eyes are partially hidden behind a pair of designer horn-rimmed black glasses, perched on the bridge of her cute button nose. Glossy, full pink lips pout as she frowns in concentration, trying to locate the desired object from her handbag.

I gulp and let my eyes wander over the rest of her.

She's quite tall—I'd guesstimate maybe five foot eight or nine with her shoes on. She's wearing a fitted blood-red shirt, open at the throat, exposing the barest glimpse of cleavage, just enough to set my pulse racing. The shirt is tucked into the high waist of a black pencil skirt that clings to her shapely arse. She's not too thin; instead, she's curvy and soft, all feminine angles, with hips to hold on to and an arse to keep you up at night. Long, toned legs lead down to three-inch red stiletto heels that make my balls clench in approval.

Her outfit choice screams confident professional. It's sexy and sophisticated yet somehow understated. She's not the usual type of girl I go for. I typically gravitate towards cutesy, petite girls who are a little on the weird side—pocket rockets you can't ignore.

But this girl ... *damn.*

Dragging my eyes back up her body, I see she's balancing a cardboard tray containing four takeaway drink cups on one hand. The sweet smell of flavoured coffee wafts up and makes me wish I'd thought to buy myself one from the café on the corner before coming to my meeting. The coffee from the machines here sucks, so I generally avoid it like the plague.

There's no ring on her finger. She's fair game.

Okay, Theo, time to work the magic. I crack metaphorical knuckles and prepare myself to chat her up. I have eight floors to get her to agree to go to dinner with me.

I open my mouth to introduce myself and hit her with one of my best lines and winning smiles, but before I can, the lights flicker overhead, and a grinding sound rumbles through the lift. The woman shuffles on her feet, her search through her bag abandoned now, and we both look up at the red number *3* that's glowing above the door. A split second later, the lights go off completely, and the lift judders to an abrupt stop.

"Oh crap," she groans.

My stomach clenches as we're plunged into darkness. A couple of seconds later, emergency lights blink and then illuminate under the handrail.

Oh, perfect. Stuck in a lift. Just what I need.

I heave a dramatic sigh and turn to face the woman as her bewildered gaze meets mine. Narrowing my eyes, I shoot her a mock accusing glare, saying the first thing that pops into my head, "Let me guess ... you didn't forward that chain message to ten people last night, and now, the karma gods have come to seek their revenge."

four

THEO

The girl laughs awkwardly at my joke, and we both look up again at the glowing floor number above the door, waiting for it to fix itself. After a few seconds, my heart sinks. This is the first time I've ever been trapped in a lift. I'll admit, I'm not crazy about it.

Reaching out, I jab the Help button over and over, my chest tightening with each passing second as the air seems to thicken around me.

Suddenly, a voice crackles through the intercom. "Hi. I know you're in there. The lift has stopped. We've got the engineer en route already. Is everyone okay in there?"

I lean forward. "We're peachy," I lie. "How long will it be, please?"

"Um … not sure. He'll be as quick as he can."

"Not gonna lie, mate, that doesn't sound too reassuring," I grunt.

"We'll have you out of there in no time," he replies, his voice full of static and echo.

I groan and turn to the girl, forcing a fake smile. The last thing I want is to be trapped in an enclosed space with someone having a freak-out. As I think about the enclosed space, my chest tightens further.

She winces, her nose wrinkling. "Last time this lift got stuck, it took them almost an hour to get the people out. That was a couple of weeks ago."

An hour? Heck no.

My upper lip starts to sweat. I reach up and wipe it.

The girl pulls out her phone and taps on the screen before putting it to her ear. "Aubrey, it's me. You will never guess where I am." She shakes her head and laughs. "I wish. Nope, I'm stuck in the lift. I'm serious! I'm stuck in the lift with a guy." She chuckles at something the other person says, and her eyes dart to me before flicking away. "Um, yes actually. Anyway, can you do me a favour? Call up to my floor and have someone tell David I'm in here? He sent me out to get coffees for his meeting, but I don't think I'll be freed in time to give them to him, and they'll be wondering where I am. The security guy has sent for someone to fix it, but I don't know how long I'll be in here. No, there's nothing else you can do. Oh, wait, hold on a second." She looks up at me and moves the phone from her ear. "Do you need me to pass a message on to anyone who's expecting you?"

I gulp, my brain not really working, and nod. "Uh, yeah. I'm supposed to be meeting with Patricia Newman. If they could send word that Theo is going to be late, that'd be great, thanks."

She speaks for a few more seconds and then hangs up, smiling awkwardly over at me. "My colleague will pass on your message."

I nod. My eyes rake over her face; she really is pretty. Her lips are full and covered in a glossy pink lipstick that makes me want to lean in and see what it tastes like.

"Is it hot in here?" I ask, feeling sweat break out on my temples now too.

Her eyes widen. "Oh Christ, you're not claustrophobic, are you?"

"No." I adamantly shake my head. "I'm just having some sort of chest and heart issue. But seriously, is it getting hotter, or is that just me?"

She gulps and sets her handbag and the coffees down in the corner as I suck in a deep breath and rub my face in a rough swipe.

"Everything's fine. This happens all the time. It's getting hotter because the air con went off with the power. There's nothing to worry about." She waves a dismissive hand. "Why don't you come sit down here with me? We can get to know each other while we wait?" She awkwardly manoeuvres in her tight pencil skirt and sits down against the wall, stretching out her long legs, crossing at them at the ankles as she pats the space next to her. "You said your name is Theo? I'm Lucie."

Lucie. I note her name, but chatting her up is now way down on my list of priorities.

Her posture is stiff and resigned. I can tell we're not getting out of here anytime soon, and she's trying to distract me from whatever freak-out is building inside me. I've never been claustrophobic before, but then again, I've never been trapped inside an enclosed space before, so who knew I wouldn't like it? Lucie doesn't look flustered though, and her cool demeanour calms my racing heart. Maybe sitting down is a good idea. My legs do feel somewhat wobbly.

I slide down the wall next to her and shrug off my suit jacket, folding it and laying it on the floor next to me. Smiling at my cooperation, she reaches over, picking up the tray of drinks, and drags them closer to her. As she does, it catches on the strap of her handbag and makes it tip over. A Magic 8-Ball rolls out, followed by a box of three Krispy Kreme doughnuts and a bunch of other junk. Her bag is like the one from *Mary Poppins*, bottomless and full of crap. The 8-Ball hits my leg, so I pick it up and smile fondly. I haven't seen one of these for years.

Instantly, I shake it. "Will we die in this lift?"

MY REPLY IS NO.

I huff a relieved sigh, and actually, stupid as it sounds, my chest does loosen at the answer. "Well, that's a relief. I still have so much to tick off my bucket list."

Lucie laughs, and I set the toy back next to her bag. "We might as well drink these before they get cold." She holds up the coffees in offering.

I nod. "So, what have we got?"

Squinting down at the cups, she attempts to make sense of the tick boxes on the side of them, reading them out.

When she says, "Mocha," I nod and call dibs.

I'm never *not* calling dibs on something again; I learned that the hard way. After dumping in a couple of sugars she produced from her gargantuan handbag, I sit back and take a sip of my coffee, closing my eyes, letting the sweetness and caffeine wash over me.

When I open them again, I see she's watching me, and there's a small worry line between her eyebrows.

I smile and tilt my head. "I'm fine, honestly. Not going to have a panic attack." *I don't think anyway.*

Her shoulders seem to relax at my assurances.

My gaze drops to the box of doughnuts half-hanging out of her bag. "Are we sharing those?"

She quickly shakes her head. "No, they're for a meeting."

"Yeah, a meeting that will likely be finished by the time we get out of here—you said so yourself. What a waste, and look at us, all cooped up and in need of sustenance and sugar to keep us alive." I reach for the box, greedily eyeing the contents. They're not merely the glazed ring kind; they're the sickly sweet kind, covered in toppings that taste like sin in your mouth.

She sighs deeply, and pink tinges her cheeks. It's cute. She looks innocent and sweet when she blushes. I like it. "Okay, admission: they're not for a meeting. They're mine."

"All three?"

"Yes, all three. Don't judge me!" She chuckles and reaches out, pointing to each one in turn. "Morning snack, lunch, afternoon snack."

Food done right. My kind of girl.

"I'm suitably impressed by your ability to eat that much sugar without going into a diabetic coma." I grin. "Come on though, let me have one. Just one? I'm starving. How about we Rock, Paper, Scissors for it? You win, you keep all three. I win, and we split them." I throw her my disarming smile that people usually find adorable. I'm not quitting until I eat at least one of these bad boys; I won't be able to stop thinking about them all day otherwise. Yes, I am *that* child.

Lucie groans. "And what exactly am I getting out of it? If I win, I get to keep something that's already mine, but if I lose, I have to give you my food. Are you high?" She takes the box from my hand and pushes it back into her bag, shaking her head, grinning good-naturedly.

"Ah, but you won't have to sit here and listen to me whine about it for however long we're trapped for. Surely, that's worth it. Come on, Rock, Paper, Scissors." I hold out both my hands, one closed fist resting on my palm, and wait.

She pushes her hair back over her shoulder and playfully rolls her eyes. "Fine, just to shut you up."

She mirrors my hands, and we thump our fists. One, two, and on three, we throw our shapes.

"Ha!" I crow, leaning over and chopping her paper with my scissors before reaching for the box.

Lucie lets out a loud groan. "The biscotti one is mine. That's my favourite. You can choose from the other two."

"Deal." I flip open the box lid and offer her the contents, watching as she takes the caramel-coloured one. "So, keep me distracted then. Tell me about you. You work here? I've not seen you around." And I certainly would have remembered.

She nods. "Yeah, I've been here for six weeks now. I'm an intern, working for David Schuh's department."

"Really?" *Interesting.*

David Schuh runs the children's publishing division; Patricia, my editor, reports to him. No wonder we were both headed to the same floor.

She nods and takes a large bite of her doughnut, her tongue licking across her bottom lip, collecting the biscotti crumbs that have stuck to her lipstick—and now, I've lost interest in my own food and my train of thought. Who knew eating doughnuts was sexy?

I swallow and force my mind back on track. "An intern? Aren't they usually spotty eighteen-year-olds? How old are you?"

"I'm twenty-six," she replies. "And me being an intern is a long story."

I grin and wave my hand around at the stationary lift. "We're not going anywhere, so we've definitely got time. You might as well catch me up, Luce."

She chuckles, and after some more encouragement and cajoling words from me, she rolls her eyes before proceeding to tell me how she has always wanted to work in publishing but how she fell for the wrong guy. She explains how they split up three months ago after he cheated on her, how she basically had to start over and was lucky enough that her friend got her the intern job here, and how she plans on working her arse off to get the junior editor position at the end of her temporary contract.

I watch her talk, a little fascinated by her drive and a lot fascinated by the fact that her fiancé cheated on her. *Is the guy blind or just plain dumb?* I've spent less than thirty minutes in her presence, and I can already see the appeal she has. If I had a girl like her to come home to, I wouldn't be looking anywhere else for sex.

"So, pretty crappy couple of months for you then," I surmise.

"God, yeah, it's sucked. I kinda wish this year were over with already. I woke up on New Year's Day and honestly thought this was going to be my year. Oh, how wrong I was." She chuckles darkly. She nods and looks down at the last doughnut in the box. "Want to split it?"

"Yeah, go on then." I smile gratefully as she tears the raspberry-iced doughnut in two and holds out the larger half to me. "Thanks. So, you sound like you need a holiday." As I say the words, a plan starts to form in my head.

This girl is cute and fun—and not to mention, easy on the eye. She's definitely someone I could spend a weekend with without wanting to kill myself. I'd like to get to know her better. Before today, I all but gave up on trying to find a date to the wedding; it was too late now to find someone—or so I thought. Maybe we could help each other out.

"I wish. I can't afford one." She sighs dreamily, sucking jam from her thumb.

Screw it. Just ask, Theo. What's the worst that can happen? "How do you fancy an all-inclusive weekend break in the picturesque surroundings of Scotland?"

One of her eyebrows rises in question, so I continue, really trying to sell it, "My brother is getting married this weekend up at Loch Lomond, and I have a plus-one. There's a five-star luxury hotel, a spa, woods to walk in, a national park, water sports, glorious weather predicted, free food, and more importantly, free drink …" I smile hopefully. "Thursday to Sunday. Come with me? I'll even pay for your flight. Everything's included. In return, you have to attend the wedding with me as my plus-one."

"This weekend?"

I nod.

Her nose scrunches. "Thursday to Sunday? Who drags out a wedding for four days?"

"My brother and his perfect fiancée."

"Uh-oh, is she not perfect? Why the animosity?"

I wish. "No, she *is* perfect—that's the issue. I want her. But she's his."

Her mouth pops open, and her eyes widen as her back straightens. "Oh, so you want me to make her jealous, break up the wedding? That's so arseholish, Theo!" She scowls at me, her anger obvious.

I scoff indignantly at her assumption. "No! I don't want to break up the wedding. I'd never want to ruin what they have. I've accepted my fate and moved on. They're great together. I just want a drinking and dancing buddy, someone to talk to and use as a buffer when people come up to me and say, *It could be you next, Theo, if you just managed to get your shit together*." I do a terrible impression of my mum and aunt and pretty much everyone else who judges me and asks when I'm going to settle down and find a nice girl who loves my quirks. Not much chance of that though. There can't be two girls as awesome as Amy in the world.

Lucie chews on her lip, curiously eyeing me, probably checking I'm not trying some form of a scam or plot to ruin my brother's big day with her as the secret weapon. "So, you want a fake girlfriend for the wedding?"

I shrug. "More like a fake date, not a fake girlfriend."

She's silent for a few seconds. I can see in her eyes that she's considering it, but then she shakes her head.

"Ah, sorry, I can't. That's insane. I don't even know you; people don't just go on a mini break with someone they met in a lift. For all I know, you're the next Ted Bundy, or you think pineapple belongs on pizza."

I don't let her rejection get to me though; instead, I reach over and snag her Magic 8-Ball from the floor. Grinning, I give it a shake. "Should Lucie come to Scotland for a free weekend of day drinking and sunbathing?"

I turn it over, and both of our eyes drop down to the window.

WITHOUT A DOUBT.

I smirk at her. "Well, that's definitive. The 8-Ball has spoken."

Lucie laughs and snatches it from my hand, tossing it back into her bag. "Traitor," she tells it.

"Oh, come on. A free long weekend? I'll pay for your flights, you'll get your own room, and you'll get plenty of downtime. All I ask is that you come to the pre-wedding party on Friday night and that you attend the wedding with me on Saturday afternoon. The rest of the time is your own. You don't even have to hang out with me if you don't want to. Though I'm not sure why you'd choose *not* to hang out with me. I'm pretty awesome." I shoot her a cheeky smile.

Her lips purse as she thinks about it. I stay quiet and mentally cross my fingers. I already accepted my fate as Nanna's bitch, so this really is my last shot. A totally unexpected shot at that.

She huffs out a breath after a solid minute of deep thought. "All right, I might be moving mad here, but … how about I make you a deal? If we ever get out of here"—she nods at the lift doors—"I'll do you a solid and come to your wedding weekend and be your fake date. *If*, the following Saturday, you come with me to a posh party at my parents' house and let me pretend I'm over my arsehole ex-fiancé. I want to make him choke. I want to look so smoking hot that he dies from jealousy while I hang all over another man. How about it?" She purses her lips and cocks her head to the side, waiting for my answer.

"Oh, I can absolutely do that."

She's already got the smoking-hot part down; I'm surprised a guy would ever cheat on her in the first place. I have no plans the following weekend, so I can let her hang all over me to make this idiot jealous.

"Deal!" I hold out my hand. She grins before placing her hand in mine, and we shake on it. "Can you get time off work on short notice?"

She shrugs one shoulder and winces. "Hopefully. I'll ask when I get back upstairs. Surely, I'm entitled to some form of recompense for the trauma of being stuck in the lift. They owe me," she jokes. "Let's swap numbers."

She reaches into her handbag and comes out with a thick organiser, pulling a business card from the plastic wallet stuck on the inside of the front cover. She hands it to me, and I look down at it, seeing her name and all the social media handles, email, plus her mobile phone number.

"*Luciella Gordio,*" I read. "What kind of name is that?"

"It's Italian. My family moved to London when I was ten."

"Ah, so that's what the faint twang of an accent is, though it's almost imperceptible." *Fiery Italian girl. Me likey.*

She smiles and nods. "Yeah, I've been here so long now that I've practically lost it. Though when I'm angry or around my family a lot, my accent comes back a bit," she answers, pulling her mobile phone from her bag and looking at me expectantly.

I reel off my number, watching as she taps it in her phone. "If you text me your date of birth later, I'll get the flights booked tonight," I say.

She nods and flicks through the pages of her organiser. I notice it's full of notes, quotes, appointment reminders, to-do lists that have all been checked off, and a buttload of other organisational crap. Stopping at a blank page, she reaches into her shirt and magically pulls a pen from her bra. I raise a suitably impressed eyebrow and am strangely jealous of the pen for having been tucked into her bra this whole time.

She clears her throat and clicks her pen a couple of times. "I think we need to have some sort of contract. Put it in writing that this is simply a friendly agreement, that it's not a real date, more like a *date stand-in* kind of situation. Just so we can be clear that neither of us is expecting more."

Her friend-zoning is subtle, and I have to admire how she slipped that in there. I nod in agreement, kind of liking how ordered she is—her and her colour-coded organiser and pen bra. It's cute.

"Sure. If that makes you feel more comfortable."

"It would. Thank you."

She gets to work, writing down a couple of lines that basically explain the exchange in services: that we'll be polite and courteous to each other's families, that this is a fake date, that I'll be paying for her trip, and that she will pay expenses for my returning the favour the week after. She loops her signature underneath and then passes me the pen, and I slash mine next to hers.

She nods approvingly down at the contract and closes her organiser, chewing on her lip. "Is this insane?"

"Definitely, but all the best adventures are." I nod, grinning.

She chuckles and starts packing up her bag again as I pull out my phone and scoot closer to her. Opening the Camera app, I tell her to smile. She looks up just as I position the phone and snap a selfie of us, but she doesn't smile. Instead, she sticks out her tongue and throws a peace sign. It's perfect.

Grinning like a moron, I head to Twitter and post the picture, tagging her account, adding the caption: *Scored a date whilst stuck in a lift. Thank you, karma gods!*

After posting it, I head to her profile and look it over. Her profile picture is a cute one of her baking; there's flour on her cheek, and her smile lights up the damn room. Her bio makes me chuckle: *Professional meme stealer. I communicate best via GIF. Unsolicited dick pics will be sold to stock image sites. All views my own.*

Out of nowhere, the lights flicker, and the elevator whirs to life. My heart leaps, and Lucie gasps.

"Thank the Lord, we're saved!" I joke, eliciting a snicker from her.

Truth be told though, I'm a little disappointed our encounter is over. But I do have the weekend to look forward to.

I push myself to my feet and hold a hand down to her. A blush covers her cheeks as her hand slips into mine, and I pull her to her feet. As the lift speeds us both up to our desired floor, I slip on Jared's jacket, and she leans down, picking up her bag and now-empty coffee cups. I don't look at her arse as she bends over—that would be creepy. Okay, that's a lie; I totally look, and I definitely like what I see.

When she has everything, she steps to my side and glances down at her watch. "Well, that was fun. And I got fifty minutes off work, so … winning!"

"Yeah, weirdly, this was kinda nice."

As we get to floor eight, the doors ping open. There's a cluster of people there, comprised of a security guard, a mechanic-looking guy, and a few random, curious staff.

Stepping to the side, I politely motion for Lucie to exit first.

She turns back to me and offers me a small smile. "I guess I'll talk to you later then, Theo. Try not to get into any more trouble today."

Her blush is endearing, and I can't resist sending her a playful wink before I wave back at the lift doors and tell the waiting crowd, "Lift, zero stars, do not recommend."

Behind me, as I walk away, Lucie laughs, and I feel it all the way to my toes.

five

LUCIE

Theo walks off with all the confidence and swagger of Conor McGregor. The damn guy knows he's hot. Meanwhile, I'm a hot mess.

I gulp in a few breaths and watch as he heads off up the corridor towards the conference rooms, raking a hand through his tousled brown hair. Around me, I don't miss the fact that all of the girls—and even some of the guys—are also watching him walk away in his grey tailored suit and retro *ThunderCats* T-shirt. Not that I can blame them. The guy is gorgeous in every sense. He fills that suit to perfection with his tall, athletic frame, strong and broad shoulders, a tapered-in waist, and long legs. And that smile? Dazzling. The best part though: his eyes. They're a light amber brown; it's like staring into a glass of whiskey. They are mesmerising and twinkle with a zest for life that I've probably never had. He's magnificent, and with his bone structure, he looks like he should be on the cover of *GQ*.

His photo would undoubtedly inspire me to purchase it.

Suddenly, I realise I don't even know why he's here. I didn't ask him what his meeting with Patricia was for. He must be an agent or an author or perhaps a bookseller. My guess would be bookseller; he's too well put-together for the shy, uncoordinated author types we get come in, and an agent looking to schmooze an editor would likely not wear a T-shirt and trainers. I don't know anything about him other than his first name and the fact that he's got an exceedingly sweet tooth and feelings for his brother's fiancée.

I smooth down my skirt and lift my chin as people's curious eyes swing back to me once he's out of sight. Turning on my heel, I drop the empty coffee cups and the full cold ones we didn't drink into the bin and head in the opposite direction, stalking towards my pokey office cubicle. I drop my bag onto my desk and flop down into my chair, taking a couple of deep breaths.

What just happened? What in the fresh hell just happened?

I've agreed to spend the weekend with someone I literally just met. It seems that, in the moment, I forgot every lecture about stranger danger my parents had ever instilled in me. Now that I'm free of the eight-foot-by-eight-foot steel cube we were confined in, I can see more clearly, and it hits me full force how utterly stupid his idea was. It's like I was trapped in some sort of weird Lift Stockholm Syndrome situation where it made sense. Now? Not so much.

"Oh God." I chuckle to myself and shake my head at the absurdity of it all.

As much as it sounded so easy and fun when he was saying it—and goodness knows I could totally use the downtime and a little sunshine—I can't go on holiday with a guy I just met.

What on earth possessed me to agree to that?

I shake my head and lean forward, my stomach clenching. I can't do it.

I'm no longer the fun-loving, free-spirited, impulsive girl I used to be when I was eighteen. Yes, pre-Lucas Lucie might have jumped on the Theo fun bus and ridden it all the way to Scotland, but post-Lucas, *adult* Lucie is more sensible, more mindful of other people's opinions and perceptions. I can't jet on out of here with a super-cute guy for a weekend of drinking and dancing … *can I?*

No.

No, I can't.

I swallow a ball of regret. Part of me wants to go, throw caution to the wind and have an adventure, like he said. And the idea of him paying me back by coming to my dad's retirement party is extremely tempting. The thought of making Lucas jealous appeals to my very soul. He deserves some hurt after what he put me through.

When I think about Lucas again, an ache builds in my chest. I miss him. Or maybe more accurately, I miss the routine, comfort, and security of him. I miss the sex on tap, the cosiness of falling asleep next to someone at night, the sound of the words *I love you* being whispered in my ear. I miss that easy life of being in a committed, stable relationship. I'm not a pushover by any means, but if Lucas came back, crawling on his knees, and said he'd made the biggest mistake of his life … I would consider it and likely cave. I love him. I'd thought we were *it*. Just because he was balls deep inside someone else doesn't mean I can turn those feelings off overnight—as much as I'd like to be able to. Hopefully, one day.

I reach up and rub at my chest as visions of walking in on him and his personal trainer screwing on my burnt-orange velvet sofa spring to mind. *Ugh! Where is the eye bleach or rewind button when you need it? I would give anything just to forget it and go back to normal.*

My life has been blown to pieces in the last three months. Everything has changed, and I'm still scrambling to try and make sense of a future without Lucas in it, trying to fill that gaping hole he's left in my life. Pretending I'm okay. Faking it until I make it.

And Theo is certainly hot enough to make Lucas burn with inadequacy if I were to take him to my dad's party with me. Lucas is good-looking, but Theo, he's all kinds of hot.

But … no … my mind is made up. I'm going to cancel. It's official; I'm a big, fat chicken.

I'll catch him before he leaves his meeting and let him know I can't accompany him after all. Or even better, I'll take the coward's way out and text him instead, in case he's annoyed I'm messing him around. Dumping via text will be much easier and less awkward for us both. Besides, he can't be too upset about it really. I mean, it was a spur-of-the-moment thing, and it's not like a hastily scribbled contract and a handshake are legally binding. And to be honest, he's probably having the exact case of buyer's remorse I am now and thinking of a polite way to let me down too.

I wheel myself in closer to my desk and reach into my handbag. I haven't even unpacked yet. When I arrived earlier this morning, I was handed a list of coffees that were required for my boss's meeting and shooed out of the building to fetch them before I even got a chance to sit down at my desk. Then, Lift-gate happened.

I pull out my Magic 8-Ball and set it on my desk to use as a paperweight. Other than a few pairs of shoes and a couple of handbags, it's the only thing useful in the three packages Lucas sent over via my parents yesterday. Everything else is pretty much junk that I'll have to get rid of at some point.

I pull out my phone and am about to compose my letdown text to Theo when a shadow falls over me. I glance up and see David, my boss, looking down at me as he sets his hand on my shoulder, squeezing supportively.

"Lucie! What a disastrous morning you've had already, and it's barely past ten o'clock. How are you?" he asks, worriedly eyeing me.

I force a smile and shrug. "I'm fine. It wasn't too bad. I'm sorry I missed your meeting." I was supposed to have taken notes.

He waves a dismissive hand and perches on the edge of my desk, pushing his glasses up his nose with one finger. "Oh, don't worry about that! I'm just glad you're okay. You were in there quite a while; it must have been awful."

It wasn't. Actually, it was quite fun. "It wasn't ideal, but I survived," I joke, grinning.

He blows out a big breath and rakes a hand through his hair, messing it up. "Lucky it wasn't me; I hate enclosed spaces. I think I'll take the stairs from now on! I might even lose a few pounds because of it. My wife is always telling me I should get in more exercise." He chuckles, patting his rounded tummy.

My mind flicks to Theo and that cute, panicked expression that crossed his face when he realised we were stuck. It made my heart clench, and I longed to reach out and soothe him and relieve his worry. In a weird way, I kind of liked that he was a little scared of being in there. With him looking the way he does—all tall, imposing, and perfect—his vulnerability made me instantly like him and put me at ease because it showed he wasn't infallible.

David stands and gives my shoulder another pat. "Good to see you're okay. Take a few minutes' breather and compose yourself a bit. When you're done and ready to start, can you head into the stockroom and have a sort-out? We've had a delivery of galley copies for our autumn releases that need to be sent to reviewers. And we have a photographer coming in to take pictures of the new Johansson book this afternoon. Would you mind assisting him to ensure we get everything we need for our socials and promotions we have scheduled?"

I nod. "On it."

As he walks away, I slip my phone into my pocket before finding all the reviewer paperwork I need to help me sort the galley copies of the books and send them out.

Heading into the stockroom (more accurately, the glorified cupboard), I close the door behind me and pull out my phone.

I need to speak to Aubrey; she's going to lose her mind when I tell her what I've got myself into this morning. I shoot off a quick text to her, arranging to meet at our favourite café for a late lunch—seeing as Theo ate my lunch in the lift.

Just as I'm about to lock my screen, a Twitter notification catches my eye. I've been tagged in a photo. Flicking my eyes around to make sure I'm still alone and not about to be busted for being on social media when I should be working, I open the notification.

It's from Theo; it's the selfie he took of us in the lift.

My eyes rake over him. *Jeez, he's gorgeous.*

His smile makes my insides clench, and every female part of me wakes up and pays attention. His hair flops over his forehead and makes me want to run my fingers through it and push it back for him. His grin is contagious, and I feel a smile creep onto my lips too.

Forcing myself to stop looking at his photo, I set to work, opening boxes and piling up books, ticking them off the inventory. It's tedious, monotonous work, but someone has to do it.

Stepping into the busy café at lunchtime, I head straight to the last empty table. I'm starving. My one-and-a-half doughnuts this morning have nowhere near filled the hole inside me, and my stomach has been grumbling for the last hour.

When the waitress comes over, I order two lattes and two club sandwiches, as I know that's what Aubrey will want too. They're the best here.

Five minutes later, just as the waitress is setting our order on the table, Aubrey bustles in, flicking her blonde curls out of her face and pulling off her oversize shades. She beams a smile as she struts over and plops into the chair opposite me, her blue eyes already probing me for answers as she picks up her drink.

"So," she says over the rim of her coffee cup, "you got stuck in the lift with a cute guy? Spill. I want all the details."

I grin, rolling my eyes.

When I called her and asked her to inform my office of what was happening, the first thing she had asked me was, "Is he cute?"

Classic Aubrey.

It's no wonder she works downstairs for Hummingbird Ink, the romance imprint of my publishing house; she's always looking for the next happily ever after, either in real life or fiction. To be fair though, it's my ultimate goal to work for Hummingbird Ink too. Romance is my thing as well; you can't beat a good romance novel that tugs at your heartstrings.

"He was *very* cute." I take a sip of my latte. "And you will never guess what I went and agreed to." I shake my head at myself and chuckle.

She sits up straighter, eyeing me hopefully. "Please tell me it's a date."

Aubrey is always nagging me about moving on from Lucas and finding someone new.

"Kind of," I admit, wincing. "He asked me to go to Scotland with him this weekend."

"What?!" Her voice is so loud, people around us stop talking and openly stare.

"Shh," I hiss, laughing as I lean in so we can talk more privately. "He has to go to his brother's wedding and needs a date, so he asked me to go with him. He sold it as basically a four-day all-you-can-drink mini break."

Her mouth comically opens and closes like a fish.

I chew on my lip and shrug one shoulder as I continue, "But I'm not going to go. I said yes at the time, but I was under duress. Now that I'm not trapped in a metal box with him, I've realised how damn stupid it is. I can't go away for the weekend with a guy I just met." I really am certifiable for even agreeing to it in the first place.

"Wait, who is this guy? Does he work for Bluebird imprint, like you?" She leans forward into my space, her eyes wide and excited, food long forgotten.

I shrug and scrunch my nose. "No, he had a visitor's badge clipped on his pocket, so he doesn't work there. I don't really know who he is. His name is Theo. He's hilarious, and he's super hot. That's all I know." I pull out my phone and open the Twitter photo, sliding it across the table to her. "This is him."

Her eyes widen like saucers, and her mouth drops open as she looks at the picture. "Oh my God. The Theo you were stuck in a lift with is Theo *Stone*?"

I shrug, taking a bite of my sandwich. "I guess. I don't know. He only told me his first name. You know him?"

She puts her hand on her forehead and does a long, disbelieving blink. "Theo Stone invited you for a weekend of sin with him in Scotland, and you're considering not going? Are you insane?"

I wince at her scolding tone.

She purses her lips. "Lucie, you're going. If you don't go, I'm unfriending you. You *have* to go, and you *have* to sleep with him!"

I almost choke on my food. "What? Shut up! No way!"

"Yes way! Have you seen him?"

"Obviously. We were trapped in a lift for almost an hour together," I say sarcastically, rolling my eyes and chewing more carefully.

"He's so damn handsome. Everyone in my office has a thing for him. When we first moved buildings last year, he got lost and wandered onto our floor, trying to find the children's division. We were all falling over ourselves to show him where it was. Now, we all try to sneak a look when he comes in for a meeting. That face! I'd like to sit on it."

I snicker behind my hand. "Aubrey!"

She sucks her teeth and plucks a packet of sugar from the bowl on the table, throwing it at me. "You're going. I need this to happen. One of us needs to screw him. I'd volunteer as tribute, but he didn't ask me to Scotland, so …" She trails off, waggling her eyebrows.

I can't contain my groan. "I'm not ready to start dating people. I'm not sleeping with him." I say it sternly, but my mind is already running rampant with thoughts of the feel of his skin under my fingertips, his mouth on my body. I haven't had sex for a while, and it's not like I'm getting a lot of offers for naked time. Plus, he is damn hot.

"Who said anything about dating him? Come on, are you honestly telling me you don't fancy him? Of course you do!" she states knowingly.

I chew on my lip and scrunch my nose. She's right; of course I do. He's melt-your-underwear hot, especially when he smiles.

Aubrey continues, "Look, you've been frustrated. This is the twenty-first century, and you're a modern woman. Go get it, girl. Sex is just sex, if you want it to be. No need to be ashamed for wanting to be satisfied. We all have needs. You can sleep with him with no regrets or strings. I'm not saying you have to marry the guy. All I'm saying is, go with an open mind. Don't beaver-dam yourself before you even board the plane."

I chuckle and take a sip of my drink.

"And don't let memories of that idiot Lucas beaver-dam you either."

I chew on my lip. I shouldn't have told her about his offer. I should have just sent my rejection text to Theo and pretended it'd never happened. Now that I've told her, she'll drone on and on about it until I change my mind and agree to go. Especially if she thinks it'll get me laid. She's already tried persuading me that to get over Lucas, I need to get under someone else. So far, I've resisted her attempts at matchmaking me with random people she knows (including her dentist and the guy who delivers our pizza), but looking at her now, I know she won't let this one go. She'll be following me around like my own personal *Just Do It* Shia LaBeouf GIF cheerleader until I cave.

"Lucie, you have to go! You deserve a free holiday with a hot guy. You're going!"

I groan in defeat and close my eyes.

"You're going!" she repeats sternly.

"Yes, Mum," I joke, sighing in exasperation. But I'm only saying that to shut her up.

I have no intention of changing my mind. It's too absurd. Yes, the idea of a holiday sounds great, and spending time with a hot, hilarious guy is appealing, but … I'm not brave enough to be that impulsive anymore. Besides, I already have a date lined up this weekend with Netflix and one of my mother's tiramisus. I'll simply text Theo a rejection later and then tell Aubrey I couldn't get time off work at short notice. That's a perfectly reasonable and believable excuse.

The rest of lunch is her raving on and on about Theo and how jealous she is. She tells me he's an illustrator. I must admit, I'm more than a little intrigued about him now, and I can't wait to get back to the office and look him up to see what books he's worked on and if he's talented. I tell her about our bargain—that in return for me going to the wedding, he'll come to my dad's party and let me pretend we're a couple to make Lucas jealous. No surprises, Aubrey loves the idea.

I feel bad for lying to her, but it must be done.

By the time lunch is finished and we're heading back to our building, arm in arm, I feel a little deflated. She's so upbeat and positive about it, but I'm back to wallowing in self-pity about losing my fiancé to a prettier, fitter, younger version of me. Putting on a brave face is exhausting.

As we flash our badges to get through the barrier at reception, the lady sitting there gives me a wide smile and holds up one finger. "Oh, wait, you're Lucie, aren't you? Lucie Gordio?"

"I am." I nod and stop by her desk, thinking she must have some more galley copies or a delivery or contract for me to sign for.

"Perfect timing. I was about to call upstairs to you!"

"Oh, really?"

She grins and reaches under her desk, pulling out a box of six Krispy Kreme doughnuts, heavy on the biscotti variety. "Someone left these for you." She makes an excited squealing noise and grins, eyes flitting from me to Aubrey.

I take the box, and my heart leaps into my throat. I don't even need to read the note that's written in black Sharpie on the corner of the box to know these are from Theo. It's too random and too much of a coincidence to be anyone else sending me doughnuts.

"Ooh, yummy! Share!" Aubrey chirps, grinning down at them, not realising the significance of them.

"They're from Theo." I take a deep breath and read his message aloud, "*Don't ever let it be said that I didn't buy you dinner.*" It's so cute that I almost do a little internal swoon as I chew on the inside of my cheek.

Aubrey excitedly claps her hands, and the receptionist gives a dreamy sigh.

And that thoughtful inside joke is all it takes to change my mind again. I open a text, and instead of letting him down ... I send him:

> *Me: Thanks for the calories! They'll all be eaten within three hours.*

And I tack on my date of birth at the end.

Screw it, I have nothing to lose. And I'm now strangely excited about my little impromptu weekend getaway. Aubrey is right; I do deserve it.

I head off upstairs to go book the time off.

STAND-IN SATURDAY

Later that night, just as Aubrey and I are sitting in front of the TV, eating my mum's reheated cannelloni, Theo texts me with our flight times and numbers and the itinerary for the wedding weekend.

I stare down at my phone in confusion for a minute and then text him back.

> *Me: Is that a joke for Friday night?*
>
> *Theo: Nope, deadly serious.*

"Oh crap, what have I got myself into?" I groan.

six

THEO

London Stansted Airport around lunchtime on Thursday is packed with eager, happy passengers ready to jet off on their holidays. I tug my carry-on suitcase closer to me as a group of young lads come in and almost trip over it, as they're not paying the slightest bit of attention to their surroundings. They're about eighteen, and they likely have just been dropped off by their mums for their first ever lads' shagfest. Probably headed to Ibiza, if the looks of them is anything to go by. They're jeering and skipping around like excitable puppies with no clue as to what they should be doing. I smile to myself and wish I were going with them. A nice, carefree holiday where I wouldn't have to watch the girl I was semi in love with marry my kin. What I wouldn't give for that instead of what I'm about to do this weekend.

I chew on my thumbnail again as nerves ball up inside me. I had to switch around my plans for today after Lucie agreed to come with me. I was supposed to be flying up with my parents and sister today but cancelled my flight and rebooked one with Lucie instead from an airport closer to where she lives for convenience—hers, not mine. Now, I'm wondering if I made a mistake. We agreed to meet here five minutes ago, but there's no sign of her. Usually, I'm the one late, but as my train got me here mid-morning today, I've already had a couple of hours to stand around and worry myself sick that she won't turn up.

We've not had much contact, just a quick message or two on the Monday that we met, merely communication about flight times and numbers, and then we had a couple of short check-in messages too—the last of which was yesterday evening when I asked her if she was done packing. It's been almost twenty-four hours since then.

What if she's chickened out?

I glance back at the wall of monitors. Our flight check-in is open now. *What do I do if she doesn't show? How long should I even wait here before I have to board without her?* I can't miss the wedding, though the thought is tempting.

I glance down at my watch again, seeing the second hand tick around agonisingly slow. I should have arranged to pick her up at her place, so we could have taxied here together—less chance of her pulling out at the last minute then.

Before Monday, I resigned myself to the fact that I would be going alone, but now that she agreed, I can't think of much worse than going to this wedding on my own. I need her. She's not only a shield, but also a distraction. I'm not sure how I'm going to feel, watching the ceremony. I'm the best man. I have to stand beside Jared and pretend like it's fine that the only girl I've ever really wanted is marrying my twin.

Hell, not only do I *need* a hot Italian distraction, but I also *deserve* one.

I shove my hand into my pocket and pull out my phone, checking for a letdown message from her, but there's nothing. I type out a quick text, asking where she is and if she's still coming, and then I delete and write again, trying to word it so I don't come across as a needy prick. Just as I have typed out something I'm happy with and am about to press Send, I glance up, and in she walks.

I feel the smile stretch across my face as relief washes over me.

Her eyes meet mine but quickly flick away. She ducks her head, wheeling her small, bright yellow cabin regulation size suitcase alongside her as her teeth sink into her bottom lip. My eyes have a mind of their own as they sweep over her. She's wearing high-waisted, skinny, cropped jeans that cling to her curves, another pair of amazing heels, and a short-sleeved red shirt with white polka dots. It's one of those fashion ones that has been cut too short and shows off a couple of inches of luscious skin across her belly. Her hair is pulled up into a stylishly messy topknot. She looks edible.

Damn. Why did I let her friend-zone me so quickly?

I gulp and swallow my inappropriate thoughts, trying not to wonder what her hair would feel like if I tangled my fingers into it while I kissed the life out of those glossy pink lips.

Lucie trots over to me, her red stiletto heels clacking on the floor almost to the same rhythm of my rapid heartbeat. She's still not looking at me. A blush covers her cheeks as she drags her luggage along. A different but still ridiculously large handbag hangs from the crook of her elbow. Stopping in front of me, she looks up, and her eyes meet mine. She seems uncertain, flustered, and pretty much terrified. I sort of feel the same.

I gulp and feel the grin slide onto my face. "I wasn't sure you'd show up."

"I almost didn't. I got up this morning, fully intending to cancel, but my flatmate was having none of it." She laughs breathlessly at the admission. "I'm sorry I'm late. Traffic was a nightmare. My Uber driver said there was an accident on the M20 that was backing everything else up." She flashes me an apologetic smile.

I wave a dismissive hand. "Don't worry about it. You're here now."

Unreasonable excitement settles in my tummy. I'm genuinely looking forward to getting to know her more. I like her. She has a bit of sass, and I like humour in a girl; it's sexy.

Reaching out, I take the handle of her suitcase from her and pull it to my side. It's half a gentlemanly gesture, but also half a kind of guarantee that she won't run away and change her mind if I'm holding her luggage hostage.

She smiles weakly and wrings her hands in front of her. "I still think this is insane, Theo," she admits, wincing. "There's still time to call off this ridiculous agreement. Have you come to your senses?"

She looks so apprehensive that it makes me feel a little uncomfortable too. I hate it when people feel awkward. I'm one of those people who likes to try and make everyone around me happy and at ease.

"I haven't. Come on, let's just do it. Live our best lives. What could possibly go wrong?" I joke.

"A lot of things actually." She gulps, probably imagining all the things that could go wrong. Her eyes flick to the exit before coming back to my face.

I give her one of my most charming, disarming, reassuring smiles. It's the smile I throw at skittish kids when I occasionally do my magic shows in hospices—yeah, I am that person. The one who pulls handkerchiefs from their hands and makes money appear from behind ears and a whole bunch of other stupid stuff in the hopes of making sick kids laugh like some dorky, rip-off Patch Adams.

"It's gonna be great. Are you hungry or thirsty? Let's check in and then get a coffee or something." I raise one eyebrow and wait, letting her think it through.

I have everything crossed that she doesn't change her mind. She's here now, so surely, it's too late to back out.

She sucks in a breath and then pulls back her shoulders and nods. "Screw it. At least I'll have an eccentric story to tell my grandkids when I'm old. *Nonna was wild once, kids; I got on a plane with a complete stranger …*"

Grinning, I shoot her a wink. "It'll make a great bedtime story. Provided I don't kill you on this trip and sink your body to the bottom of the loch, of course." As soon as I say it, I wish I hadn't. That's not really a good joke to make to an anxious woman who you're trying to convince you're not a serial killer.

But she obviously likes my humour because a chuckle escapes her lips and she rolls her eyes. Stepping closer to me, she loops her arm through mine and tugs me towards the waiting attendant. It breaks the ice a little more.

After checking in, we're ushered through the body scanners, and Lucie is pulled for a random pat-down. I grin at her exasperated eye roll and watch, kind of jealous of the female security officer who gets to run her hands over Lucie's thighs and under her breasts.

As she steps to my side and slides on her shoes, she leans in and frowns. "I always get the pat-downs. I must have one of those untrustworthy faces or something."

"It's the glasses. They give you a bad-girl edge." I can't help but chuckle at her disgruntled face.

We head towards Departures, and I nod in the direction of the food court. "Do you want anything to eat? They won't serve food on the flight; it's too short."

Lucie groans and shakes her head, pressing a hand to her stomach. "No. I'm too nervous to eat."

I smile sadly and step closer to her, trying to catch her eye as I touch her wrist with my fingertips. "What can I do to make you less frightened of me?" I genuinely want to know; I don't want her all kinds of nervous the whole weekend.

She shakes her head. "It's not you. Now that I'm mentally committed to going, I'm kind of over it. What will be, will be," she replies. "Now, I'm just worried about the flight."

"You don't like flying?"

"I'm not overly keen, no."

My insides clench. "Why didn't you say? We could have driven up instead. I mean, it's, like, ten hours, but if you're not a good flyer, we could have done that. A couple of friends are driving up today; we could have hopped in with them."

Tim and Heather wouldn't have minded a couple of extras in their car. Heather doesn't like flying either, apparently.

Lucie waves a hand. "I fly. I travel to Italy all the time to see family, so I've flown loads since I was a kid. I've just never really got used to it, and I get really nervous about it beforehand. Normally, I take a Benadryl, but as it's only a short flight, I thought better of it. It's the take-off I don't like. Once we're going and the seat-belt sign switches off, I usually feel better. Let's maybe get some Dutch courage first, huh?" She nods at a bar, and I grin.

A day drinker. Add a tick to the *my kind of girl* box.

The bar is busier than I expect it to be on a Thursday afternoon, so we have to weave through the crowd. Her hand is fisted into the back of my T-shirt, so we don't get separated as I try not to run over anybody's feet with our carry-ons.

I clock the eighteen-year-old wannabe wolf-pack gang from earlier in here, too, drinking their Stella Artois. Lucie follows me to the bar and leans against it. As the group of boys all watch her arse, I step closer and set my hand on the small of her back—a clear sign for them to back the fuck off. I get it though; her arse is spectacular, all J-Lo rounded, and it's like it pulls your eyes down there with its own gravity. With the denim hugging every inch of it, I can't even blame them for looking.

I order a Corona Light because I'm driving once we get off the plane in Glasgow, but Lucie opts for a whiskey sour. I'm suitably impressed.

We manage to snag the last empty table, and I lean in closer to be heard over the busy hubbub around us. "I had a bet with my mate as to whether you'd stand me up today."

She laughs and sips her drink. "Oh, really? He didn't think I'd show?"

"No, he did. I didn't." It's a joke laced with truth.

She laughs, and the sound makes my insides clench. She's so easy-going; it's nice.

"You'd just better not be using me as some sort of pawn in a plan to break up this wedding, Theo. If I get there and find out that this is part of some scheme, you'll be in so much trouble. I'm not afraid of jail time; I will decapitate you."

"Savage." I chuckle but then see the hard glint to her eye. She's serious. I lean back and cross my finger over my heart. "Honestly, it's not like that; you'll see. I'm happy for them. Besides, Amy and I never would have worked anyway; we're too similar. It's just ... it takes a while to stop wanting someone, you know?"

Her smile falls, and she nods. "I know exactly how that feels. And it sucks."

Her eyes are sad, and I suddenly realise she's likely in the same place as me, mentally. She's not over her cheating ex, and I'm still hung up on Amy. How tragic.

We chink glasses and cheers to our pathetic love lives.

"Did you and Amy ever date?" she asks, sipping her drink, watching me over the rim of the glass.

"Nope, never." I take my own swig. "I just liked her, but she never knew, and then she got with my twin brother."

She gasps and then winces. "Your twin? Ouch."

"Yeah, serious ouch. But it's okay. I'm over it—well, mostly. Um, Lucie ... obviously, it goes without saying that I don't want this stuff to be common knowledge. No one knows that I have a little, inappropriate crush. If you could keep that to yourself, that'd be great." I eye her hopefully, but she doesn't strike me as the sort of person who would intentionally cause trouble for the hell of it.

She smiles and sets her hand on my arm, squeezing gently. "I won't say anything. I'm not an arsehole."

"Excellent. Well, to not being an arsehole then." I grin and nod, holding up my bottle, offering her an air cheers.

By the time we finish our second drinks, they're boarding our flight. The closer we walk towards our gate, the paler Lucie becomes. Her breathing is shallow, and her eyes are darting over every surface as we step onto the plane. The stewardess shoots Lucie a worried look and then glances at me questioningly as we step over the threshold. Smiling reassuringly, I reach down to grip Lucie's hand. It's warm and clammy, and she clings to me so hard that my fingers creak and mash together painfully. I should worry about it really; my fingers are my livelihood, so I have to look after them, but instead, I quite like that she's using me to anchor herself. I'm so messed up.

Lucie allows me to dumbly lead her down the aisle.

When we get to our seats, I motion to them and take her bags from her hands. "You want aisle or window? I'm easy."

She gulps and shrugs. "Okay if I have the window?"

I nod and move aside, so she can slide in. Then, I stow her handbag and our carry-ons up in the overhead compartment.

As I slide into the seat beside her, I glance over to see her fumbling with her seat belt with shaky hands. "Here, let me."

I reach over and gently push her hands out of the way, fastening the belt for her, tightening it to fit. I don't miss the fact that the back of my fingers accidentally brush across the exposed skin of her belly. I also don't miss the fact that her breath catches the same as mine does. My mind wanders to inappropriate places, but I force it to stop. This is simply a friendly weekend; that's what I promised her. I just need to try and keep my mind out of the gutter and off her arse and amazing rack. Then, maybe we can just have a good time together and enjoy a free holiday. Every male part of me is finding that hard though—likely because every female part of her draws my attention.

"Looks like it's my turn to distract you from a panic attack," I joke, winking at her. "Come on, it's only an hour and fifteen minutes of your life. It'll soon be over."

I place my hand over hers and give it a little squeeze, trying to get her fingers to relax from the white-knuckle grip they have on the armrest. She smiles at me weakly, and I motion with my head to the back of the plane, grinning mischievously.

"Fancy joining the Mile-High Club? That'll keep your mind off it."

Still pale, she playfully raises one eyebrow. "But what will I do for the other hour and twelve minutes?"

I can't contain the laughter that rips from my throat.

seven

LUCIE

Of course, we don't join the Mile-High Club. And we don't crash and burn in a fiery wreck either. In fact, the whole flight is actually kind of nice—well, after the initial take-off anyway. Theo is hilarious in a weird but cute way. He's not like Lucas at all; in fact, he's pretty much the opposite of my quiet, well-to-do ex-fiancé who is always about image and status. Theo is incredibly chatty and friendly and just all-round sweet. The way he looks after me throughout the flight makes my stomach flutter.

He holds my hand the whole of take-off, not even complaining about me probably breaking his fingers. And then we joke around and talk about random nothingness for a while, sipping on coffee and eating plane-bought sweets. And when it becomes time to descend, he silently holds his hand out in offering, and I don't hesitate to take it.

It's so unlike the times when I flew with Lucas and he would just tell me to calm down and stop being foolish. Lucas isn't exactly the most patient or empathetic person on the planet. In fact, he's the one who started me on the pre-flight Benadryl train. He'd heard from friends that it made you drowsy and suggested I give it a try. So, they became a regular thing when we travelled together. I don't like taking them; they make me feel all muffled and groggy for hours after. That's the real reason I didn't take one for the flight today. Not because it's a short flight, like I told Theo, but because I didn't have Lucas to press a pill into my palm and insist I take it so I wouldn't embarrass myself—and him.

When the wheels finally touch down, I gratefully beam over at Theo as I release his hand. He makes a show of wincing dramatically and unclenching his fingers a couple of times, and I chuckle and resist the urge to clap for the pilot and cheer just because I'm still alive.

Theo grins, and when he finds a gap in the traffic of eager beavers wanting to get off the plane first, he stands and reaches up to grab our bags from the overhead compartment. As he does so, his white *Top Gun* homage T-shirt—emblazoned with a pair of aviator shades and the slogan *Talk to me, Goose*—rides up a little, and I blink as I catch a quick glimpse of his tanned, toned stomach and a small smattering of hair.

Holy hell.

Gulping, I swallow the wave of desire that pulses through my body. I knew he was good-looking, but no one ever knows what's hiding behind a well-cut suit or loose T-shirt. I didn't exactly expect him to have a dad bod, but I wasn't expecting flat, sculpted yumminess either. That one inch of exposed stomach has set the tone for the whole weekend. It's now my life's mission to get that shirt off him and snap a picture, so I can show an envious Aubrey because she will lose her mind.

"That bag is almost as big as you."

While I'm off in fantasy Theo-land and not paying attention, my handbag accidentally hits me in the face as he dangles it in front of me.

I giggle awkwardly and slip it onto my shoulder, standing and half-kneeling on my seat as I force my dirty mind away from thoughts of what the rest of his chest might look like. No doubt I'll see over the weekend. It's the height of summer after all, and he did promise me sunbathing. I shouldn't be this excited about the prospect.

We fall in line with the other passengers, and by the time I get to the exit door, I'm beaming so wide, my cheeks ache. I practically skip down the gangplank, excited to start the weekend. Weddings aren't exactly my thing, but it's only one afternoon, and like he said, the rest of the time is my own. I've never been to Scotland before, and I Googled Loch Lomond on Monday night with Aubrey, so I know the place we're headed to is stunning. This break is a long time coming.

Following the signs, we head through customs and up to the car rental desk. While Theo leans on the desk and talks to the assistant about his pre-booking, I take a moment to study him. Now that I know there's a real body under there, I can't help but want to see more. He's in his *Top Gun* T-shirt, a pair of cream shorts, and well-cared-for white trainers on his feet. His shoulders are broad, his legs long and toned, and his forearms have that muscled, vein thing going on—I never knew I liked those before today.

He's decidedly more casual than in the suit I first met him in. He looks better like this though, more comfortable, more himself. There's a faded three-inch scar on the shin of his right leg. I ponder it, wondering how he got it. When he turns, I'm still mid-examination of him, so my eyes zero in on his crotch, and I'm too slow to drag my stare away. Face burning with embarrassment, I startle, wrenching my gaze away, hoping I've not been caught on crotch watch.

"Right, all sorted. Come on then. Let's go." He nods over my shoulder, looking pleased with himself as he pockets the rental keys and hands me the paperwork, which I fold and shove into my bag. He's still wheeling my suitcase for me as we follow the assistant. It's adorable.

As we walk through the airport and out the door, our arms accidentally brush against each other, and I feel my stomach flutter as I resolutely stare at my feet, knowing my face is likely beet red.

"How'd you get that scar on your leg?" I ask, needing to think about something else.

"Car accident about a year or so ago. Broke my leg, and the bone came right through. I had to have it pinned and—"

I squeal and throw my hands up to cover my ears as I squeeze my eyes shut, trying not to picture it. I've always been squeamish. "Oh my God. Stop!"

"You big baby." He chuckles at my side, and we follow the assistant to parking bay three, where we are confronted with a tiny blue car. Theo scowls at it and inspects his keys, reading the label and checking it against the registration number. "A Citroen C1? Don't you have something bigger?"

The assistant guy smiles apologetically and shrugs one shoulder. "I'm sorry. We're fully booked. You got the last car. It's always busy this time of year."

"Am I even going to be able to fit in this? I hate small cars." Theo's scowl deepens, and he rubs at his forehead.

He already told me his choice was to either hire a car or get the bus ... and I absolutely *do not* want to get on a bus in this heat if he changes his mind now, so I step forward and put my hand on his back. "It's only a thirty-minute drive, you said. This will be fine. It's not like we have a load of luggage that won't fit. It's just the two of us. Just scoot the seat all the way back."

He nods, seemingly reluctant, and heads to the boot, stowing our cases as I slide into the passenger seat. When Theo opens the driver's door and leans in to depress the seat button and slide the seat back as far as it will go, I smile and watch the show of him trying to fold himself into position. He's so damn tall, probably about six foot one or two. Even though the seat is as far back as it will go, his knees almost touch the steering wheel. He looks so exasperated; it's almost comical. I can't resist a little chuckle, which earns me a scowl.

"Maybe you could drive?" he suggests, looking at me hopefully, but then his face falls. "Ah, crap. You had those whiskeys." He lets out a groan and adjusts himself in his seat, shuffling, tilting the seat back to try and get another precious inch of legroom.

"I wouldn't be able to anyway, even without the drinking. I never bothered to learn. Living in London, it's easier and quicker to get to places on the tube or walk. And parking—don't even get me started on the parking." I roll my eyes and remember nights where Lucas would complain and grumble about having to drive round and round the block, looking for spaces to park his precious Audi, if we took his car anywhere.

"I don't drive much either. Cambridge is mostly set up for bikes, and everything I want is basically within walking distance or a short taxi ride away." He nods in agreement and pulls a scrap of paper from his pocket with a postcode scribbled on it. He punches it into the satnav, and we watch as it calculates the route for us.

Twenty-nine minutes.

I smile brightly, imagining being there.

Theo takes a deep breath, his hands gripping the wheel tightly, seeming to ground himself. Then, he grinds the clutch, and the engine revs too loudly, as he can't quite manoeuvre his legs right in the tight space. We bunny-hop out of the space. I chuckle behind my hand, which earns me another dark look.

The drive is nice despite Theo swearing every time he has to change gear because he's struggling to adjust his legs, and whenever we stop at traffic lights, he either stalls the engine or bunny-hops off the line so hard, my head bumps back against the headrest.

I turn on the radio, and we both hum along while the satnav directs him to wherever we're going. I don't even know the hotel name. I don't even care. He could be taking me anywhere right now, and I wouldn't even object to it; I'm so serene and chill.

My eyes are trained out of the window on the hills, trees, and all the green that surrounds me. As a city girl, my eyes are wide and excited at the lush scenery, my heart is in my throat, and stupidly, I feel a teensy bit emotional.

When the satnav tells us to pull into a sweeping gravel driveway flanked by trees, I sit up straighter and look around excitedly. At the end, it opens into a car park, and Theo swings into a space, breathing a sigh of relief as he cuts the engine.

I grin over at him. "You're a terrible driver."

One of his eyebrows rises. "But did you die?" he jokes before glancing at his watch. "It's almost six. I'm getting hungry. Fancy getting checked into our rooms and then meeting back downstairs to grab some food? I could smash a burger and chips right now."

I nod in agreement, feeling my tummy clench now that he's mentioned food. "I could eat."

When I climb from the car, a blast of warm air hits me in the face now that I'm out of the air-conditioned vehicle. The air smells amazing, so clean and fresh and so unlike the city smell I'm used to. A little sigh of contentment leaves my lips.

Theo is busy stretching his back and legs on the other side of the car, so I walk forward a few steps and look over the little wall. Shielding my eyes and squinting against the bright sun, I see the loch for the first time. I don't know what I was expecting, but it wasn't anything near this beautiful. My breath catches at the sight. It's magnificent. The expanse of water glimmers, reflecting the fluffy clouds and bright sun. Mountains rise in the distance on the other side of the loch, silhouetted against the bluest sky I've ever seen.

It's the most perfect place to get married. Amy is so lucky.

If Lucas and I were still engaged, after seeing this, I would unquestionably be trying to convince him we needed a Scottish wedding. My heart gives a pathetic squeeze when I realise that will never happen. Maybe I'll never get married now. Maybe I'll never fall in love again. Who knows?

Pulling out my phone, I snap a photo of the view. I'm about to take a selfie next when Theo walks over and lets out an appreciative whistle as he looks out over the water too.

"That's not too shabby."

Reaching out, I grab his T-shirt and pull him to me, holding out the phone and lining up a selfie of us with the view behind. His arm goes around my waist, and he pulls me closer to him, tucking my side tightly against his hard chest as he smiles at the camera, his eyes twinkling. I snap a picture and then grin down at my screen, trying not to notice how nice we look together as I send it to Aubrey to let her know we arrived safely. She replies almost immediately with a string of heart-eyes emojis and a message.

> *Aubrey: Not sure which view is finer—him or the scenery! Have you shagged him yet???*

I chuckle and send back an eye-rolling GIF.

"Oh, I hope my room has a view of the loch." I sigh wistfully, slipping my phone back into my bag. I'm already in love with this place.

"Let's go find out." Theo nods towards a beautiful-looking three-story hotel right on the edge of the loch.

Unable to take my eyes from the view, I blindly follow behind him, my heart in my throat. I wasn't aware places looked like this in the UK. I've only ever really holidayed in Italy. I've never even ventured outside of London for anything other than the occasional work meeting. I'm a Londoner; city life is what I've grown up in. This is so tranquil and picturesque that it steals my breath. A little beach edges the loch in front of the hotel, and I'm itching to take my shoes off and feel the sand between my toes.

A sigh leaves my body as I allow myself to feel perfectly happy and content for the first time in three months.

The inside of the hotel is gorgeous, all stone walls, hardwood floors, high ceilings, exposed beams, and rustic decor. We stop at the reception desk, where we're greeted by a smiling lady with a severe ponytail and a lovely Scottish lilt to her voice.

"Hi," Theo says. "We have two rooms. Theo Stone. We're here for Jared and Amy's wedding."

"Oh, I could have guessed who you were by looking at you!" She marvels over him for a few seconds and then turns her attention to her computer.

I ponder her comment. *Does that mean he and his twin look alike? Maybe I should have asked.*

"Let me look you up, and then we'll get you settled." She taps away at the screen. Her smile faltering is my first clue that something is wrong. The second clue is when she says, "You said, two rooms?" Her tone is too polite as she carries on clicking away.

"Yeah."

"I'm sorry. I only have you down for one. A deluxe double room." She frowns apologetically and looks between us.

Theo shakes his head and rests his forearms on the desk, leaning in and trying to look at the screen. "No, there should be two for me. Jared told me I could have one of the floating spare rooms he booked for people in case they changed their minds and decided to attend last minute. He said he had a room block booked as part of the wedding package. There should be spare rooms."

Understanding crosses her face. "Ah, I'm sorry. The wedding party room block you're talking about is booked for Friday and Saturday nights only. We're fully booked up tonight."

"You're kidding, right?"

"No, sir, I'm afraid I'm not."

"Shit. Jared! Bloody idiot," he groans and grips his hair in his hands. "Wait, a deluxe *double* room. You mean, just one bed, right?"

She nods, her eyes again flicking between the two of us. "Yes, sir."

Theo turns to me, his eyes wide and almost frightened. "I didn't do this on purpose. This isn't one of those seduction things where I'm trying to get you in my bed, I swear." He holds his hands up innocently.

A nervous giggle escapes my lips because he looks truly horrified. "I believe you." And I do.

He turns back to the receptionist and runs a hand through his hair. "Could we switch to a twin room at least?"

"No, sorry, sir. As I said, we are fully booked tonight; all rooms are accounted for. However, all our deluxe rooms are equipped with a sofa bed. They're very comfortable. If you call down to reception when it's a convenient time, we'd be happy to have one of our staff pop in and make up the bed for you. I know it's not ideal if you were expecting two rooms, but there appears to be some crossed wires somewhere along the lines. Tomorrow, I'll be happy to allocate you another room from the pre-booked wedding block."

Theo looks back at me as if waiting for me to make the decision.

I don't see any other choice, so I shrug. "Sounds okay to me. It's only one night."

I categorically will not be telling Aubrey about this little room situation though; I already know what she'd try and Shia LaBeouf talk me into.

Resigned, Theo gives a nod to the receptionist, who instantly brightens.

"Excellent. Well, here is your key. Your room number is twenty-eight. It's located in this main building, on the top floor. The lifts are there." She points at the back of the lobby and then slides two white plastic wristbands across the desk. "And these are your wristbands. You're a tier one guest of the wedding, which means everything is included in your stay—food, drink, sunbeds. You simply flash the wristbands and tell them your room number." She patiently watches as we both awkwardly attach them to our wrists. "If you need anything else, just dial zero from your room telephone to come straight through to me or dial one to order room service. The hotel reception and kitchen are twenty-four hours, so if you need anything, please do give us a call." She hands over a small cardboard folder with a map of the hotel and two keycards inside. "Is there anything else I can help you with, Mr Stone?"

He huffs a breath. "I suppose not. Can you tell me where we can get some food?"

She smiles broadly and points off to the left. "Our restaurant is just down there, next to the bar. I believe some of the wedding party are already in there, and some are in the bar area, if you're looking to meet up."

"Thanks," Theo mutters, turning and wincing at me apologetically. "I swear I didn't do this on purpose. Jared told me there would be spare rooms when I spoke to him on Monday night. If it makes you uncomfortable, I can bunk in with my parents or something for the night instead."

Unconsciously, his face scrunches in distaste, and I can tell how much he doesn't want to do that.

I wave my hand and shake my head as we make our way to the lifts. "It's fine. But if you snore or fart in your sleep, you're getting smothered."

He laughs loudly, and the sound makes the hair on my arms stand up and my tummy flutter.

When we get to our room, Theo pushes open the door and waves me inside first. The room is lovely, decorated with sumptuous grey wallpaper and a huge king-size bed with a purple tartan thrown over the end. A matching tartan sofa is situated next to it. The furniture is all dark wood and polished to perfection. As I step further into the room, my eyes are drawn to the opposite glass wall, and the view of the loch is spectacular. There's even a little balcony with a table and chairs. My teeth sink into my bottom lip as I take it all in, just imagining watching the sun set or rise from the comfort of my bed.

Smiling happily, I turn back to Theo and head over, taking my suitcase from him, knowing I need to freshen up before we go eat. As I walk past it, my eyes again take in the plush-looking bed. Glancing from it to the sofa, I frown. The sofa doesn't look particularly *un*comfortable, but compared to the luxurious-looking king-size bed, it's not something I want to get personally acquainted with.

"So … who gets the bed?" I ask.

We both look over at it longingly.

Theo doesn't answer, just holds out his fist on his palm and raises one eyebrow. I laugh and match his gesture, and we Rock, Paper, Scissors for it.

He groans when I beat his scissors with my rock.

"Best of three?" he pleads.

I shake my head. "Best of one. You lose, sucker." I throw my suitcase on the bed and giggle at his disgruntled face.

eight

LUCIE

After a quick bathroom trip to freshen up, touch up my make-up, and change my top for a more evening-appropriate one, leaving on my high-waisted jeans, I head back into the room to see Theo sitting on the edge of the bed, watching TV with his back to me, dressed and ready to go. He's changed his top too; he's now wearing a short-sleeved black shirt. The room smells of aftershave that makes my skin break out in goose bumps and my scalp prickle.

"Ready to go smash those burgers?" I joke as I slip on some blue heels in place of my red ones.

"Heck yeah."

He flicks off the TV and stands, turning to face me. He freezes, and I don't miss the small, barely perceptible widening of his eyes or the tightening of his jaw as he sees me. His Adam's apple bobs, and his lips press into a thin line before he finally clears his throat and nods, huffing out a long breath, eyes still on me. The way he's looking at me makes me shift on my feet and chew on my lip. Aubrey would call what he's doing *eye-fucking*. I certainly feel thoroughly eye-fucked—and I like it.

"Wow, Lucie. You look great. Really great."

"Um … thanks. You do too." *Understatement.*

I chuckle awkwardly and look down at myself, feeling my cheeks burn at his compliment.

My top is a cute off-the-shoulder baby-blue crop top that shows some midriff and my shoulders. It's new. One of the many things I treated myself to with my first wage packet after Lucas and I split. I wanted a fresh start, and I wanted to wear stuff I liked rather than things Lucas had thought were suitable. Our—or more correctly, *his*—circle of friends we hung out with when we did venture out to posh dinners or high-end bars were more sophisticated than my own friends. They were into their brand names and wouldn't be caught dead in high-street bargains like this one. This shirt is not something Lucas would have said looked great; in fact, the last time I wore a top that showed off a bit of tummy, he regarded me as if I'd lost my mind and kindly reminded me that we were going to brunch with his parents and not a hooker convention. Then, he politely suggested I might like to revisit my choice of attire before he kissed my forehead and playfully swatted my bum. I cried myself to sleep that night and threw away my shirt. When we broke up, I bought as many belly-revealing tops as I could get my hands on as a giant *eff you* to him. Not that I've seen him since the split, but it's more of a mental *eff you*, and it makes me feel empowered.

As I look at Theo now, seeing his obvious approval, it makes me feel a hundred feet tall.

"Let's go then," I say, staring at my shoes as I push my glasses up my nose, cheeks still flaming.

Silently, he grabs the keycard from the sideboard and heads to the door, opening it and holding it for me to walk through first. We walk side by side to the lift, the air thick with unspoken attraction. I can feel his eyes on me, and I can't stop smiling. I've no intention of doing anything about it, but the way he just looked at me made my thighs clench and my heart race.

"If you're nervous about meeting my family, don't be. They'll love you," Theo says as he sets his hand on the small of my back.

His thumb strokes across the exposed skin there, and I feel a little shiver tickle up my spine that I fight hard not to show.

"I'm not nervous." That's the truth. I'm merely a fake date.

After this long weekend, I'll never see them again, so I don't need to worry about making a good impression or fitting in with them. As we agreed, I'm here for the vitamin D, the alcohol, and the free food he promised me.

And maybe some no-strings naked Twister if he keeps touching my back like that …

I am, however, curious about Amy. I can't help but wonder what Theo's type is. This girl must be something special if she's hooked him and his brother so easily. I imagine she is a beautiful, tall, blonde goddess with legs up to my belly button.

We stop at the reception on the way past and ask them to make up the sofa bed in our room while we're out, and then we head to the restaurant. As we step inside, I hear a girlie squeal and look around with wide eyes as a little girl of about seven or eight springs from her chair and races over, shouting Theo's name at the top of her lungs. At the table she vacated is an older couple, and they both look over with undisguised interest. I watch, shocked, as Theo's face breaks out in a grin, and he bends just as the little girl leaps into his arms and hugs him tight.

"Hey, squirt. I take it, you've missed me?" he teases, tickling her.

"Yes! God, it's been so boring here all afternoon. Why didn't you get the plane with us? You said you were gonna." She pouts and fiddles with the collar of his shirt.

He shrugs, his eyes quickly flicking over me before looking back at the little girl. "Had to go pick up my date."

Her eyes suddenly widen as she looks over at me for the first time. "Is this your girlfriend?" she stage-whispers comically from the corner of her mouth.

I chuckle, but Theo doesn't look fazed.

"No, we're just friends," he stage-whispers back, mirroring her. He sets her down on her feet and puts his hands on her shoulders as he turns her to face me, his grin that of a proud father. "Carys, this is Lucie. And this little ball of fun is my favourite niece, Carys."

She slaps his stomach and frowns. "I'm your *only* niece."

Theo nods. "Hence, my favourite."

I give her a nod and a big smile. "Nice to meet you, Carys."

The woman who was with the girl at her table is walking towards us now, and a megawatt smile covers her face as her eyes flick between Theo and me. She's probably mid-fifties, and she actually looks like Theo a bit; they have the same colour hair and bright smile. There's a baby sitting on her hip—a few months old, I'd guess. The gentleman at the table finishes the last of his drink in two gulps before he follows behind her.

"Hey. You made it," the lady greets, leaning in to kiss Theo's cheek and give him a one-armed hug.

"Hey, Mum. Hi, Dad." Theo grins happily and nods, instantly—and somewhat expertly—plucking the baby from his mother's arms, nuzzling his nose against the baby's cheek until the baby grins and grabs two fistfuls of Theo's hair.

I slow-blink. *Well, goodbye, ovaries! It was nice knowing you.*

If I thought he was hot before, throw in a baby, and my underwear seems to have melted. *If Aubrey could see this ...*

Theo's hand rests on my back again, his thumb doing that soft sweep thing across my skin, and I silently wonder if he can somehow tell what I'm thinking because he looks smug as hell.

"Lucie, these are my parents, Deborah and Kenneth. And this little fella"—he tickles the baby again, garnering another giggle that makes my heart stutter—"is Finley, my nephew." He turns the baby towards me. "Cute, right?"

I nod dumbly. "Very cute." And I'm not just talking about the baby.

Deborah steps forward and beams a smile at me before opening her arms and pulling me into a tight hug. It's the type of hug you give someone you know, not someone you've just met. Awkwardness overcomes me, and I pat her back and wince in Theo's direction, but he just laughs and shrugs one shoulder, his eyes twinkling with mischief.

When Deborah pulls back, she clutches my shoulders and looks right into my eyes. It's like I can almost see her joy fizzing. No wonder Theo was so desperate for a date. By the looks of this woman's expression, she's likely the one who keeps asking him when he's going to find someone and settle down, like he told me during Lift-gate.

"It's so wonderful to meet you, Lucie! How was your flight? Are your rooms nice? How beautiful is this place?" She puts her hand on her heart, and her eyes well with tears. "The wedding is going to be so beautiful." She sniffs, and Kenneth sighs heavily, pulling out a handkerchief from his pocket and passing it to his wife, who takes it gratefully and dabs her eyes, laughing. "Sorry. I'm just so happy at the moment."

Carys stage-whispers again, "She keeps happy-crying *all* the time. The plane ride was *so* fun." She rolls her eyes, and I fight a chuckle.

Theo steps closer to me, probably sensing my unease. "Flight was good. Rooms are great. The wedding will be beautiful." He holds up a hand and waves at someone at another table. "We're gonna grab some food and then hook up with Jared and Amy."

Deborah sniffles. "Oh, if I'd known you were coming to eat, we would have waited, and we could have all eaten together. It's even lucky you came in when you did. A couple of minutes later, and you'd have missed us. We're just on our way out for a walk along the beach; we promised Carys we'd explore. We're on babysitting duty while Emily and Chris enjoy the night off."

"And by night off, you mean, they're in the bar, getting blathered?" Theo raises one eyebrow knowingly, and Deborah chuckles and nods along. "Thought so. Anyway, don't let us stop you. Go enjoy your beach walk." He leans in and gives his mum another one-armed hug before passing Finley back to her, dropping a kiss on the top of the baby's head and ruffling Carys's hair. "Have fun." He and the little girl do a fist bump, and he pats his dad on the shoulder as they walk past.

"You could have warned me your mum was a hugger," I say quietly, waving at her again as she waves Finley's chubby arm from the door.

"We're all huggers. Get used to it." His arm casually slips around my waist as he guides me forward and towards an empty table.

We both order cheeseburgers. He gets a beer, and I order a glass of wine. Dinner is lovely, and the company is even better. Conversation flows freely. He jokes around and makes me laugh. At one point, I laugh so hard that wine dribbles down my chin, but he doesn't seem to care; he just seems proud of himself. The more I talk to him, the more I see how great he is. This weekend is going to be fabulous, and I'm so pleased Aubrey forced me to come.

"Shall we get dessert?" Theo asks as our empty plates are cleared away.

And even though I just pronounced that I couldn't possibly eat another bite, my mouth waters. I can't say no to dessert, just ask my arse and thighs. Thigh gap? Hell no, I have a pie gap—as in no gap, blame the pie.

"Hell yes. What kind of question is that?" I reply.

He grins. "An unnecessary one, clearly."

I nod and sip my wine. "Exactly. Don't ever ask me such a stupid question again."

We order. I go for death-by-chocolate cake, and he orders a caramel sundae. When they arrive, they look like heaven.

As I dig in and the sweetness hits my tongue, I moan in appreciation. "You know, if it were socially acceptable, I'd eat dessert first."

A smile twitches at the corner of his mouth as he scrapes the caramel sauce that's running down the side of the glass with his finger and sucks it off. "Same. You know, maybe we're soul mates," he jokes. "Maybe that lift meeting was good karma, not bad …"

I roll my eyes. "If it were good karma, I wouldn't have had to share my doughnuts with you."

He points his spoon at me and grins. "Ah, but you got extras in return, so you lucked in. Case closed. We're meant to be."

He sends me a wink, and I try so hard not to let it make me giddy, but I just can't help it. I haven't been flirted with for months—hell, maybe even years. It seems like a lifetime ago when Lucas used to flirty-banter with me like this.

When we've finished gorging ourselves, Theo signs to add the bill to our room, and then we head to the bar next door.

As we step in, my eyes instantly land on his twin. I'm momentarily startled when I discover they look exactly alike. They're not just twins; they're *identical* twins. I gasp, and my mouth drops open. When Theo said "twin brother," I didn't expect an actual body double. Damn, two of their hotness? It's almost too much. Two killer smiles and those twinkling amber eyes? Jesus, their mother certainly outdid herself by creating not one, but two fine specimens in one go. I really should congratulate her on her achievement next time I see her.

My eyes rake over Jared as we walk over to him, and I can't help but wonder how Amy chose between the two of them. If they look exactly alike, how can you fall in love with one and not the other? How would you know which one of them you wanted to be with and marry if they were exactly the same? It seems so weird. An impossible decision, surely.

Jared is standing in front of the bar, drinking a pint of beer, talking with two other guys. They all smile over at us as we step up next to them.

"Started without us?" Theo gives them all a handshake/chest-bump greeting and then introduces me to his brother Jared; his brother-in-law, Chris; and one of Amy's best friends, Tim.

Jared's handshake is a firm grip as he nods a hello to me, and Tim is grinning from ear to ear and already looks a tad drunk.

"Where's the soon-to-be Mrs?" Theo asks Jared as he waves to get the barman's attention.

"Causing mayhem, as usual." Jared motions off to one side with his pint.

I notice that his eyes soften when he does, and a small, wistful smile twitches at the corner of his mouth when he looks at his fiancée. *That's what love looks like.* It makes my heart ache.

I look over too. There are three women standing and laughing together. I pick out their sister, Emily, immediately. They all have the same shape to their noses and the same warm, rich brown shade to their hair. My eyes rake over the other two—one is tall, the other short. My eyes zero in on the tall one, and I nod in understanding. She's gorgeous. Her make-up is on point, cheeks and nose contoured flawlessly. Long, shiny raven hair cascades around her face and down her back. A tight dark purple dress hugs her body to perfection, showing off long legs and a flat stomach.

Now, I know what Theo's type is—stunning.

Theo grins and cups his mouth, shouting over the music playing in the background and the other people standing around the bar, talking. "Oi. Don't I get a hello? Rude! I mean, I am the second-most-important man in the wedding, you know!"

The girls' conversation stops immediately. His sister and the gorgeous model-like girl send him a wave. The other one, the short girl with the pale pink hair, beams and marches over excitedly; she's all bouncy steps and flouncy arms. Her smile is radiant; it's one of those contagious smiles that you can't help but reciprocate. She's wearing Converse, jean shorts, and a short-sleeved grey top that says, *Warning: may contain alcohol*. I already like her.

"Hey!" she greets, throwing her arms around Theo. As she pulls back, her eyes meet mine, and they sparkle excitedly. "Ahh, you must be Lucie! Oh, bloody hell, I still can't believe you got stuck with this one in a lift for almost an hour. How did you not murder him?" she jokes, teasingly elbowing Theo in the stomach. "I would have done it if he'd basically guilt-tripped me into giving up my doughnuts."

Theo chuckles and rolls his eyes, and Jared wraps his arm around the girl's waist, gently pulling her to him. Her hand goes to his stomach, and she strokes absentmindedly, as if she can't keep her hands off him, as he leans in and drops a kiss on the top of her head.

The metaphorical penny drops with a loud clang. This girl is Amy, not the tall, leggy girl with the perfect make-up and killer dress. No, this shorter, gorgeous, smiley girl is the one who has Theo tied in a knot.

Hmm, interesting.

I take her offered hand and give it a shake. "Hi. Yeah, it's nice to meet you. Thanks for letting me crash your wedding. Though it's not like I had much choice in the matter; he basically wouldn't let me say no," I joke, rolling my eyes.

"You're welcome," Theo chirps, winking at me.

The other two girls come over then. The tall stunner I incorrectly assumed was Amy steps up close to Tim and leans against him. I'm introduced to everyone again, and finally, the barman stops at our group.

Amy's smile widens. "Guys, it's Thursday. Seeing as it's a special occasion, I think, just this once, we can extend the tradition to include all of you. What do you think, Hev?" She nudges the raven-haired beauty.

Heather nods in agreement. "Just this once."

I frown in confusion as Tim and Jared both wince and turn their noses up.

"Tradition?" I ask.

Amy excitedly rubs her hands together, her blue eyes twinkling. "Tequila Thursday. Let's get them shots going. One shot every fifteen minutes. First one to puke loses."

One hour and four shots later, the first one to puke is their brother-in-law, Chris. Emily escorts him back to their room, and we all playfully boo and shame them out of the bar. I'm having a great night. Amy and her friend, Heather, are hilarious, and Theo bounces off the two of them like they're in a sparring word match.

As I watch the group interact, it's a little strange to see Jared and Theo sitting next to each other. While they look exactly the same, Jared, I've noticed, is quieter and more reserved than his loud, outgoing twin. Don't get me wrong; Jared is funny, too, but his jokes and one-liners are delivered in perfect precision for maximum impact rather than Theo's all-round friendly banter that doesn't seem to stop. They're so different but yet the same. It's kind of fascinating to witness.

And Amy? Well, let's just say, I can see why Theo is attracted to her. She's gorgeously cute and witty, and she never stops smiling. I might even have a tiny crush on her myself by the end of the weekend. She's amazing and the type of girl you want to be best friends with.

I'm also relieved to finally be able to stop worrying about Theo's intentions in bringing me here. Seeing them all together, it's clear that Theo really doesn't seem to want to disturb or cause problems with the loved-up couple. I now believe he genuinely just didn't want to come to the wedding on his own and brought me here under innocent pretences. Thank the Lord for small mercies because I really didn't fancy jail time for murdering him.

At around half past ten, the tequila shots and travelling seem to be catching up with me, and I can't stifle my yawn, so I try to discreetly hide it behind my hand.

"Tired?" Theo asks, leaning in, his hot breath blowing down my neck as his fingers brush across the top of my shoulder.

I nod and turn my eyes to his, seeing he looks exhausted too. His eyes are slightly droopy. It's a good look for him. "Yeah."

"Let's call it a night and get some sleep. Then, tomorrow, we can do something fun," he suggests. "There's this little village I Googled that's not far away. They do all sorts of water activities there, like kayaking or paddle boarding or waterskiing. Fancy that?" he asks, but then his face falls, and his eyes tighten. "Or do you just want to be away from me and sunbathe on the beach or walk in the woods on your own? Like I said, your time is your own. If you don't want to hang with me, that's fine, honestly."

Water sports? Oh, heck yes. I'm more than up for that.

I used to love that kind of stuff and never really got to do it with Lucas. He didn't like activity days. Our holidays were more the *sunbathe and dip your toe in the pool* type. He wouldn't even let me ride the banana boat last time we went away—too dangerous, he said. You can imagine how much I rolled my eyes at that. Lucas's idea of danger was ordering something from the Thai menu that he'd never tried.

"Hell yes! Let's do that. And if I'm too hungover tomorrow to do anything, we can get a two-person kayak, and you can paddle me around the loch while I hurl over the side and feed the fish."

Theo's grin dazzles me. "Great. It's a date then."

I scrunch my nose and wave my hand in a so-so gesture. "Fake date."

He laughs and nods. "Fake date," he agrees before turning back to everyone else. "Guys, we're gonna turn in."

We all say our goodbyes, and I smile as I push myself up to my feet. When the world tilts slightly inside my fuzzy head, I wobble, and Theo's arm snakes around my waist, holding me steady. After my afternoon whiskey sours, a couple of glasses of wine, and the tequila shots, I now regret my stiletto heel choice.

The walk back to the room is in relative silence, but it's not an uncomfortable one. When we stumble in through the door, I notice the sofa bed has been made up, as we requested.

"Okay if I use the bathroom first?" I ask, clutching my pyjamas to my chest, silently thankful that I brought nice ones with me instead of a raggedy pair or something revealing.

"Sure." He nods and absentmindedly looks through his own suitcase.

I head in, changing, wiping off my make-up, and doing my business. When I step back into the room, Theo has changed already; he's wearing loose-fit shorts and T-shirt pyjamas and is sitting on the edge of the bed, watching the door. He turned off the overhead light, so the bedside lamp casts a soft glow over everything.

I smile awkwardly because I didn't expect to be sharing a room with him tonight. Only a handful of people get to see me without make-up, and hot guys I barely know are not among the few.

As Theo goes into the bathroom, I put my phone on to charge next to the bed and then slip between the sheets. A sigh of contentment falls from my lips as the soft mattress caresses my body to perfection. I scoot to the middle and starfish, revelling in the space. After sleeping the last three months in an uncomfortable second-hand bed, this is like actual heaven. I can't temper my happy smile as my eyes already start to get heavy.

Minutes later, Theo returns and climbs into the sofa bed. He lets out a groan, and I roll to the side, propping myself up on one elbow, watching him as he wriggles, punches his pillow, and tries to get comfy. He's so tall; his feet comically hang off the end.

"Well, my TripAdvisor review of this place just took a sharp decline," he grumbles, shifting uncomfortably again as he rolls his eyes.

I chuckle as the springs creak. "I don't want to rub it in or anything, but this bed is like sleeping on a cloud."

He throws me a dark look, and I giggle, flicking off the lamp and settling back against the pillows. A few minutes later, he's still moving around, trying to get comfortable, and I start to feel slightly bad for him. Those sofa beds are probably designed more for kids, not hulking six-foot sexpots. The trouble is, I won the bed fair and square, so I can't relent now. If I do, it'll set a bad precedent for the weekend, and he'll expect me to cave on all my decisions. No. He can suffer for the night. Tomorrow, if for whatever reason we can't get another room sorted, I'll switch with him, and he can have the bed.

Just as I'm about to drift off, he speaks, "Thanks for coming with me, Luce. I really appreciate you being here. It honestly does make it easier."

Luce. I like it when he calls me that. It's familiar and kind of intimate.

I smile into the darkness, trying to make out his shape in the gloom. "Well, thanks for bringing me. So far, I'm having a blast."

"See you tomorrow."

"Night, Theo."

nine

LUCIE

"Well, good news: I didn't wake up dead, so I obviously don't snore or fart in my sleep," Theo jokes.

I smile, my eyes still closed as I stretch and let out a little groan, letting the last fog of sleep ebb away before turning my head to see him sitting on the sofa bed, propped up against his pillow. His sketchpad and pencils lie abandoned next to him. He's sipping from a mug, still in his pyjamas. His hair is messed up, sticking out everywhere, and there are lines of sleep still on his face, a shadow of short stubble covering his jaw. He looks delicious.

"Morning," I greet, rolling to my side and automatically reaching for my glasses.

"I made you a coffee. I didn't know how you take it, so I left that up to you to sort out." He nods at the bedside cabinet, and I see a black coffee next to a sachet of milk and four sugars.

He made me coffee in bed? Well, that's adorable. "Thanks. How'd you sleep in the end?"

He reaches up and roughly rubs a hand over his face. "Wasn't too bad once I eventually drifted off. There isn't much that can wake me once I'm under, so …" He shrugs and gulps down his drink as I stir sugar and milk into mine. "Still up for checking out the water activities this morning?"

"Try and stop me."

His grin widens. "Excellent. I'm gonna jump in the shower, and then I'll head downstairs, so you can have some privacy to get ready. I'll sort out getting my own room while I'm down there."

As I sip at my coffee, I can hear him in the shower. He's humming, but I can't make out the song. It's cute.

Less than fifteen minutes later, he steps out of the room, dressed in black swimming shorts and an old-school *Ghostbusters* T-shirt, looking refreshed and all kinds of glorious.

"I'll be in the lobby. I'll grab us some croissants and stuff to take with us. It's already past ten. If we leave too late, the sports centre might be too busy to fit us in."

"Good idea."

I have a quick shower, taking care not to wet my hair. Once dry, I slather myself in sun cream and shimmy my way into my black bikini. Then, I shove on denim shorts and a loose vest top over the top. I apply a quick swipe of tinted moisturiser and some waterproof mascara, and then I insert a pair of disposable contact lenses, so I can forgo my glasses today. After scraping my hair up into a topknot and grabbing my handbag and two towels (because I didn't see Theo take one with him), I head down to the lobby to meet him.

He's sitting in one of the plush armchairs with his back to me. As I step to his side, I put my hand on his shoulder to get his attention. It's solid under my fingers, like steel muscles under silky skin.

"Hey. I'm ready."

He looks up at me and grins as he pushes himself to his feet. "Great. Here." He holds out a takeaway coffee cup and a *pain au chocolat* wrapped in a napkin. "Milk, one sugar, right?" He purses his lips and looks from me to the cup in my hand.

My eyes widen in surprise, and I nod. "Perfect. Thank you." Clearly, he watched me this morning as I added my sugar to my cup. I didn't even notice. "Have you eaten already?" I ask, watching as he nods in answer. "And what about the room? Did they have a spare one today?" I ask, biting into my pastry and moaning appreciatively at the taste. It's so fresh; it's still warm.

"Yeah. Once the people check out of it today, they'll give it a clean, and I can get in this afternoon. It's right next door to ours actually." He grins over at me, fiddling with the car keys as we walk across the car park. "I'll pack up my stuff later."

I greedily cram in the last bite of pastry and brush the crumbs from my shirt before I slide into the passenger seat of the car, again watching the show of Theo trying to contort himself in behind the steering wheel. I can't stop smiling.

As he reverses from the space and the car lurches and splutters, he keeps his eyes firmly on the road as he says, "Don't you dare say a word."

"I didn't. I am totally not judging you." Chuckling darkly, I mime zipping my mouth closed.

The village he mentioned isn't far away at all; it only takes a few minutes to get there. As we step out and head over to the wooden hut, I pull the towels from my bag and hand Theo one.

He blinks at it. "Thanks. I didn't even think about a towel. Actually, I didn't bring dry clothes or anything either. Shit." He winces down at his black swim shorts and T-shirt.

Dry clothes? Oops. "Oh crap, I didn't either. Looks like you'll get revenge on the small car after all."

We stop next to a blackboard announcing what's on offer and the prices. My eyes skim over it, and I gasp in excitement as I see one in particular.

"Oh my God. They have a banana boat!" I squeal, jumping on the spot and clapping my hands like a toddler. I've wanted to try one for the last couple of years, ever since Lucas categorically told me that no, I wasn't allowed. I haven't been this excited since the Jonas Brothers announced they were getting back together.

"Yeah? Epic! Let's do that first. What else do you fancy?" Theo asks, pursing his lips as he looks over the board too. "Ooh, want to try waterskiing too? I did it once when I was younger. I pretty much sucked arse at it, but it was fun."

He turns and raises one eyebrow in question, but I shake my head.

"Nah, I'll pass on that and watch you. I'm doing banana boat and maybe the stand-up paddle boarding."

"Excellent choices." He beams down at me and playfully offers me his arm.

Grinning, I slip my arm through his, and we head over to the hut to check availability and book in.

Getting into a wetsuit is harder than they make it look on every surfing movie I've ever seen. There's a lot of wriggling, jumping, and grunting involved. At one point, I'm pulling on it so hard to drag it up my thighs that my hand slips off, and I accidentally slap myself in the face. Imagine trying to squeeze yourself into a pair of skinny jeans that are two sizes too small; that's probably pretty close to the effort this requires. Eventually, I manage to crowbar myself into it and get it half-zipped up the back. I feel like a fat seal and don't dare look in the mirror. After storing my handbag into the locker, I head out of my changing cubicle and see Theo leaning against the wall, waiting for me, our life jackets at his feet.

He certainly does not look like a fat seal.

The soft material clings to his shape, and I see thighs that make my breath catch. I've never been attracted to anyone in a wetsuit before. I silently wonder if Theo has just given me a new fetish. I force my eyes away as I feel my cheeks flood with heat. Hopefully, I can pass it off as sunburn.

There's sand under my toes, and I dig them in, grinning moronically. When the instructor waves us over, Theo passes me my life jacket, and we start to walk over to the jetty to meet up with the three other people who are also going on the banana boat with us. We all say our quick hellos.

Suddenly, there's movement at my back. I feel Theo's fingers brush against my skin for the briefest second before my wetsuit tightens against my chest as I hear a zip being pulled up. I smile gratefully over my shoulder before slipping my arms through my life jacket, doing up the clasps.

The banana boat looks the same as the one I wanted to go on in Italy. Basically, a giant, inflatable yellow-and-red banana gets pulled along by a speedboat. *Fun!*

The three other people take the first spots, leaving Theo and me with the two at the back. My excitement peaks as I half-climb, half-fall onto it. When my foot accidentally goes into the water, I gasp at the shock of cold.

"Holy crap, it's freezing. Am I going to fall in?" I look at Theo for his opinion as I scoot back to the last spot, so he can be the one to sit with his crotch basically touching a stranger's arse, not me.

He chuckles and clambers on in front of me. "Definitely."

"Oh God."

When all five of us are seated, the instructor gives the boat a wave, and it starts up, moving slowly, taking up the slack of the rope attached to our inflatable. We meander along at a leisurely drift until we're at a safe distance from the jetty.

"Ready?" a guy on the speedboat with a megaphone shouts.

We all cheer in response. I giggle excitedly. I hear the engines of the boat roar and feel the snap of the rope as it gives a sharp tug on the inflatable. The banana shifts under my legs as it suddenly jerks forward ... fast ... but my body doesn't go with it. Instead, the speed propels me backwards, and I half-somersault off and crash into the water within one second.

I come up, spluttering and laughing, gasping for breath. The cold water makes my whole body spasm in shock. About thirty feet away, I can hear rambunctious laughter. Turning in a circle, I wipe the water from my eyes and spot my banana buddies a little ways away. The other four managed to hold on, and they're all now practically wetting themselves with laughter. Grinning wildly, I swim over to it.

Theo's eyes are shining, and his grin is so big, he gets little dimples in his cheeks as he shakes his head. "She wasn't readyyyy!" he teases.

I burst out laughing, watching as he scoots back to the last spot and motions for me to sit in front of him this time. He holds down a hand, and I grip his wrist tightly, as he does mine. With my free hand, I reach for the strap, and with Theo's help, I manage to drag myself back onto it in an extremely unladylike fashion. I don't even care. This is my new favourite thing.

As I settle back onto it again, Theo scoots closer to my back. "You have to hold on. Squeeze it with your thighs," he says, reaching around me and playfully pressing on the outside of my knees to show me how to grip it.

"Oh, you have to hold on?" I say sarcastically, rolling my eyes as we both snicker.

"Ready?" the guy on the boat calls again.

Again, we all cheer. This time, I manage to stay on longer.

When our time is up, I'm exhausted. It was much harder work than I'd expected it to be. Sometimes, I managed to stay on, but a lot of times, I flew off—we all did. The corners were the worst, and I swear the driver was doing it on purpose just to watch us all try to clamber back on board again. Wicked bastard.

When we're back on dry land, my legs feel like jelly, and my arms ache from hauling my body weight back on board. At one point, I even regretted putting on those extra ten ice cream pounds Aubrey and I added after my break-up. I'm in reasonably good shape, I go to spin classes and do hot yoga, but I also follow them up with Chinese and a glass of wine. It's all about balance.

I sigh contentedly and smile over at Theo as I attempt to re-bun my wet, snarled hair. I've had the time of my life here today. I've loved every second of it.

He returns my smile and rubs the small of my back. "Are you okay? You did great. I mean, I was only concerned for your life for, like, the whole time," he says dramatically.

I chuckle and slap his life jacket with the back of my hand. "I did do great. My legs are like limp noodles now though. Damn, what a workout. I'm having extra dessert tonight because of that."

"Yeah, I'm shattered." He roughly rubs a hand in his hair, sending water droplets in all angles, some of them hitting me in the face. His hair is a mess after. Weirdly, I sort of like it. "Are you thirsty? We could get a drink." He nods back at the hut, where they serve ice cream and cold drinks.

"Are you kidding? I think I swallowed half the loch. At this point, I'm ninety-five percent water." I unclasp my life jacket, pulling it away from my throat so I can breathe a little easier. I can barely move in it; I feel like the Michelin Man.

"What do you want to do now? I'm too tired for waterskiing. Do you still want to do the paddle boarding, or maybe if you want something more chilled, we could go back to the hotel and lie on the beach for a bit?" He looks somewhat hopeful when he suggests the beach.

"Ooh, the beach sounds good." I nod eagerly. That sounds perfect, and my muscles rejoice at his suggestion.

"And we can get some lunch. It must be time to eat. My stomach is starting to digest itself."

"Probably all the water you swallowed." Theo laughs and casually slings his arm around my shoulders, leading me back to the changing rooms. "We don't have to leave to get our flight home until, like, one thirty on Sunday. If we have time, we can come back and try the paddle boarding in the morning before, if you want."

I grin excitedly and nod along like a bobblehead.

After managing to pry myself from the wetsuit (it's slightly easier to take off, thank God), I use the towel to try and dry some of the water from my bikini before putting my clothes over the top of it. My hair is unsalvageable, so I don't even bother trying. It'll likely get ruined again on the beach anyway. I'll have a nice, long shower tonight and even vow to leave my conditioner on for the recommended two minutes as a treat.

Looking in the mirror, I grin at myself. It's nice to feel so carefree for a change. This feels more like the person I used to be when I was younger—before I had to adult. Theo is so easy to be around, and because I'm not trying to impress him or date him (contrary to Aubrey's numerous text messages of encouragement this morning), I don't have to worry about putting on an act or behaving how people might expect me to. This is the type of freedom I've only ever really had with Aubrey. It's lovely.

Ten

LUCIE

Back at the hotel, we gorge on cheese toasties, crisps, and chocolate chip muffins, and then we head up to our room to pack for the beach. I don't bother to change my clothes. I just grab us fresh towels and my book, stuffing them into my oversize beach bag.

Theo glances at it and smiles. "Why are all your bags always so massive?"

"They make my bum look great." It's a joke, but his eyes drop straight down to it as he purses his lips.

"To be honest, I think it's your bum that makes your bum look great." He turns away and shrugs, picking up a sketchbook and pack of pencils from under his pillow.

My face flushes with pleasure.

He pushes his items into my bag too. Then, he walks to the mini fridge and pulls out cans of Coke and 7UP.

"Do you take your sketchpad everywhere?" I eye it, itching to peek inside. I know his drawings are incredible. After I learned who he was, Aubrey and I looked him up—stalker-style—his socials, his website, his published books.

"Yeah, pretty much. I love drawing. I'm lucky I get paid to do something I'm passionate about."

"That's why I want to be an editor. Imagine being paid to read." I sigh dreamily.

Plucking my sun cream from the side, I head to the bathroom and slather myself up in all the places I can reach. When I come back out, he's doing the same, rubbing oil into his legs. I resist the urge to offer my assistance.

Once ready, we head downstairs to the hotel's private beach on the edge of the water. I can't keep the smile from my face. It's a brilliant, sunny day, and the setting is idyllic. As I step onto the small beach and my toes sink into the sand, I let out a content sigh.

Straight in front of us, closer to the water, Emily and baby Finley are sitting on a blanket in the shade of a beach umbrella. There's no sign of Carys or her dad though. Theo's parents are asleep on a couple of towels off to our left, hats over their faces, one of them snoring rather loudly. On our right, Heather is sitting on a white plastic sun lounger. There are a group of loungers all pulled together with towels on them, indicating they're reserved, and two spare empty ones. Theo nods at them, and we head over, quickly snagging them before anyone else comes along.

"Hey, where's everyone else?" Theo asks Heather, shielding his eyes and looking around.

She motions with her head back towards the hotel. "They've popped to the bar to get drinks."

I lay out our two towels and then shuck my shorts and vest, folding them and stuffing them under the seat. As I turn to Theo, I catch his eyes roving my body; when he sees me looking, he politely averts his gaze and digs in my bag for a can of drink.

"You have any preference?" He holds up the two cans. When I shake my head, he pops open the 7UP and takes a couple of gulps.

Settling down onto the lounger, I look out over the water. The sun is beating down on me, warming my skin.

There's no breeze. It's perfection. I'm conscious of burning though, so my factor fifty will be reapplied studiously every hour and a half. No one wants to be tomato red in wedding photos.

"Theo, would you mind rubbing some sun cream on my back?" I smile sweetly and offer him the bottle.

He nods, chewing on his lip as he arches one eyebrow at me. "Okay. But don't blame me if I get hard. I haven't been laid in a while."

"I haven't either. This will be the closest I've come to sex with anyone other than myself in three months. Make it good, will you?" I joke.

"I'll try my best."

He laughs and slides onto the sun lounger behind me, legs on either side of my body so I'm nestled against his crotch. Hot breath blows across my shoulders, and I feel a shiver of appreciation tickle down my spine.

It started as a joke, but as soon as his hands are on me, rubbing the cream into my skin with firm, confident strokes, my insides turn to goo. It feels so intimate, so sexual, that my stomach clenches. Against my backside, I feel him getting hard, and my eyes widen in shock as my pulse skyrockets.

It's then that I realise, to my horror, that I'm actually growing wet. From him rubbing in sun cream. He has a talent; that's for sure.

His hands on my body are heaven. I never want it to end.

When his magic fingers have worked all the cream into my skin and there's a significant ache of longing between my legs, he leans in, his chest pressing against my now-slick back as his arms rest across the top of his legs. His hands are so teasingly close to touching my thighs, it makes my breath catch.

"So, was it good for you?" he whispers in my ear.

"It was great for me." I giggle.

I turn to look at him over my shoulder as I deliberately press further back into his warm, hard body, needing to feel closer to him. His face is merely a couple of centimetres from mine, his mouth so close that I can almost taste the citrusy drink on his breath as it blows across my lips. Every nerve ending in my body is alive and singing.

He reaches out and smooths a few stray hairs back into my bun, his fingertips teasing and light. He doesn't take his warm, playful eyes from mine; it's like I'm trapped in his gaze as I become aware of every place that our bodies touch. He's doing that eye-fucking thing again as his teeth sink into his bottom lip. It makes my knees weak, so I'm glad I'm already sitting.

His thumb lazily traces across the side of my thigh, and my whole body prickles and braces for impact when his mouth slowly starts descending towards mine. I hold my breath, my heart jackhammering against my ribs. I've never wanted to be kissed more.

"Uncle Theo!"

We both startle just as our mouths were about to connect, and he jerks back, whipping his head to the side as Carys comes bustling out of the hotel, hurtling towards us, everyone else following behind her with drinks in their hands. My mouth drops open, and I blink rapidly in shock because of what almost happened. We were about to kiss.

Theo pushes himself away from me slightly. There's a fumbling against my back as he rearranges himself downstairs, and then he stands and grins at his niece. They hug, and she basically drags him by the hand away from me and over to her mum and Finley.

My heart still hasn't stopped racing.

Heather looks at me over the top of her sunglasses, her eyebrows in her hairline. "Good grief, that was hot. Damn. So much sexual tension. I might have to go for a cold shower." She vigorously fans her face.

I chuckle and nod, puffing out my cheeks and dramatically blowing the air out. "Me too."

Amy plops into the lounger next to me and looks between Heather and me as she sips her Coke. "What did I miss?" She frowns, clearly sensing the charged atmosphere.

Heather opens her mouth to speak, but I shake my head, trying to look innocent. "Nothing."

I settle back and get comfy, pulling my knees up and slipping on my shades. Theo comes back then and starts exchanging some stupid banter with Amy, but I don't hear any of it because at the same time ... he also removes his shirt. It comes off in one smooth, sexy movement, inch by inch, exposing tanned, toned skin, abs, pecs, shoulders, muscles. He even has the V-line thing going on.

Holy moly.

My thighs clench, and my mouth goes dry. My eyes seem to have a mind of their own as they zero in, taking in every damn fine inch of it, committing it to memory. He's beautiful, all tall, sculpted perfection. I want to lean in and press my face against his chest, tickle my nose on that small spattering of hair he has below his belly button, let my tongue follow that V line ...

He stows his shirt with mine and pulls on a black baseball cap before turning to go back to his niece.

Oh, good Lord, the back view! I didn't even know backs could be sexy until now.

Sucking in a ragged breath, I look around to see if anyone else is feeling this ridiculous attraction, but they're all simply going about their day like nothing's happened. No one even glances in the magnificent man's direction. Meanwhile, I feel like I've been hit with a frying pan—right in the vagina.

I can't drag my eyes from him at all. And when he plucks Finley from his sister's arms and starts playfully throwing him up in the air and catching him, a big grin on his face, I feel like every womanly part of me explodes with longing.

"Theo is a professional uncle," Amy jokes at my side.

I startle because I was so in my own little pervert fantasy world that I forgot she was there.

"We could hire him out to kids' parties. He even does magic tricks."

"Shut up. Magic tricks?" I look over to her to see if she's joking. And now, I want to see one.

Amy nods, sipping her drink through the straw. "Yep. He's a right dork." She doesn't say it like it's an insult though; the fondness to her voice is easy to spot. "So, listen, tomorrow morning, we're having girlie time before the wedding. Heather, Emily, and I are getting our nails done and having massages. Want to come? I can tell them at reception that we'll be adding one more."

A wave of affection washes over me that I'm being included. She is adorable. I can see why Theo likes her so much. I hate that I'm a tiny bit jealous of that knowledge now. "Oh, that would be great. Are you sure you don't mind me crashing?" I would love a bit of pampering.

Amy waves her hand, as if it's nothing. "Course not! Theo will likely be busy talking Jared down from the edge tomorrow, doing his best-man duties, so you'll be able to come and hang with us."

"Great, thanks." I grin happily and look back over to recommence Theo Watch.

He's now in the water, up to his knees, bending so Finley's little toes dip in, as he and Carys run around, making loads of noise and splashing each other. All three of them are laughing, and I can't keep the smile from my face.

It's bloody adorable.

After a little while, Emily takes the baby back into the shade, and Theo and Carys start building sand castles, bantering back and forth as they make it bigger and bigger, even adding a moat around the edge, which Carys attempts to fill by going back and forth to the water with a bucket.

Suddenly, she stops and puts her hands on her hips. "Mum, I'm hungry!" she calls, pouting.

Emily sighs and digs in her bag, coming out with a pack of Oreos, which she tosses in Theo's direction.

"Oh, score!" He grins as he catches them.

Carys does a happy jig as he tears them open for her. They both take one. Theo twists the top from his. Then, I watch in absolute fascination as he brings the cream-filled half to his mouth, and his tongue strokes across it.

My whole body tightens, and my skin prickles with sensation. Leaning over, I pick up the magazine Amy's discarded and open it across my knees, pretending to read. Thank heavens my sunglasses are mirrored, so no one can tell what a damn pervert Theo Stone has turned me into.

I can't take my eyes from it. It's probably the sexiest thing I've ever witnessed, and all he's doing is eating a biscuit. Jeez, who knew I was into voyeurism? Not me—that's for sure.

He stops torturing the poor biscuit (and my libido) and finally pops it into his mouth, chewing. I let out the breath I was holding and feel my body relax ... until he reaches for another.

Oh, dear God.

Somewhere in the deep depths of my mind, I know I should probably pull out my phone and record this, maybe play the Diet Coke advert "I Just Wanna Make Love to You" song in the background just to sex it up that little bit more, but I can't move. I can barely breathe.

He repeats it over and over, twisting off the top and licking the cream from each one, and I have never wanted to be a damn foodstuff more in my life. I clench my thighs together, trying to relieve the building ache.

I know it's not supposed to be erotic, but try telling that to my vagina.

I can't tear my eyes from him, his mouth, his tongue, his shoulders, his abs, his skin ...

I continue to slowly turn the magazine pages for show.

A soft kick to my shin makes me jump.

"Stop staring," Amy says.

"I'm not staring. I'm reading!" I splutter indignantly.

"The magazine is upside down, Lucie."

What? Shit!

I look down at it, and she's right.

"Crap. Busted." I giggle and feel my face flame as I flip it the right way up and shake my head.

Amy giggles darkly and holds out her fist to me. Dying inside, I raise my own, and we bump. Girl solidarity. She knows he's hot; she's marrying his body double tomorrow.

The whole time we're on the beach, Theo never stops and relaxes. He's either playing with the kids, talking to someone, or playing Frisbee with Jared and Tim—oh, and did I mention that Jared is shirtless, too, and they look exactly alike? Well, almost exactly alike. When shirtless, they're easy to tell apart. Jared has a large slash of a scar down the centre of his chest that looks so precise, it must be surgical. I can't help but wonder if it's linked to Theo's scar on his leg that he said was from a car accident.

I've given up the charade of the magazine now. Instead, I'm lying on my belly, chin propped on my hands, as I watch the show. It's like free soft porn. If it were on TV, I'd record it, so I could watch it on repeat. With the beautiful loch behind them, the view is spectacular. And I'm not even looking at the scenery.

Amy is watching unashamedly too. It makes me like her even more.

When guests start arriving for the wedding, Amy and Jared, Theo's parents, Emily, Chris, and the kids all disappear inside to say their hellos to people. Heather and Tim head in, too, Heather announcing she wants a nap before she has to start getting ready.

I glance at my phone to check the time. It's only just before five. "Theo, what time is this pre-wedding party starting tonight?"

He walks over and flops down onto the lounger next to mine. "Not until seven thirty. We have loads of time."

I nod and close my eyes again, soaking up more rays, already nervous about this party. It's a little out of my comfort zone—something I would have found amazing when I was younger, but now, not so much.

When I hear pencil scratching on paper, I lazily turn my head to the side to see Theo sitting cross-legged, facing me, his sketchpad balanced on his knee. His baseball cap has been flipped backwards, and his eyes skim over my face before darting back to the paper again, his hand moving rhythmically.

"Are you drawing me?" I ask, shocked.

He nods, chewing on his lip in concentration.

Grinning, I take off my shades, turn a fraction towards him, and lie back suggestively, dipping my chin and throwing my arm across the top of my head, striking *the* pose. "Draw me like one of your French girls," I joke.

He bursts out laughing, and a thrill prickles over my whole body.

eleven

THEO

The two of us spend another three-quarters of an hour down at the beach. It's nice, companionable, easy. I sketch her the whole time. She's a pleasure to draw—her face, the lines of it, the way the shadows fall across her cheekbones, the subtle freckles sprinkled across her nose, the way her long eyelashes fan across her cheek when she closes her eyes, the shape of her chin, and the curve of her neck and shoulders. She's an artist's dream; I could draw her every day and not get tired of it. In fact, I would give anything to paint her. I'm not really a paint kind of guy. I usually prefer pencil or charcoal, and I use inks a lot for work, but for her, I would like to crack out the oils and see what happens.

I enjoy the whole experience way more than I should, spending more time than necessary getting her bikini *just so*. The way she fills the damn thing makes my upper lip sweaty. She's all luscious curves and soft skin. I knew there was an amazing hourglass figure under her sexy pencil skirts and belly tops, but I didn't expect her to unveil Marilyn Monroe curves encased in a sexy black bikini. I had to distract myself for the last couple of hours with anything other than sitting next to her because every time I look at her, she gives me a boner. So inappropriate—and talk about uncomfortable.

I shift in my seat now, making sure my sketchbook covers my arousal, as she sits up and checks the time on her phone.

"Do you think we should head up now?"

Her gaze flicks to me; those brilliant green eyes meet mine, and I lose all train of thought.

She tilts her head, watching me. "Theo? I said, should we head up now? It's gonna take me a while to wash and dry my hair and get ready for the party tonight."

I clear my throat and nod dumbly. "Oh, right. Yeah. Sure. We could order room service, if you'd like."

She grins that cute little smile, luscious, full lips pulling up at the corners as she nods along with my suggestion. "Perfect."

Actually, you might just be, Luce.

She points at my sketchbook. "Can I see? It's not one of those caricature things, where I've got five chins and a hook nose, is it?" She laughs and chews on her lip as her eyes flick up to mine hopefully.

I'm not one to be precious about my drawings, so I hand the sketchbook over to her, watching her reaction. As she looks down at it, she gasps, her eyes widening and her mouth dropping open. Her expression is awed, and pride swells inside me like a balloon.

"Oh, wow, this is amazing." She hasn't taken her eyes from it yet. "I've seen some of your drawings. You know … because of work and stuff." Her cheeks pinken, and she doesn't look at me. "You're incredible. This is beautiful. I mean, I look amazing."

She laughs incredulously as if I somehow falsified her or enhanced how she looks. I didn't. It's pretty much as accurate as I could get it. She *is* amazing.

My ego inflates at her compliment. "Thanks. And you do look amazing." I stand and quickly turn my back, awkwardly adjusting myself so I don't show her just how damn amazing I think she is. Shrugging on my T-shirt, I pick up the towel from the sun lounger and half screw it up, using it as a shield to hide my crotch.

I turn and watch as she sets my sketchbook down, picking up her own clothes from the sand and shaking them out. Every couple of seconds, her eyes dart back to the drawing, and a smile tugs at the corner of her lips as she pulls on her clothes too.

Once we've collected everything, we trek across the warm sand and climb the steps to the hotel.

"Let me go see if that extra room is ready." I nod towards the reception desk as we walk inside.

The lady beams over at me, obviously already knowing what I'm about to enquire about because she brandishes a keycard and seems pleased with herself.

"Ah, great, thanks." Even to my own ears, my voice sounds flat.

I'm disappointed they fixed the room issue so quickly. I liked sharing a room with Lucie—minus the shitty sofa bed with the broken spring, of course. I enjoyed waking up and seeing her, watching her sleep like an absolute creeper, and then drawing her while she was unaware of it. No, that beach sketch wasn't the first I did of her. But in my defence, I couldn't help myself this morning. There was a strip of light bleeding in through the curtains, slowly sliding across her face; the shadows it created were fascinating, and before I knew what I was doing, I was searching my luggage for a pencil and paper, so I could try to re-create it. I'm going to miss the opportunity to do that again tomorrow morning. Not going to lie, she's a lovely thing to wake up to.

"Can we order room service from here, or do we have to phone it in?" I ask the receptionist.

"I can certainly help you with that." She smiles and picks up a couple of menus, sliding them across the desk to us.

Lucie and I scan the menu for a minute or so and then put in our order, asking for it all to be delivered to her room, seeing as I'm going to be in there, packing up my stuff for a while.

Just as we're finishing up, someone shouts my name from the other side of the lobby.

I turn, and my stomach dips when I see who called. So far, I've managed to get away without this interaction, but it appears my luck has finally run out.

"Oh shit, Luce, I need you to pretend we're dating." My fingers curl around her hip, and I pull her to me, pressing our sides together tightly.

"What?"

"Theo, hi!"

Amy's mum and nanna are both waving excitedly as they walk towards us, each clutching a large glass of wine. If the pink on their cheeks is anything to go by, they aren't on their first glass. I gulp as Nanna's eyes make a slow, appreciative sweep of my body. She looks at me like I'm an injured antelope and she's the lioness waiting to take me down.

I lean in closer to Lucie. "Please, please help me out here. Save me from the clutches of a randy, old lady who is actually adorable and hilarious but way too flirty for her own good."

I shoot her the begging face, and she chuckles, her eyes twinkling with humour as she catches on.

"I got your back." She sends me a wink and wraps her arm around my waist as the two women stop in front of us.

I clear my throat and smile. "Hi, ladies. How are you both? Long time, no see!" I lean in and give them each a kiss on their cheek, trying not to wince as Peggy, Amy's nanna, turns her head at the last second, so her mouth connects with the corner of mine.

"Hi, Theo. You're looking nice and relaxed. Did you catch some sun?" Amy's mum asks, smiling affectionately.

I nod and brush a finger over my cheek. "Probably. We've been on the beach." I pull Lucie closer to me and slide my arm up from her back to drape over her shoulders to make it glaringly obvious that we're together. "Luce, this is Amy's mum and nanna. Anne and Peggy." I motion to them both in turn. "Ladies, this is my date, Lucie."

"Hi. It's so lovely to meet you," Lucie greets warmly, raising her hand and slipping it into my one that rests casually over her shoulder.

Nanna Peggy catches the small, possessive move, and I see disappointment flash in her eyes.

I grin happily. "So, where have you two been hiding all day? I've been keeping my eye out for you both." That's not a lie. I was keeping watch, so I could either run in the other direction or use Lucie as a human shield.

Peggy sets her hand on my forearm and squeezes gently. "Oh, Jared booked us on this amazing couples spa day as a treat! It was wonderful. We've been massaged, steamed, and mud-wrapped. Then, we drank Prosecco in an aromatherapy spa bath ... well, until they confiscated it anyway—"

"We weren't supposed to drink in there, of course. That's why they took it away." Anne, Amy's mum, rolls her eyes and motions with her head towards her own mother, clearly indicating who is to blame.

Peggy leans in closer, her eyes twinkling mischievously as she talks directly to Lucie, "I also had a Brazilian."

I look at my feet and try not to think about it or show my horror at the thought of her eighty-something-year-old lady bits being waxed.

"A Brazilian and then you went in a spa bath? Won't you get, like"—Lucie scrunches her nose and waves her hand at her crotch—"a rash or some sort of reaction?"

Peggy dismissively waves her hand and looks at her over the top of her glass. "Oh no, dear, not a wax. My masseuse was Brazilian. Antonio he was called." She fans her face and sends Lucie a conspiratorial wink. "Twenty-four. Hands like the devil. Bum like a—"

"Mum! Will you behave?!" Anne cuts her off.

"Oh my God. You're the best!" Lucie bursts out laughing. It's loud and free, and I can't help but laugh along with her even though I'm dying inside.

Anne clicks her tongue. "Don't encourage her."

I smile at the exchange; Lucie is still shaking with laughter under my arm.

"Lucie and I should probably get going. We just ordered room service, so don't want to miss it. I'll see you both at the party in a bit. Can't wait to see your outfits!" I smile sweetly, sending them a wave as I guide Lucie away.

"You'll save me a dance tomorrow night at the wedding, Theo?" Peggy calls as we walk away.

I turn back and nod. "Of course. I think it's my duty as best man to dance with both of you actually."

Lucie sets her free hand on my stomach, and the warmth of it seeps into my skin through my T-shirt. "That's if I let him go, of course. I might have to fight you a little bit." Lucie playfully raises her eyebrows at Peggy, and I send her a grateful smile.

Anne chuckles. "Oh, you'd likely lose against my mum."

"I think you're probably right," Lucie agrees good-naturedly. Her smile is radiant.

"See you in a bit." I send them both a wink. I know I'm not helping myself, but I genuinely do really like them both; they're great.

When we step into the lift and the doors close, I huff out a breath and look at the ceiling. "Thanks, Luce. I owe you."

She grins and steps out from under my arm. I hate that I miss the contact already.

"You owe me big. Was she one of the reasons why you needed a date so desperately that you were willing to bring along a virtual stranger under offer of an all-inclusive weekend bender?"

"One of them, yes." No point in lying.

She chuckles, and I pull out my phone.

"I'm gonna call Tim. I need to pick up my outfit for tonight. It wouldn't fit in a suitcase, so they offered to bring it with them, seeing as he and Heather drove up yesterday instead of flying."

Lucie nods and chews on her nail as I quickly talk to Tim and arrange to make a quick stop at their door to pick up my excess luggage.

By the time we get to our room, me carrying my box and grinning like a fool, the waiter is literally just coming out of the lift with our ordered food.

Lucie plops on the bed, digging into her pizza, so I sit on the opposite side and take a large bite from my wrap.

"So, are all the wedding guests going to be at this party tonight? Is this in place of a hen and stag night?"

I shake my head. "No, we had those last weekend. I think this is more like a pre-wedding get-together for everyone else, a kind of thank-you for travelling so far. Only close family and friends arrived on Thursday, but tonight, everyone else should be here."

"How many people are coming to the wedding?"

I watch as Lucie gets a string of cheese stuck to her chin, and she sheepishly pulls it off. It's too cute. "Um, I think Jared said there are about eighty people in total. Friends, family, work colleagues of both Jared's and Amy's. Though mostly, the work friends are Amy's. Not many people like Jared at his work, apparently."

Lucie frowns. "Why not? He seems so lovely."

"No idea." That's a lie. I *do* have an idea.

Anyone who has ever tried to plan anything near Jared and has had him take over everything knows the reason. He's basically an evil dictator in disguise, a stickler for details. I'd hate to work for him; in fact, if he were my boss, I'd secretly put laxatives in his morning coffee and rub his favourite pen across my nutsack at every given opportunity. His superiors probably love him though; he's the type of dependable, proactive, hardworking perfectionist who bosses jizz their pants over.

"Poor Jared." Lucie pouts and frowns.

"He'll get over it. He likely gives exactly zero shits what they think of him."

She nods, picking at her pizza. "You know, when you texted me the itinerary for the weekend, I was wondering why on earth someone would choose a fancy-dress theme for a party. But now that I've met Amy, I get it. It makes total sense."

I grin and nod. "Right?"

Lucie's lips purse as she looks up at me. "She's so great. I can see why you like her."

My breath catches, and I clear my throat awkwardly. "Er … yeah."

"So, what are you going as tonight?" She inquisitively eyes my cardboard box. "Can I see?"

I nod and wipe my fingers, pushing my empty plate onto the side as I pull the box closer to me and peel off the tape. Lucie leans over, and we both peer in at the vibrant green, blue, and red inside the box. When she doesn't get it, I stand and pull the outfit from the box, holding it up against my body.

As she realises what it is, she bursts out laughing. "Oh my God, that's bloody brilliant! I love it."

I look down at the outfit and grin. It took me forever to choose what I wanted. After six weekends of trudging around all the cosplay shops I could find within driving distance (and several failed online orders that were subpar), I finally found the perfect outfit. It's Mario riding Yoshi. The top half of my body is Mario's red T-shirt and blue dungarees. There are fake padded Mario legs that start at my hips. Then, around my middle, there is a large stuffed Yoshi head and body, complete with big, wide eyes and tiny, padded arms. Mario's fake legs hang over Yoshi's sides, so it looks like he's riding him. My legs are green and are supposed to be Yoshi's. I even have Mario's hat and a fake moustache to complete the outfit. It's pretty damn genius, even if I do say so myself.

Folding it up carefully, I put it back in the box and cock my head. "Let's see yours. Who are you going as?"

"Uh, no, you can have a surprise."

I shrug in acceptance. I like surprises. I can wait. Silently, I wish we'd conferred and gone as a couple, maybe Bonnie and Clyde, or Han Solo and Leia; that would have been amazing.

"Fair enough. Were you running around, frantic to find a hire shop after I texted you Monday night with the itinerary?" I wince apologetically.

I definitely sprang it on her and purposefully didn't tell her until after she agreed and I booked her flight. Less chance of back-outs then!

She shakes her head. "Actually, no. Surprisingly, I already had a costume. For my twenty-first birthday, I had a girls' night, fancy-dress-themed bar crawl. I only wore it the once and then leant it to my best friend, Aubrey, for her work's Halloween party one year. She just kept it at her place after that because I had no use for it. Luckily, it was hanging in the back of her wardrobe. I just hope it still fits." She winces and looks down at her body. "Maybe I should have tried it on before bringing it. I've, um, filled out a little since I was twenty-one. That's probably the politest way of saying that my tits and arse are bigger now."

At the casual mention of them, I fight with everything in me not to let my eyes drop down to said tits and arse. "And likely better …"

She chuckles and shrugs one shoulder. "Well, you're a man, so obviously, you think that. All men like a bit of T and A."

"Solid fact." I nod in agreement and hold up a hand for a high five.

Her blush is adorable as she slaps her palm against mine. "I should really start getting ready. Do you need help packing up your stuff? If not, I'm going to hop in the shower." She stands and scrunches up her napkin, pushing her plate onto the side as she looks at me hopefully.

"You go in the shower. I'll pack up and then head next door to my room. I'll call back for you at seven thirty, and we'll go downstairs to the function room."

She nods and throws me a smile as she heads into the bathroom, locking the door behind her.

It takes me less than a couple of minutes to gather my stuff and leave her in peace. Once in my room next door, I flop on the bed and flick on the TV. There's still a little over an hour left to go before we're due to meet up. It won't take me long to get ready. I'm going to forgo the shave again—screw it, stubble is on trend right now. I'll fix it tomorrow before the wedding. Basically, just a shower and change of clothes—twenty minutes, tops.

Sometimes, I love being a man.

My outfit is epic. I'm grinning like a moron as I look at myself in the full-length mirror. It was worth the hours of searching to find the perfect costume. Mine is undoubtedly going to be the best costume of the night. I might even get a prize. Hopefully, Amy's doing prizes.

At precisely seven thirty, I'm so excited to see what Lucie's wearing that I practically skip to her door and knock.

"Theo, I'm not quite ready!" she calls from inside. "I don't want to make you late to the party. Shall I meet you down there in a few minutes?"

I frown at the door. "Is everything okay?"

"Yeah. It's just taking me longer than I thought to get ready. I'm sorry. I won't be long though. You go and get us a round in, and I'll see you in a bit."

I step closer to the door in case people can hear me and close my eyes. "Luce, you're not going to stand me up, are you? The deal we made was for the Friday night party and the wedding …" I hold my breath and wait.

Screw the deal. I just want to spend some more time with her. If she doesn't come tonight, I'll be gutted. The more time I spend with her, the more I like her.

I hear her laugh before she calls back, "I remember the deal, Theo. I'll be there in a few, I promise. I'm just finishing up with my hair. I'm almost done. Ten minutes, tops. I'll see you down there."

Happier now after her reassurances, I smile and step back, brushing a piece of lint from Yoshi's stuffed head. "Okay. See you in a bit then."

As I'm about to step into the lift, I remember I didn't pick up my phone. I left it on charge in my room. I quickly head back to get it, spending an extra couple of minutes to add some more glue to doubly secure my fake moustache to avoid any embarrassing costume mishaps.

The hallway is deserted as I walk down it and get into the lift—the lobby isn't though. As I step out of the lift in my costume, people stop and stare, smiling, laughing, and pointing me out to their friends. I grin proudly when a stroppy-looking teenager lifts his head from his phone and takes a picture of me. The receptionist's eyes follow my every move, her mouth hanging open. Clearly, I'm the best dressed so far. My chest puffs out smugly.

The function room for the party is at the back of the hotel. When I step inside, I'm a quarter of the way across the room before I notice that everyone is in dark suits, shirts and ties, and nice dresses.

Perplexed, I look around at a few faces to check I'm in the correct party. Maybe I've unwittingly wandered into someone else's celebration instead. But nope, there's my mother, gawping at me with her hand covering her mouth, and there's Aunt Theresa, choking on her drink.

I spot Jared and Amy with a group of our mutual friends, all standing around, talking. Jared is in one of his nice suits; I know it well, as I've borrowed it enough times. Amy is in a long, sparkly black dress, her hair pulled back into an elegant twist.

What the hell are they all dressed as? Is this some joint *Men in Black* effort or something? If so, their effort is piss poor. I'm definitely getting a prize.

As one, the crowd falls quiet, and then the tittering and whispering begin as people stare at me with wide eyes while I swan over to my brother.

When I get to him, Jared is openly gaping at me, his mouth and eyes wide. Amy is grinning like a madwoman. Heather is just slow-blinking at me. Tim is snickering and biting his knuckle to stifle it.

Jared reaches out and puts his hand on my shoulder, his mouth now pulling up into a massive smile as he lets out a little snort-laugh. "What the hell are you dressed as? Theo! I said dress fancy, not fancy-dress!"

Realisation hits me like a bucket of ice water.

Oh Christ, I've fucked up.

Suddenly, people's attention moves from me to the door. The shocked gasps and whispers double. My heart sinks, and I turn just as Lucie is walking in the door. Her eyes widen and then narrow accusingly as they zero in on me. The muscle in her jaw twitches, and her hands clench into fists at her sides.

"I am so dead," I groan.

Twelve

THEO

I raise my hand and wave. I actually wave at her—you know, just in case she can't see the fucking green dinosaur with the fat little Italian plumber perched on top of it among the sea of posh frocks and suits. In my defence, I'm not thinking straight. A man can only think with one of his heads at a time, and right now, seeing her in her outfit, the head below my belt is in charge, not the one attached to my neck.

Luciella Gordio looks smoking hot.

I gulp and stare.

She's dressed as Wonder Woman—not the new, modern one, but the old classic '70s TV show one. Her strapless, fitted red top hugs and clings to every curve and has the gold Wonder Woman logo emblazoned across her breasts; the blue skirt with white stars on is short, just kissing the tops of her shapely thighs. It makes my heart stutter and my balls clench. She even has the little gold Lasso of Truth tied to her hip along with knee-high red-and-white boots, wide gold cuff bracelets at her wrists, and the gold tiara. Her hair is blown out big, like the actress on the show I used to watch reruns of with my dad when I was a kid; it flows down around her shoulders and back. There's so much skin, so many curves, so much ... bombshell ... that I'm worried I might pass out due to lack of blood because it *all* seems to have flown straight down south. She looks like Comic Con gone wild. It's perfection.

I've never been more attracted to anyone—*ever*. My dick has gone from sleeping to full salute so fast that I'm surprised it's not cut Yoshi's head clean off.

Scratch what I said earlier—*she* should win the best-dressed prize. She wins *all* the damn prizes for this outfit.

Hell, Luce, here, take everything I own. Take my heart, take my body. You win; it's yours. They think it's all over; it is now ...

She's an actual Leonardo DiCaprio in *Wolf of Wall Street* fist bite in this outfit.

Behind me, Tim loses the battle against stifling his laughter, and I shift on my feet, knowing this is going to be bad.

I've fucked up spectacularly here and obviously heard what I wanted to hear when Jared said "dress fancy." What is wrong with me?

Lucie stalks towards me, her strides measured and calculated, her hands still in fists. She hasn't taken her eyes off me and ignores everyone who ogles her as she walks past. I'm not sure she's even breathing. She looks like she could spew fire. I'm actually concerned for my life.

Fuck. I'm in trouble here.

"Theo, close your mouth," Jared whispers helpfully from my side. But I note that he takes a step away from me, obviously clearing the blast zone in case shit goes down.

I snap my mouth shut and gulp just as Lucie stops in front of me. I can't help but notice that she looks even better up close. Her make-up is flawless, the skin of her shoulders is creamy and smooth, and her figure is all hourglass curves. I want every inch of it wrapped around me like a boa constrictor—I wouldn't even care if she crushed me to death at the same time. At the moment, I can't think of any way I'd rather go.

Her eyes finally leave my face and flick around the group I'm standing with before coming back to me again. I flinch at the hardness to them. What confuses me is the polite, tight smile on her mouth.

"So, it's obviously not a fancy-dress party like I was led to believe." It's a statement, not a question.

I wince apologetically. "I'm sorry. Christ, I'm *so* sorry. Jared apparently said dress fancy, and I heard fancy dress and ... shit. This is all my fault. I'm sorry." I awkwardly shuffle on my feet, hating that her eyes seem to be a little glazed.

Is she about to cry? Oh, man, that hurts.

Amy and Heather step forward as one and crowd her, Amy's arm supportively going around her waist.

Heather shakes her head, and her lips pull down at the corners. "Oh, Lucie, I'm mortified for you. Oh my God, I can't believe this has happened. Theo!" She turns to glare at me, eyes narrowing accusingly as she punches me in the shoulder so hard that I'll likely wake with a bruise in the morning. I can't even blame her.

Amy reaches up and takes hold of Lucie's shoulders, stepping closer to her. "You look absolute fire right now. Just incredible. So bloody hot. Don't even worry about this. You're stunning. Own it, girl. You're killing it." She gives her a little shake and firmly nods her head. "Seeing you in this, I'm actually jealous. I wish this *were* a bloody fancy-dress party." She turns to Jared and pouts, a frown lining her forehead. "We should have had a theme for tonight. What a missed opportunity."

Lucie's smile doesn't change; it's polite and obviously fake. It's the smile Dolores Umbridge gives when she makes people write with the blood pen. She's plotting my murder behind that smile.

The people around us are still staring, enjoying the spectacle. They probably think we're the entertainment for the evening. As I look around, I notice that almost every male guest at the party is lustfully staring at Lucie—either outright or discreetly so as not to get caught by their significant others. People laughed at my costume, but they're lusting after hers. I hate it. Noah, one of my best friends, is full-on checking her out, his eyes predatory as his gaze rakes over her body so slowly that I want to karate-chop him in the fucking throat. I can almost see the cogs in his head turning. He wants to make a move. A zing of jealousy and possessiveness hits me and makes my back straighten. I've not felt passionate like this in a long time. I hate them all for looking at her and thinking they have a chance.

I shoot Noah a glare and subtly shake my head, warning him off, letting him know she's with me.

Lucie awkwardly clears her throat. "I could use a drink right now. Did you get that round in, Theo?" she asks as she looks at my empty hands.

I shake my head and drag my attention back to her. "I didn't have time. I only got here a minute or so before you did."

The muscle in her jaw twitches again.

Behind her, someone bustles through the crowd, pushing horny guys out of the way who have converged, trying to get a better look at Lucie's arse. (I must admit, I want to see her from behind too.) It's Amy's nanna. Her eyes are wide and fixed on Lucie as she stops at her side and obviously looks her up and down, wrinkly lips pursed in consideration.

When she's finished her examination, she clicks her tongue. "Well, I'm glad I decided last minute not to wear my Wonder Woman outfit; that would have been embarrassing if we'd both worn the same thing." She shoots Lucie a wink, and it breaks the hard, bleak look in her eye.

Lucie erupts into laughter, and I feel my muscles loosen slightly.

Peggy loops her arm through Lucie's. "Don't you dare even think about changing. You look marvellous! Jeez, if I had a body like yours, I'd be walking around in spandex all day, every day."

A blush covers Lucie's cheeks, and somehow, it makes her look even better.

"Thank you, Peggy. Can I keep you? Hire you to follow me around and shower me with praise all day?" Lucie jokes, shifting on her feet.

Amy nods in agreement. "Oh, please say you're not changing. Please leave them on. You guys both look amazing! I love them! Please?" She beams a smile over at me, and I can see the happiness twinkle in her eyes as she looks back at Lucie hopefully.

I don't want Lucie to change either. I want her to wear this outfit for the rest of her life and never leave my side.

Lucie cringes, but when Amy begs her some more, she finally nods in agreement.

I step closer, looking into Lucie's eyes. I don't reach out and touch her like I'm desperate to; she's liable to break my fingers or something. "Luce, I'm so sorry. I messed up. I'm sorry."

"It's fine."

"Really?"

Her mouth is saying fine, but her eyes are saying, *Die in a fiery wreck …*

"Sure. It's fine; don't worry." She waves a dismissive hand. "I'm going to get that drink. Are you staying here, or do you want to come with me?" One of her eyebrows rises in question. She sets a hand on her hip, the movement making her skirt rise half an inch.

I still can't really think straight. She looks so hot; it's like the outfit has melted my brain.

I blink dumbly. "Um …"

She laughs quietly, and the sound makes my body relax a fraction. Maybe I'm not going to die tonight after all. "It's not a trick question, Theo. You can do whatever you want."

Behind her, Jared's eyes widen, and his back stiffens. He shakes his head and is mouthing something at me. I frown and give an imperceptible tilt of the head to let him know I don't understand.

He mouths it again. It looks like … *Tits a slap*?

What? Is he high? Slap her tits? Like that's not going to inflame the already-volatile situation.

Lucie raises her chin and turns to walk off, thankfully rendering my reply unnecessary because I have no clue what's happening right now. She's muttering something in Italian under her breath. My eyes drop down to her arse, and I grunt in appreciation. The damn thing sways from side to side like a pendulum as she walks away, the short skirt swishing around it teasingly. It's exquisite.

As soon as Lucie is out of earshot, Jared steps to my side and grips my elbow, squeezing tightly. "Oh Jesus, you gotta fix this quick. She's seething mad." He almost looks afraid now too.

I shake off his hold because his fingers are digging in too tight. My eyes are still glued to Lucie. "She said it was fine."

Jared makes a scoff in the back of his throat and shakes his head. "Word to the wise: the words *it's fine* or *don't worry* coming out of a woman's mouth should terrify you to the very core. She said both of those. And the whole *do what you want* thing? You do not ever do what you want. That's a trap."

Oh, trap, not slap! That's what he was mouthing. It's a trap. That makes more sense.

Tim nods and steps to my other side. "Get over there and grovel, or she'll be using your nutsack for a handbag before the night is over."

Jared winces. "You know I speak Italian. You don't even want to know the translation of what she said as she walked off. Let's just say, it has something to do with your arse and a cactus." He laughs and shoves me towards her so hard that I almost stumble.

As I stop at her side next to the bar, she doesn't even turn to look at me as she speaks, "I can't believe this. I really can't believe I'm standing in a bar, surrounded by people glammed up in cocktail dresses, and I'm wearing a Wonder Woman outfit that's two sizes too small. Why does this crap always happen to me? Honestly, I'm almost not even shocked." Her shoulders slump, and she covers her face with her hands.

I lean against the bar next to her. "Stuff like this happens to me too. I usually just roll with it." I wince, feeling awful. "I'm so sorry. I'm an idiot. I didn't do this on purpose, I promise."

"I know you didn't." She huffs a breath and turns to face me, her eyes raking down my body, and I notice the tiny twitch to the corners of her mouth. "At least you actually look pretty good," she says grudgingly.

I raise one eyebrow. "You look better than pretty good." That's the truth. "You look amazing. I'm almost not even sorry I misunderstood the dress code. Seeing you in this is *so* worth the castration you're liable to do to me because of this. You look phenomenal."

She chews on her lip, her eyes meeting mine, and I want to do a celebratory jig when I see the hardness beginning to fade from them. She forgives me a little. "Yeah?"

I nod and step closer—as close as the Yoshi head sticking out a foot and a half in front of me will allow. "Definitely. Your costume is sick; your body is killer. You're positively lethal tonight, Luce."

She rolls her eyes, but a smile tugs at the corners of her mouth now. "Keep the compliments coming," she tells me, and as the barman stops in front of her, his eyes firmly fixed on the swell of cleavage spilling over the top of her sweetheart neckline, she holds up two fingers and tells him, "And keep the vodka shots coming. Two, please."

I chuckle and lean in closer, so no one else can hear me. "Thank heavens I'm not wearing spandex, too, because my approval of your outfit would be clear for all to see." I motion down to Yoshi. "His head is full of wood."

She bursts out laughing and slaps my chest with her hand, but it's playful and not vicious, so I take it as encouragement and keep going.

"Luce, you look like something out of my Comic Con fantasies. I'm literally—" I make the mind-blown hands next to my head with an explosion sound effect.

Her eyelashes flutter closed as she chews on her lip, a blush blooming on her cheeks. "You're kind of good for my ego."

Feeling brave, I reach out and touch the material of her skirt; it's soft satin between my fingers. A groan escapes my lips. "This is the stuff wet dreams are made of."

Lucie laughs and rolls her eyes, picking up one of the shots as the barman sets it down in front of her. She turns back to me and purses her lips. "Okay, rules. You do not leave my side the whole night. If I'm staying in costume, so are you. And let's get absolutely rat-arsed to mollify this embarrassment."

I nod in approval and signal the barman for two more shots as I pick up mine. "Solid plan. Here's to a good night. Cheers." I chink my glass against hers, and we grin before knocking them back.

Thirteen

LUCIE

As I slowly drift into consciousness, the first thing I notice is the ferocious pounding in my head. It's like someone is savagely jackhammering the inside of my skull. I wince and reach up, raking a hand over my face. As I move, a wave of nausea makes my stomach roll. My mouth is so dry, my tongue feels like sandpaper. And … what the hell have I been eating? Or is that the flavour of morning-after vodka regret? It tastes like a sewer. I feel like death warmed up. Positively awful.

Rhythmic, heavy breathing from my right draws my attention, and I turn my head, confronted by Theo's gorgeous face. He's lying on his front, arms bent and tucked under his head, face all peaceful and childlike. He looks adorable while he sleeps.

"Aww, cute." I get the weird urge to reach out and jokingly boop the tip of his nose with my finger. I smile to myself and let my eyes rake over his features, drinking him in.

Wait … what the …

I gasp as I realise this isn't right.
Theo is in my room ... in my bed?

I sit up quickly, clutching the thin sheets in my fists. I move so fast, another wave of nausea squeezes my stomach. I fight the urge to vomit. It's then that I catch sight of my bare breasts.

Oh God, am I ...

Closing my eyes, I count to five and hope I'm still dreaming this. But when I open them and carefully lift the sheets to peek underneath, I know I'm not dreaming.

I'm naked. Butt naked, apart from the fact that I'm still wearing the knee-high red plastic Wonder Woman boots from last night.

Embarrassed heat floods my face, and I glance back over at Theo. He's still sleeping peacefully. Around his neck, a flash of gold material catches my attention. I lean in closer for a better look and realise it's my Wonder Woman elasticated crown; it sits around his neck like a gaudy necklace. There's more gold at his wrists; he's wearing the gold bracelet cuffs from my costume too.

What is happening?

I gulp, and my eyes trace across his naked back, noticing flawless skin encasing muscles; he's broad, tanned, perfect. My eyes rake further down, following the line of his spine right down to where the sheets bunch at the small of his back.

I have to know. *Is he naked too?* I carefully lift the sheets—and there's his butt.

My eyes widen. It's a damn cute butt, all firm and tight. You could bounce a penny off the thing; it's so toned. He must squat.

Wait, this is no time for distractions, Lucie.

I'm beginning to freak out. I can feel the panic and mortification taking over. We're both naked. That means ...

But no, wouldn't I remember if we had sex?

As I press my knees together, the skin at the inside of my thighs rubs and burns. Frowning, I lift the sheet again and look down. My face flushes when I see red chaffing on the insides of my thighs. *Dear Lord.* I know instantly what it's from. Moving my leg to the side to get a better look, I spot something black and furry on my skin. My brain instantly fires the word *spider* at me. Squealing, I slap at it blindly. Two seconds later, after it sticks itself to my finger, I realise what it is ... Theo's Mario moustache.

My fraught squealing and thrashing wakes Theo.

He groans loudly and rolls to his back, throwing an arm over his eyes. "Ugh, I'm never drinking again!" he moans. "I feel like a microwaved turd."

I gulp and decide to confront this head-on. We don't have much choice in the matter. "Theo, did we ... Theo!" I shake his shoulder to get his attention, as it appears he's already drifted off again.

He licks his lips and finally moves his arm, turning his head to face me with a sullen grunt. He squints and blinks a couple of times, as if he has no idea who I am, and then a smile of recognition tugs at the corners of his mouth. "Hey." He sits up awkwardly, holding his head, letting out a long, pain-filled groan. "Am I naked?" He lifts the sheet, and I get an eyeful of sculpted chest, and—oh my God, he has a semi. An impressive semi too.

I hate the flush of excitement that pulses through me.

I nod and wince. "I'm naked too. Apart from my boots."

He chuckles and rubs his eyes with his fists. "Kinky."

"I think we might have done it." I shift my body, and as soon as I do, I know for a fact that we screwed last night. I can feel the slight ache between my legs when I move. It's been a while; I'm definitely out of practice, and I can feel the difference.

"Did we?" Theo winces as he speaks, rubbing at his temples. "Ugh, I need to pee. I'll be right back."

He swings his legs out of bed, and I see a glimpse of glorious arse crack as he manoeuvres and reaches for the tartan throw from the bottom of the bed, wrapping it around his waist like a kilt as he stands up.

"Eww! What the hell?" Suddenly, he comically hops on one leg, grimacing as he reaches down and peels something from the bottom of his foot. "Well, I guess that answers that question." He looks back at me helplessly as he holds up what he stood on.

A used condom.

Oh God. I gulp. "At least we were safe." That's more than I dared to hope for. Lucky one of us had the forethought to use protection.

He peers at it. "Looks like I got my happy ending. Not sure about you though."

I close my eyes and feel my face flush. "I have beard burn on the insides of my thighs. I'm pretty sure I got mine too."

"Oh, nice." He laughs and reaches over, holding up his hand for a high five.

I raise one eyebrow. "Now is not a high-five moment, Theo."

He nods, his hand dropping to his side, though his grin is broad, and he's obviously proud of himself. "You're right; that would be totally inappropriate." His eyes move to the Wonder Woman wristbands he's wearing, and he reaches for the crown that's tight around his neck like a choker. "What the hell happened? Do you remember anything at all?" He pulls off the crown and frowns at it, and then he tosses it onto the sideboard.

I shake my head, racking my brain. I think back to the last thing I remember: the party, the drinking, there was dancing and singing and stumbling and lots of laughing.

"Shit, I gotta pee so bad." He darts around the corner and goes into the bathroom.

The sound of a steady stream of urine hitting the water permeates the air, as he's not bothered to close the door. I'm too hungover to care.

"Jeez, it's a mess in here. Whatever we did, we definitely had some fun in here. Either that or you're the messiest chick alive!" he calls from the bathroom.

Mortified, I quickly climb from the bed and grab the fluffy hotel robe from the hook on the wall, shrugging it on and tying the belt at the waist so he doesn't see me naked. Which is ridiculous, considering, apparently, we've already been intimate, and I have his stubble rash on my cooch.

My head gives another throb, so I push my glasses on and then dig in my toiletries bag to find the sweetest treasure a hungover person can be confronted with—paracetamol. Snagging a bottle of water from the fridge, I gulp down half and swallow two pills before setting another bottle and two more pills on the side for Theo.

"Your phone was on the side in there. It's dead. I'll stick it on charge for you," he says as he comes back into the room and walks around the bed to the bedside cabinet, where my charger is. He picks it up and plugs it in for me before heading back to the dresser and flicking on the kettle.

"Thanks. Water and tablets on there for you." I nod at it.

He smiles gratefully. "Sweet. Ta."

I slump onto the edge of the bed and frown down at my boots. I barely have the energy to attempt it, but my feet are sweating in the plastic, so they need to come off. As I grip the foot of one and pull, Theo chugs his water and pills. I growl in frustration and try the other foot. The damn things are welded on. I might have to call down to reception and ask for them to send up some scissors to cut them off.

Theo chuckles and walks over, dropping to his knees in front of me. He's still wrapped in just the throw, so his sculpted chest is on full display. My fingers itch to reach out and touch it.

My body heats up. I get a little flashback of him on his knees, smiling up at me devilishly, his eyes sparkling with lust. My core clenches, and the skin at the nape of my neck prickles.

"Let me have a go." He takes hold of my calf and lifts one leg.

When his fingers curl around the back of my knee, I get another flashback—this one of his hands caressing my skin, our bodies pressing together, the weight of him on top of me, his eyes meeting mine as his breath blows across my face.

I blink and have to look away. It's so intimate and hot that it makes my body ache. I can't remember much, but I can sort of remember what those lips feel like against mine, what his teeth feel like scraping against my skin. An involuntary shiver of lust tickles down my spine as he finally works one boot loose and then starts on the other.

"There you go, miss." He smiles up at me as the second boot slides off my foot. It's a cute smile, not a smirk or a gloat because we did the nasty last night.

"Thanks." I smile back weakly and then flop back onto the bed, staring up at the ceiling, trying to breathe through my nausea.

The shots last night were a mistake. The sex was also a mistake, though because I can't remember it, I can't bring myself to feel too bad about it.

Theo makes us coffee while I lie there and watch the muscles in his back and shoulders contract and expand whenever he moves. It's hot. The smell of coffee just adds to said hotness.

Needing to know the time because I agreed yesterday to meet the girls for our little pre-wedding pamper session at ten thirty, I drag myself up the bed and prop up against the headboard as I reach for my phone. There's enough power in it now to turn it on, so I blink at my screen, waiting for my eyes to focus.

It's just after nine. Hopefully, I'll feel more alive by the time I have to meet them.

A pop-up tells me the internal storage of my phone is full, and my cloud has stopped syncing. I frown, confused.

As the phone connects to the hotel Wi-Fi, notifications start arriving one after the other: Instagram, Twitter, text messages, WhatsApp. My phone goes crazy in my hand, and I quickly switch it to silent before it makes my head explode.

"Someone's popular," Theo jokes, flopping down next to me and pinching the bridge of his nose with his thumb and forefinger.

I click on the Instagram notifications first because I know the messages will all be from Aubrey, and I'm not ready to deal with her level of intensity yet. Theo has tagged me in numerous posts.

I frown at my screen and click on the first one. "You've tagged me in videos."

"What?" He leans in, and we both watch the screen.

It's a TikTok video of us attempting some funny voice-over, mime routine. It's terrible, and by the end, we're both just laughing. The next is worse; we're attempting the Carole Baskin dance together. I click them one after the other. They're stupid and ridiculous and yet bloody hilarious. Some of them are in the function room; you can see the party going on around us, people watching us like we're crazy. Some of them are outside on the patio with the loch behind. The last one is us in the lobby. We're clearly hammered but having a blast.

I chuckle and shake my head. The comments are people basically adding laughing/crying faces and calling us idiots. There are lots of comments about how fit I am, how amazing we look together, how stellar our outfits are, lots of people asking Theo if I'm his new girlfriend.

"Do you even remember making these?" I ask Theo, watching as he sips his coffee.

He rubs at his forehead, shrugging one shoulder. "Sort of. Maybe. Down in the bar, we were fooling around, I think." He frowns as if unsure, so it must have been towards the end of the night.

I nod along and then open my Photos app, intending to delete them. They've obviously clogged up my memory. A video that's over three hours long is the last thing I recorded.

I frown down at it. "Ugh, what's this one?"

I open it and click play.

It's Theo and me in the bathroom in my room. I can tell it's mine because my make-up bag and toothbrush are on the side next to the sink. We're laughing hysterically. Theo is holding my phone, and he's filming us in the mirror. We're both still in our costumes. We look a little worse for wear—sweaty, mussed up, and uncoordinated.

"Oh God, this one's gonna be epic," I hear myself say from my phone.

I wince because hearing yourself on video is painful. I hope I don't sound that screechy in real life.

"I bet we go viral." That's Theo. "You ready?"

There's more giggling.

"Let's do this."

In the video, I fiddle with Theo's phone that sits on the counter, and a song starts up: "Flip the Switch" by Drake. I gasp as I realise what we're doing—the Flip the Switch challenge. I actually can't wait to see the results. Now, I know why Theo is wearing my wristbands and tiara—we swapped clothes! I'm pretty sure we're doing it wrong though. We're not even in the TikTok app. This is just a normal video. Inebriated Lucie and Theo are clearly idiots.

In the video, I start dancing to the beat of the song, swaying my hips seductively. When it gets to the *flip the switch* part, Theo turns the light off, and the screen goes black, but the camera doesn't stop rolling. I can hear laughing, banging, the rustle of clothes.

"I need to turn the light back on. I can't see jack and can't get this off with one hand!" Theo chuckles. "I'll just put the phone down, and we'll let it roll on. Then, we can edit it before we upload. It's gonna be *so* good."

The light flicks back on. Theo props the phone up against the mirror, camera facing towards us now. The angle is awkward. Most of the screen is taken up by the ceiling, and we're in the corner, but I see myself struggling to pull off my wristbands, handing them to Theo and grinning like a loon as he puts them on. When I yank down my top, bunching it around my waist, ready to shimmy it down my hips, Theo's eyes widen as he stares at my strapless, lacy red bra.

"Damn. Wow, nice!" he compliments.

I glance over at the real Theo, squirming.

He nods in agreement with his drunken self. "Very nice."

Chuckling, I look back at the screen. Theo is unfastening the Velcro on the back of his outfit, pushing it off his shoulders and down his waist. I get a great view of his arse in his tight black Calvin Kleins as he bends. When he tries to step out of the bulky Yoshi part of his costume, he trips and loses his balance. His hands reach out and grab me, and we both go down, disappearing from view.

The giggling intensifies, and then suddenly, there are a few beats of silence before ... sounds of noisy, sloppy kissing.

My eyes widen. Theo and I both lean in to get a better look at the phone screen.

"Oh shit, please don't tell me we made a sex tape." I groan loudly.

Seconds later, we both reappear. I stand first and then Theo. We're grabbing at each other, frantic, bumping into stuff as we stumble against the wall, Theo's body pressing against mine tightly as my hands scratch at his back and fist into his hair. We kiss like we're trying to kill each other.

"Well, that escalated quickly," Real Theo says beside me.

My face burns, and I can't contain my bubble of laughter.

In the video, Theo picks me up, and my legs wrap around his waist. When he manoeuvres us towards the camera so I'm sitting on the counter, blurring the image with a close-up of my back and my bunched-up costume, my possessions go everywhere, make-up scattering onto the floor as we fumble awkwardly, obviously pawing at each other.

Just when I think it can't get any worse, it does.

"Ouch. Okay, you're a biter." Video Theo chuckles. "Bed or counter?"

"I don't care where we do it as long as you get inside me right now!" I sound so breathless and excited in the video that a wave of shame washes over me.

"Bed then. More room." He picks me up again, and we're on the move, bumping into the door on the way out of the bathroom.

The camera continues filming the empty room, but in the background, though fainter now, you can hear us kissing, moaning, and giggling. Video Theo is humming the Wonder Woman theme song.

"No, leave the boots on, Luce. They're hot as shit." His video voice is all gravelly and filled with lust. It makes my breath catch and my whole body ache with longing.

I wince and jab at the screen, stopping the video. My face feels like it's on fire. "That's quite enough of that!"

Theo's mouth pops open. "No, come on. I wanna listen. Don't you wanna hear how it ends?" He reaches over and tries to take the phone from my hand, his eyes excited.

I shake my head and hold it out of reach. "No! Jeez, it's over three hours long. It's filled my whole phone memory. I'm deleting it. I don't even want to know what we got up to; denial is a much better idea. What we don't know won't hurt us."

He rolls his eyes. "Three hours? I'm not even gonna try to blag and say I can last that long. I got thirty, maybe thirty-five minutes of solid rutting at the most. Drunken fumbles … probably less than half that. Three hours? No way. We'd be dead."

My body stiffens at his words, and I raise a disbelieving eyebrow. Thirty-five minutes. Is that a joke? I quickly filter through my sexual encounters with Lucas over the years.

They're all essentially the same—some foreplay, then seven or maybe eight minutes of actual screwing, if I was lucky. Thirty-five minutes? No way.

Theo presses a hand over his crotch and shifts uncomfortably. "I know I shouldn't get turned on from watching us have a drunken hook-up, but damn, that looked hot. I wish I could remember it."

He looks at me and grins, laughing as I slap his chest with the back of my hand. I don't disagree with him though.

A sudden surge of panic grips me. "This had better not be uploaded anywhere!"

I quickly do a scan of my socials and his, but it appears this one was just for us. *Thank God.*

I breathe a sigh of relief and look over at Theo. His eyes twinkle as he looks at me over the rim of his coffee cup.

I gulp and know this needs fixing. We get on great, and I don't want that to change because of a drunken mistake neither of us remembers. Well, sort of don't remember … I get another micro flash of his mouth on my body, skin on skin, but I force it away.

"Listen, I don't want to feel awkward about this now. The wedding is today. I don't want to be walking on eggshells or feeling self-conscious about this the whole time. Neither of us remembers it, so I think we should pretend it never happened and move on." I purse my lips and wait to see how he feels.

He nods in agreement. "Okay. We're both adults. We can agree not to let this get weird."

"Great." I grin and reach for my coffee, taking a big gulp. The pills are kicking in now. I already feel a tad more human.

I turn my attention back to my phone, and just as my finger hovers over the delete button, Theo says, "Ah, come on, Luce. Before you delete it, can't we hear how it ends? Please? Come on, you know you want to." He nudges me in the ribs with his elbow, his bottom lip jutting out pleadingly as he bats his eyelashes. "Let's play for it. I win, we skip to the end and listen before deleting. You win, we straight-up delete and never mention it again." He holds out his fist on his palm, ready for another ridiculous round of Rock, Paper, Scissors.

A chuckle escapes my lips. "You do realise this isn't how all adults make decisions or settle debates, right?"

He grins and waits, one eyebrow raised. Giving in, I put my coffee down and then match his gesture, and we thump our hands and throw our shapes.

"Yes!" He crows happily as he defeats my scissors with his rock.

I groan and roll my eyes. Though I must admit, I'm more than a little curious myself. I pass him my phone and gulp the last of my coffee as he slides his finger across the screen to skip to the last five minutes. I hold my breath, strangely excited. It feels naughty, and I kind of like it.

When he presses play, soft snoring emanates from the phone.

"Oh, what an ending!" I burst out laughing, shaking my head, deciding a nice, hot shower is in order. I can't keep the smile from my face.

fourteen

THEO

While Lucie busies herself in the bathroom, I turn my attention back to the video. I'm not ready to admit defeat. I need to hear it. Does that make me a pervert? Probably. But it's not like I'm watching someone else … I have every right to check and see if I managed to make her moan my name. I scan through the video, stop-starting every few minutes, trying to find the highlights. When I find them, hearing her moan my name and begging me not to stop, it's so hot that I'm instantly hard as steel. I press my hand against my crotch to try and relieve the ache, but it doesn't help.

Damn, why can't I remember this? And why the heck didn't I take the phone into the room with me? I bet this looks even hotter than it sounds.

My mouth is dry. I would give anything not to have been this drunk, so I could remember every second of this encounter. What a damn waste. She looked that hot, and I got her naked, yet I can't recall a single second of it? Life isn't fair.

The trouble is, now that I've heard it, I'll likely never be able to get that sound out of my head again: her breathy moan, the little mewling hums she made, the rhythmic movement, and skin-on-skin noises. I want it again and again and again.

When we finally finish (seventeen minutes later—go, Drunk Theo!), I turn the video off, and my finger hovers over the delete button. It's like actual torture. I don't want to delete it, but I know I have to because that's what Lucie wants. I close my eyes and take a breath before sending the homemade porno to video heaven.

Huffing out a breath, I force myself to get up, finding my discarded underwear carelessly strewn under the dresser chair. I slip them on and gather up my phone, wallet, and costume from last night. I don't bother putting it on as I head to the bathroom door and knock gently.

"Luce, I'm gonna head to my room and get showered and then go find Jared. You're meeting the girls this morning, right?"

"Yeah!"

I can hear water running, and I try not to think about it cascading down over her naked body. I'm already hard enough without picturing that. I desperately want to go inside, climb in the shower with her, soap her back. Heck, as far as I'm concerned, that'd be saving the environment—conserving water and all that. It's probably even my civic duty. Go green!

I force the fantasy away and close my eyes. "Okay, well, I'll see you at the ceremony this afternoon at two. I'll be the one in the tux at the front."

But then I frown, wondering if she'll be able to tell me apart from Jared if we're both wearing the same. Our suits are practically identical. I kind of hate the thought that she wouldn't be able to tell me from my twin. I don't want to lose another girl if she falls for Jared's quiet calm.

"See you in a bit!" she calls back.

As I step out of her room and into the corridor, arms full of fancy-dress costume, I spot a waiter dropping off some room service a couple of doors down. He looks up and catches my eye, sending me a knowing smirk, so I tilt my chin in acknowledgement of his silent praise. If I were closer, he'd have fist-bumped me for my conquest, no doubt.

In the safety of my own room, I flop on the bed and pick up my phone, going to my Instagram and replaying the videos I posted last night. They're hilariously stupid, so of course, I love them all. I reply to a few comments. When I get to one asking if Lucie is my girlfriend, I'm not expecting the sudden pang of disappointment when I answer no. Lucie is great. I lucked in when that lift got stuck on Monday. She's made this whole weekend not only bearable, but also fun. I owe her big time.

When I can't put it off any longer, I head into the shower and let the water pound across the back of my neck and shoulders, massaging away the last of my hangover. I'm still thinking about Lucie, but my mind moves to distinctly dirtier places, like her naked skin, her red lace bra from the video, her legs wrapped around my waist ...

Before I know it, I'm hard as steel again, and I can't get out of the shower until I've indulged in a little self-satisfaction, replaying the sounds of her moans over and over as I stroke myself to climax.

After the three *s*'s (shit, shower, and shave), I head downstairs to Tim's room, where the guys from the wedding party have agreed to meet and get ready together. We all eat brunch, have a couple of pre-game drinks, and then get dressed up into our posh wedding attire before heading downstairs.

The wedding ceremony itself is being conducted on the patio outside. As we step out of the glass double doors, my eyes widen. It looks spectacular. A white-and-cream tartan-patterned carpet forms the aisle down the centre of the patio, leading towards a large, circular metal altar with pink and white roses woven around it. Behind that, the loch and mountains will form a stunning backdrop as people watch my brother and his fiancée exchange their vows. White wooden chairs tied with a pink silk sash are set out in straight lines on either side of the carpet. The sun is shining; there's not a cloud in the sky. They couldn't have asked for a more glorious day or more perfect setting to get married.

A few people have already arrived, filling the chairs, chattering excitedly among themselves. Jared, Tim, my dad, and I make our way to the front, stopping every couple of steps to shake hands with people and for them to wish Jared luck. Our mother is already crying happy tears as she hugs Jared and then me so tightly that it feels like I'm being crushed. Aunt Theresa gives me a hopeful smile, and I can already read her expression—*This might be you one day if you hurry up and settle down!* Emily is gnawing on her lip furiously as she absentmindedly bounces Finley on her lap and mumbles to her husband that she hopes Carys is behaving and not causing trouble for Amy. She keeps looking at the door, obviously waiting for them to arrive. A few friends tell Jared to make a quick getaway before it's too late.

I throw out a few jokes, trying to distract everyone from the fact that with each step taken, Jared's shoulders seem to tighten a little more and his face is paling.

"Well, we'd better go take our places." I grip my brother's elbow and guide him to the flower-arch thing at the front, stepping closer to him so no one else can hear.

He's shifting from foot to foot, his eyes darting from the guests, to the door, to his watch, and back to the door again. This is not the cool, composed, unflappable Jared I'm used to.

"All right, mate? How are you feeling?" I ask.

He turns to look at me, his face pallid. "Sweaty."

I burst out laughing and clap my hands on his shoulders, massaging a little through his suit jacket. "Not getting cold feet, are you?"

If he does, I'll punch some sense into him. There's no way I'll let him mess this up and lose Amy over some last-minute doubts.

Jared shakes his head fiercely. "No, I'm one hundred percent sure I'm doing the right thing and that I've chosen the right girl to spend my life with."

A smile twitches at the corner of my mouth. I admire his confidence in his decision-making skills. I'm not sure I've ever known what I want in life with that much clarity. Hell, I sometimes struggle to choose what I want to eat, as I'm so indecisive, but here he is, ready to tie himself to someone for life. We're so different.

"Why are you being so weird then?"

His eyes meet mine, and I can see genuine concern there. "What if Amy's changed her mind overnight? I haven't spoken to her since yesterday. What if she stands me up at the altar? What if she decides that, actually, she doesn't want to marry a grumpy bastard like me?"

I scoff at the ludicrous things spewing from his mouth. *That's why he looks like he's about to have a prostate exam? Jeez, talk about ridiculous.* "She won't change her mind! Amy is utterly smitten with you. She's been harping on about this damn wedding and getting all jazzed about it since you put that engagement ring on her finger. I can hand-on-heart promise you that Amy will not change her mind about marrying you."

The tension in his shoulders seems to loosen at my words, and he huffs a breath and rakes a hand over his face. "Thanks, Theo. I'll be happier once I have my other ring on her finger."

"Any minute now, buddy. Stop worrying. Today is going to be great."

"I hope I don't pass out," Jared grunts, taking a deep breath and looking up at the cloudless sky.

I chuckle and pat his shoulder. Tim gets out of his seat near the front then, rendering my next assurances unnecessary. He's tapping away on his phone as he stops next to Jared.

"Heather's just texted me. Amy's not budging on her decision about her entrance. She wants to walk herself up the aisle." His eyebrows pull together, and I notice the disappointed slump to his shoulders.

Amy's dad has never been around; instead, she was raised by her mum and nanna. With no father figure to speak of, I know Tim has offered several times to give her away, but she's rebuffed all advances, claiming she is a strong, independent woman who can walk of her own volition.

Jared nods. "I told you. She said if it's good enough for Meghan Markle, it's good enough for her." His smile is proud as he tweaks his already-perfect tie and brushes non-existent dirt from his lapel. He's such a perfectionist. At least his colour is coming back now though.

More people arrive, and each time they do, my eyes swing in the direction of the door. I don't want to admit to myself that I'm looking for Lucie, but I totally am. When she finally does step out of the door, her arm linked through Peggy's, the smile on her face is so radiant that it brings one to my own.

I can't take my eyes off her. She looks incredible. Her hair is up, elegantly twisted at the back of her head. She's not wearing her sexy glasses, so I assume she's donned contacts again. Her lips are painted a bright ruby red, which makes them look so kissable that my mouth starts to water, just thinking about it. Her dress is pale blue with small flowers on it. It has spaghetti straps, is fitted across her bust and waist, and flows out from her hips down to the floor. As she walks, a slit on one side from the floor to mid-thigh shows a flash of skin that makes my pulse race. The material is all floaty and flowy; it's perfect. Tall, strappy silver sandals complete the outfit. She looks like a knockout.

Amy's nanna leads her over to the front row on the bride's side, and I watch her every move. When she perches on a seat, she finally looks up at me, and we make eye contact. Her smile almost knocks me sideways. I'm having trouble staying at the altar and not going to her side.

Hi, she mouths to me.

Hi, I mouth back. I point to her. *Beautiful.*

Our conversation is silent, but I can practically hear her thoughts as her cheeks flush a gorgeous shade of pink, and she grins down at her lap.

When she looks up at me again, I send her a wink and force myself to turn my attention back to Jared, so I don't neglect my best-man duties. The last few people file in. I see Amy's mum slip into her seat next to Peggy, and then the music starts.

There are collective gasps and murmurs of excitement as everyone stands and turns, wanting to watch Amy's entrance. I watch Jared, setting a hand on his shoulder and squeezing supportively as, first, Carys and then Heather make the walk up the aisle, both grinning broadly in their pretty pink bridesmaid gowns. The tension leaves Jared's body as soon as Amy steps out of the door. He lets out an appreciative groan, and his whole face lights up. He's beaming with happiness and pride, and I've never seen him look so elated. It makes my stomach clench.

I turn my head, wanting to see her too. Amy holds her head high as she walks slowly down the carpet towards us, carrying a pretty bouquet of pink and white roses. I smile as I catch sight of her.

Of course, she didn't choose a conventional white dress. I should have known.

Her dress is sleeveless and has a lacy white V-neck top. Then, there's a pink ribbon tied around her waist that matches the shade of her hair pretty perfectly. The bottom of the dress is made of layers and layers of blush-pink-coloured tulle; it flows and cascades like a waterfall down to the floor and swishes as she walks. It's gorgeous. She looks stunning, just like a princess.

As she Meghan Markles herself down the aisle to marry my twin, grinning and saying hello to people as she walks past them, I realise that I'm not as devastated as I thought I'd be. In fact, I'm not devastated at all. I thought this would be agony, watching the girl I wanted to be with marry my brother, but instead, I'm just incredibly happy for them both.

It's then that I realise that maybe it was never *her* that I was hung up on but the *idea* of her. All this time, perhaps it was never actually Amy I wanted but more that I wanted my own Amy. Someone to look at me as if I'm the centre of her world and like I'm the person she can't live without. Someone who completes me, like Amy completes Jared. I've never had that. I've had a few girlfriends over the years. One or two of them turned semi-serious, but they soon tired of me when they realised I was basically an unambitious child trapped in a man's body.

All this time, I thought I was jealous because I wanted Amy for myself, but really, I was jealous of what Jared has with her.

The epiphany hits me just as Amy steps to my brother's side and smiles up at him, letting out a little sigh, as if she's now home.

I want that.

I want to be that to someone.

My eyes unconsciously flick back to Lucie. She's watching Amy and Jared. Her hands are clasped together under her chin, and her smile is huge as her teeth sink into her bottom lip. As if she knows I'm watching her, she glances back at me, and our eyes meet. The soft green to them captures me, and I can't look away as I get a warm, fuzzy feeling inside.

That's when I have my second epiphany ... I like Lucie. I like her *a lot* actually—not just in a friendly way.

And that's a big problem because we're only an agreement, merely a two-weekend, *help each other out of a sticky situation*, friendly agreement—complete with a signed contract stating that clear as day. Plus, I know for certain that she's still in love with her cheating ex because our whole relationship started owing to the fact that we were both hung up on other people and we needed a fake companion to help us navigate through our situations with our respective crushes.

So what if I think she's adorable and being around her is as natural as breathing? So what if she makes me laugh until my stomach hurts? So what if I think she's hot as sin? I can't have her because that's not the agreement we made. This whole thing is almost over. Tomorrow, we'll go our separate ways, and then I'll see her just one more time at her father's party, where she plans on using me to make her ex jealous.

The knowledge hurts more than it should. I'm genuinely gutted.

fifteen

LUCIE

Oh, man, I'm crying!

Amy's mum leans over and hands me a tissue when I sniff in a very unladylike fashion. I smile a thanks, and she grins back before letting out a watery sob of her own and dabbing at her eyes.

It's crazy really. I met these people less than two days ago, and now, I'm crying because I'm over the moon for them.

I let out a little dreamy sigh and look back to the happy couple. With the water behind them and the sun shining, it's the most beautiful wedding I've ever been to. Amy looks incredible, and aside from the colour of the skirt and the pink ribbon, her dress is not too dissimilar from the wedding dresses I used to fawn over when planning my own nuptials to Lucas—though I would never have chosen to wear a pair of lacy Converse as my wedding shoes like Amy has. A small pang of regret and sadness hits me out of nowhere as I realise that this would have been me next spring if Lucas had managed to refrain from bumping uglies with his hot personal trainer.

Amy and Jared are so cute together. Looking at them now makes my whole body break out in goose bumps. Jared is staring into Amy's eyes as if she's the most amazing thing he's ever seen, and she's beaming up at him like he's the winning lottery numbers. They're holding hands, his thumb absentmindedly tracing over the back of her hand, her body unconsciously leaning into his. It's almost like there are magnets pulling them together. Their chemistry is palpable, and their happy smiles make my heart ache. I must admit, more than once in the last couple of days, I've been a little envious of the way that Jared looks at his fiancée. It's everything. He clearly adores her; it makes me wish I had that with someone.

Watching them now, I can't help but wonder … did Lucas and I look like that to outsiders?

Even at the start of our relationship, I don't think so. Even though I was only eighteen when we first got together, he was five years older and at a different stage in life, so we totally skipped the randy-as-teenagers and stupid-in-love stages of a relationship and went straight to the serious, long-term stuff. At the time, I didn't mind. I had known Lucas for pretty much most of my life, so when our relationship evolved from friendship to romantic, it felt like the natural next step. But now, looking at Jared and Amy as he pushes the ring onto her finger and then loops his little finger around hers, dipping his head, brushing his nose across her cheek and whispering something in her ear that makes her chew her lip and her eyelids flutter closed, I can't help but feel a bit cheated.

In our eight years together, Lucas was never like this with me. Never affectionate in public or romantic, never spontaneous. He never looked at me like he wanted to rip my clothes off. Behind closed doors, our sex life was satisfying, and I had no complaints, but even in private, there was never the hand-holding, touching, snuggling on the sofa, or the desperate need to *rub over each other like animals* sort of thing that I can see in Amy and Jared's eyes. We were never wild with lust for each other.

I hadn't known I wanted that.

My gaze flicks to the best man, checking to see if he is okay. Poor Theo. Today must be hard for him, considering he has a thing for Amy, but I can't see any signs of it on his face. He was his fine, comical self this morning when we woke up, and he doesn't look like he's about to have a mental breakdown now. He's hiding his hurt well. I hate that I feel a little jealous about it.

As my eyes wander over him, I swallow down a wave of lust. Theo in a tux is the stuff that dirty fantasies are made of. He was wearing a suit with a T-shirt under when I first met him, but this three-piece suit is a masterpiece on his body. The waistcoat under his jacket with the pale pink tie combo, paired with his killer smile and hair that flops like it has a mind of its own? Perfection. *This* is the photo I should be sending to Aubrey. I commit it all to memory, every damn fine inch of it. Talk about swooning and wanting to rip someone's clothes off! I've never seen a guy look more attractive. He could be in movies, looking like this, and would even give Tom Hardy a run for his money. I want nothing more than to slowly take him out of his suit, peel it from him inch by delectable inch.

Although I had a lovely, relaxing pampering session this morning with the girls, today has actually been tough. I've been getting hot, inappropriate flashbacks of our night together all damn day, and it doesn't help that my body aches a little too. I must have used muscles last night that I barely even remembered having. I can't stop thinking about it: his cute, firm butt I saw this morning, the planes of that chest, the stubble chafing I have on the inside of my thighs, which meant his mouth was on me there. Jeez, I wish I could remember that part. It's only, like, my most favourite thing *ever*.

I'm getting flustered again. I shift on my seat as the ache that's been lingering between my legs all day intensifies, and I force myself to stop thinking about him naked.

My eyes bounce between Jared and Theo. When I first saw Jared on Thursday night in that bar, I remember wondering just how it was that Amy could have chosen between them. With them looking the same, I wondered how she could pick one over the other and fall in love. Now, I know. It's so weird. They might look exactly alike, but personality-wise, they're on different hemispheres. Jared is all quiet composure, neat edges, whip-smart, dependable, and adorable. In contrast, Theo is a loud, wild spirit. With Theo, you'd never know where you were going to end up—but he'd guarantee you would enjoy the journey. Looking at him leaves me a little breathless and giddy. It's kind of like that scared exhilaration you get when you're on a roller coaster, that thrill that causes your heart to race and makes you feel alive. It just so happens, I love roller coasters.

The rest of the wedding is beautiful. After the guests have emptied their boxes of confetti over the happy couple as they walk up the aisle, hand in hand, Theo steps to my side. His teeth sink into his bottom lip as he reaches out and catches a stray hair that's escaped from my French twist, pushing it back into place, his fingers lingering against the shell of my ear. My whole body breaks out in goose bumps at the small, intimate gesture.

Does he know how hot that is?

I hold my breath and tilt my head to look up at him. His eyes burn into mine, making me feel a little weightless.

"Hi," he whispers.

Bloody hell, can you come from one word? Because I think I just might have done it. "Hey."

"You look amazing. Really beautiful." His eyes slowly rake over me. It's the kind of look that makes you feel like you're on fire; his gaze is almost a caress as it glides down my body. "Maybe you should have toned it down a little today, Luce. You know, it is the bride's day after all. Surely, it's bad etiquette to roll in, looking this hot and sassy with that delicious-looking slit up to your thigh, and hog all the limelight."

My breathing is shallow. I'm not sure I've ever been this turned on in my whole life—and he's not even touching me. "I'm pretty sure no one is looking at me." My voice comes out in an embarrassing, husky mess.

"I am."

My heart squeezes at the sweetness, and I press my thighs together and clench my core to try and ease some of the pressure. I want nothing more than to drag him upstairs and get naked and sweaty.

Feeling bold, I reach out and touch his tie, needing to ground myself a bit because I'm fast melting into a puddle at his feet. The tie is pure silk and slips against my fingertips as I smooth it down against the hard planes of his chest. "You look great too. How's the head?" A blush creeps across my cheeks.

"Thankfully better. Yours?"

"Good now."

My hand is still on his chest. He looks down, catching it and bringing it closer to his face to look at my new powder-blue manicure with the flower art decals. One corner of his mouth kicks up into a sexy smirk.

"Nice nails. Did you have fun with the girls?"

I gulp and nod, struck mute as he slides his hand into mine, interlocking our fingers. Motioning behind him with his head, he gives me a gentle tug to get me moving. My legs feel slightly wobbly as he leads me over to the table the waiting staff has set up at the back of the patio. When we stop to each pick up a fruit-filled glass of Pimm's, I press against him and revel in the feel of his hand wrapped around mine. It's nice. His hand is soft and warm, and it dwarfs mine. My mind is instantly making the connection between the small skin-on-skin contact and other places he could put that hand on my body. A little shiver tickles down my spine.

We have drinks on the patio, casually chatting with his friends and family. He holds my hand the whole time. As I laugh along with his aunt about something, I realise that everything about Theo Stone is easy and effortless. This entire situation should be uncomfortable and awkward, but it's not because it's almost impossible to feel awkward around Theo. He radiates a positive energy that's easy to get swept away in. Standing there with his friends and family, with his hand in mine and his thumb absentmindedly tracing a pattern around my knuckle, I realise I love spending time with him. As much as I didn't want to admit it to myself, I missed him all morning. We've pretty much spent two whole days in each other's pockets, getting to know each other. I've fast grown used to his company and adorable, witty banter.

When the function room is ready, we're called to take our seats. I gasp as I step inside. It's gorgeous. The carpet on the floor matches the cream tartan aisle Amy walked down outside, and the tablecloths covering the round tables are crisp white cotton. There are pink napkins, little pink table favours wrapped in silk, pink ribbon sashes tied around the back of each white wooden chair, shiny silver cutlery, and real crystal glasses. Beautiful flower arrangements sit in the centres of each table. Behind the top table, the wall is covered in white voile with fairy lights behind it. The whole effect is spectacular.

Theo strides confidently across the room, guiding me along, heading for the long, lavish table at the head of the room.

My breath catches, and my eyes widen when I realise that's where I'm going to be sat—with everyone watching me eat. Talk about awkward.

"Shit, am I sitting at the top table?" I mumble, squeezing his hand and gently pulling him to a stop.

He nods and looks down at me. "Well, yeah. Where did you think you'd be? The cheap seats at the back? I'm the best man and twin. I deserve prime seating." He grins that panty-wetting smile, and it momentarily dazzles me.

"I know but …" My cheeks are burning as he tugs gently, getting me moving again.

As he stops at the long table at the head of the room, he grins and pulls my chair out for me in a gentlemanly gesture that makes my heart stutter. Sitting, I notice that his name card is printed in fancy script while mine is written in black Biro. I chuckle as I pick it up and show Theo; it's a little reminder of just how insane this whole idea is of me being here. I only met this man five and a half days ago, yet it feels like I've known him forever already.

It takes a while for everyone to take their seats, and then the bride and groom come in, Amy practically skipping along at her new husband's side. She looks like she could burst with happiness.

Once all the guests are seated and the waiting staff has filled everyone's glasses with champagne, Theo is discreetly handed a microphone.

He grins moronically. "Speech time."

I chuckle. "Have you got note cards?"

He wrinkles his nose and shakes his head as he reaches into his inside pocket and pulls out a scrap of paper with four bullet points on it. He smooths it out and puts it on the table in front of him. "I'm not a planner. I'm just gonna wing it."

My eyes widen in horror as I grip his forearm. "Theo, I feel like this is one of those things in life that you definitely shouldn't wing."

The fact that he's not planned it gives me mild anxiety. He might not be a planner, but I certainly am.

"I got this." He sends me a little wink that makes my stomach flutter as he taps his glass with his knife and stands up.

Jared groans loudly. "Theo, keep it clean. And don't make it weird."

"Weird, me?" Theo puts his hand over his heart and feigns offence.

The crowd quietens, and everyone turns their attention to him. Theo doesn't even look nervous; I'd be a quivering wreck, having to speak in front of all of these people.

"Good evening, ladies and gents. For those that don't know me, I'm Theo, and I'm the best man. I'm thrilled to be here to preside over the only five minutes of today that Jared has completely no control over." He smirks down at his brother, who rolls his eyes good-naturedly. "I'm gonna keep this short because I can already see he's starting to sweat, just imagining things I could say about him today. Now, in case you can't tell by our matching suits, Jared and I are twins, so obviously, I've known him a long time. I've definitely got the goods on him, but he's made me promise not to say anything too bad about him in my official speech today. Therefore, I'll be doing an *un*official speech later by the bar to anyone who buys me a drink."

There are titters of laughter and a few cheers from the rowdy group of friends at the back table.

"When Jared asked me to be best man today, I was pleased but not surprised. After all, he doesn't have any friends." He waits for the laughter to die down before speaking again. "I've never been a best man before, so in preparation for my role, I looked up speech guidelines on the internet. Apparently, the format is: introduction, few jokes at the groom's expense, compliment the bride, leave off on a positive note." He ticks them off on his fingers, and I notice they're the four bullet points he has on his notes. "So, here we go with the roast."

He turns to Jared and smiles wickedly, microphone still at his mouth. "Don't worry, buddy; I know you have some work colleagues and your boss here, so I won't mention anything about that time you got your ballbag caught in your zip and cried like a little girl at the hospital, or that time we were fourteen and tried weed and you got so out of it that you accidentally set Mum's curtains on fire, or when you got so drunk that you puked in your own shoe and then wore it home."

The crowd erupts into laughter as Jared winces and shakes his head, laughing quietly.

Theo turns back to the crowd as if nothing happened. "Jared has always worked hard—first at school, then university, then with his career in ... what is it you do again?"

I chuckle behind my hand, and some others in the room laugh too.

"In all that time, he's pretty much been single. But don't worry; don't be feeling sorry for him. He was single by choice. The girls just chose not to date him."

Ripples of laughter tinkle through the room.

"Jared always looks on the bright side of life. He can put a positive spin on anything. For example, his commendable charity work. Let's have a little round of applause for Jared's amazing charity work." He claps, and people in the room clap too. Amy is beaming with pride. "You guys know all about it, of course. Every six months, we get the dreaded group email, asking for sponsorship money because he's running a half marathon ... again." Theo teasingly rolls his eyes. "But seriously, that's a perfect example of how to put a positive spin on stuff. I mean, *I ran a half marathon* sounds so much better than *I quit halfway through a marathon*. Am I right? Glass half-full."

The room erupts into laughter.

Theo grins and takes a sip of water before continuing, "In all honesty though, growing up with Jared, I always felt like I was the luckiest guy in the world. Not only did I have my best mate twenty-four hours a day, but he could also step in and take my exams for me. I still owe him for my maths and science GCSE results. It worked the other way though too, like me stepping in to ask Cassie Bennet to the prom for him because he was too chicken or me passing his driving test for him. Joke. That one's just a joke, Mother, jeez," he says as his mother gasps in horror. *It's not a joke*, he mouths to the crowd when she's not looking.

There are more chuckles from the guests.

"Jared's dependable and hardworking, and he achieves anything he puts his mind to. But he was born a grown-up, and he can certainly be a grumpy git; he's always worked too hard and taken life a little too seriously. But then he met Amy. Smart, wonderful, quirky Amy who, let's face it, definitely could have done better." He winces playfully in Amy's direction, but Jared nods along in agreement. "Theirs was a chance encounter outside a coffee shop, a proper meet-cute. From the moment he met her, I could tell this was serious. Jared changed overnight. For example, he started smiling. Shock horror."

People snicker.

"Amy brought out the fun in my brother. They're the perfect couple. They complete each other actually. She's his fun-loving, carefree side, and he's her adult."

More laughter.

"To finish off because I know we're all checking our watches, waiting for the food to be served, I just want to say, I couldn't be happier for my twin. He deserves to be loved the way Amy loves him. I've never seen him so relaxed and content. Amy did that. And now, I also get a fun sister-in-law to go do crazy stuff with." He sends Amy a wink, and she grins and nods in return.

"So, please join me in raising a glass. To Jared and Amy. May your arguments be short, and may your sex be long, and may you always be as happy and in love as you are today. You are couple goals."

"To Jared and Amy," the crowd repeats as one.

I swallow the ball of emotion that's lodged in my throat and pretend to take a sip of my drink. I'm so proud of Theo that I want to hug him. Knowing how he feels about Amy, that must have been hard for him, but he didn't show a single hint of jealousy or malice in his speech. It was perfect.

He sits down next to me, smugly slipping his arm across the back of my chair, seeming incredibly happy with himself.

I grin and lean in conspiratorially, my side pressing against his chest as I set my hand on his thigh. "That was brilliant."

He smiles and turns his head to face me, his eyebrows suddenly shooting up. "Aww, Luce, are you crying … again?" His expression is teasing as he reaches out and cups the side of my neck, the pad of his thumb wiping the tear that slid out without my permission.

I chuckle and blink a couple of times to try and clear my blurry vision. "So, I like weddings. So what?"

His thumb moves down to trace the line of my jaw, eyes twinkling. "You're a secret, soppy romantic, aren't you? I've found your weakness."

I place my hand over his and shrug unashamedly. "It wasn't a secret."

"You're utterly adorable." Grinning, he leans in and plants a kiss on the tip of my nose.

My eyelids flutter closed, and I desperately want to tilt my head up, so our lips connect, but I resist the urge. As he pulls away a fraction, our eyes meet, and I get trapped in the depths of those whiskey-coloured pools. This close, I can see there are flecks of green and gold around the pupil. They're beautiful. His breath blows across my lips; I can almost taste the sweetness of the fruit and the Pimm's he was drinking earlier. My lips tingle, and I see his eyes flick down to my mouth. He's debating on kissing me, the same as I am him. That knowledge sends my hormones spiking.

I know he's using me right now. Making himself feel better about the fact that Amy just married his brother by hitting on me, burying the pain with something nicer. I'm simply a butterfly stitch, something to stop the bleeding and momentarily attempt to heal his wounded heart. To be honest, I don't mind that at all. Because I want the same from him. Both of us are bruised; we both have battle scars. This is merely a little stage make-up to cover them for a while … and I'm okay with that. Like Aubrey keeps telling me, we're both adults, and if we go into it with our eyes wide open, where's the harm?

Before Theo has the chance to kiss me, Jared stands, his voice resonating through the microphone as he starts his speech. I gulp and pull back, realising how totally inappropriate our little moment was. Theo blinks a couple of times, his lips pressing into a thin line before he leans back, too, looking over to his brother with a fond smile on his face. His arm stays across the back of my chair.

Jared makes a beautiful speech, gushing about how wonderful Amy is before he hands out presents to the bridesmaids—much to Carys's delight—and then Anne makes a speech in lieu of the father of the bride. I struggle to concentrate on them all though because the whole time they're doing their thing, ninety-nine percent of my brain is zeroed in on Theo's fingers, which are absentmindedly tickling a line across my upper arm, moving rhythmically back and forth, melting what's left of my brain and incinerating my underwear.

When Anne finishes her speech, Amy's nanna, Peggy, tries to take the microphone, but Anne looks horrified and refuses to let go of it. Amy and Jared are watching with wide, terrified eyes as Amy shakes her head at her mum, doing the *hand slashing across the throat* gesture, universally recognised as *no fucking way, shut that shit down immediately.*

I can't stop giggling, just imagining the things that would come out of the old bird's mouth. She is as savage as she is hilarious. After Theo, I think she might be my favourite person in the room.

sixteen

LUCIE

After speeches, dinner is served. The food is delicious, top-notch, and Theo tells me halfway through the starter of tomato and mozzarella tart that these are his mother's recipes and her sous chef is in the kitchen, preparing the food. It turns out, his mother is a head chef at a high-end restaurant. It also turns out, Lucas and I ate at her restaurant in Ely once when we were on a business trip. Small world.

By the time my dessert comes out (chocolate truffle cake with Chantilly cream), I'm almost in a blissed-out coma because it's so good. I groan and lick the back of my spoon, wanting to savour every morsel. "Yeah, sex is cool, but have you ever tried this cake?"

Theo bursts out laughing and looks down at my plate. "Is it that good?"

I flick my eyes to the passion fruit cheesecake he chose and grin. "You messed up big time."

His spoon darts out towards my plate, and I gasp, slapping the back of his hand as he tries to cut off a chunk of my dessert.

"Ahh, come on, share? There's no way that dessert is better than sex. Maybe you've been doing it wrong?" He playfully raises one eyebrow.

My insides quiver, and while I'm distracted, he steals a chunk of cake from my plate, devouring it before I can protest.

His eyes narrow, and his head drops back. "Holy crap, that is the most perfect cake in the world. Nothing can taste better than that. That's the pinnacle of cakes. All other chocolate cakes should be ashamed to even share its name. Why didn't I order it?" He pouts down at his cheesecake that he was wholly content with less than a minute ago.

I chuckle and send him a grin as I shrug one shoulder and start eating again. His eyes watch my every move as I finish every last crumb of it; it's kind of sexy.

After we're finished eating, Jared and Amy cut the wedding cake and pose for numerous photos before they have their first dance. Theo resumes stroking across my arm, and it makes my whole body sing with pleasure.

After a couple of songs, he stands and holds down a hand to me. "Dance?"

I can't very well say no and leave the best man hanging, so I slip my hand into his and let him lead me to the dance floor. There are a few other couples dancing, only the important ones, like parents and bridesmaids. As Theo pulls me closer to him, I hold my breath and look up at him through my eyelashes. Tingles spread through my whole body as he wraps his arms around me, setting one hand on the small of my back and the other on the bare skin at the nape of my neck. His touch sears its way through my skin, heating my blood.

It's romantic as we sway to the beat of the song. My chest is pressed against his, my hands curl around his shoulders as he dips his head, and our cheeks brush together, his hot breath blowing down my neck. I get another of those inappropriate scorching flashbacks of his lips on my neck, my ear, my collarbone, and I shiver as desire pools in my belly. I desperately want him to snog me silly, right in the middle of the dance floor with everyone watching.

Luckily—or maybe unluckily, depending on how you look at it—the song comes to an end before my lust spills over and drowns us both. Theo is immediately dragged off by Anne. He throws me an apologetic look as he dances with the mother of the bride, then his own mum grabs him for her turn, and then he dances with the bride herself. I watch that one for signs of his heart breaking as he dances with Amy, but there's nothing—no lingering touches, no yearning looks or signs of pain on his face. They simply laugh and talk the whole time. He spins her dramatically, the pair of them behaving ridiculously as people around them grin and watch the spectacle. It just looks like a fun dance between friends and family. The fist that has been gripped around my stomach the whole time seems to loosen, but I don't even want to think about why or what caused it.

Theo's eyes keep flicking to me as I dance first with Tim and then with some guy called Noah, who flirts shamelessly with me and barely manages to keep his hands off my arse and eyes from my cleavage. When the dance finishes, I excuse myself to the toilets quick smart, spending a couple of extra minutes checking my hair and reapplying my lipstick so he'll move on to someone else. Not that I'm not flattered by his attention, but I'm just not interested.

Returning to the room, I note the music has become more upbeat '80s classics. Jams to get people up on their feet blast from the speakers. The dance floor is almost packed full now, mostly ladies dancing around their handbags. Out of nowhere, Theo's hand closes around mine, and he tugs me into the fray. His grin is dazzling. I laugh, bopping along to the beat, generally having a great time. Carys joins us, too, grabbing her uncle Theo and making him do outlandish dance moves with her that are obviously well-practiced routines. It's too cute, and I can't contain my grin. He melts my heart with how he is with her.

When Emily comes over and hands baby Finley to Theo, my ovaries feel like they erupt as he makes stupid faces and dances with him on his hip.

I'm so done for.

I have a fantastic night even though Theo and I barely get more than five minutes alone. Mostly, I dance or chat and gossip with his family and Heather, getting mildly drunk and laughing the whole night.

Occasionally, Theo escapes the clutches of one of his family members, and we make a break for the bar together, rehydrating. He's so sweet with the way he watches out for me, making sure my drink is topped up, asking if I'm hungry, joking around so much that I shake with laughter. But then his attention is demanded elsewhere, and off he goes again, sending me an apologetic, pained look. It's adorable, and it makes my tummy quiver.

I have a blast, and I'm immensely grateful to Theo for bringing me here. This whole weekend has been amazing, and tonight is the best night out I've had in years. As much as I might miss Lucas and our relationship, things with him were never this carefree and fun; our rare date nights were more structured entertainment—pub quizzes, dinner parties with his snooty friends, cocktail bars. I can't remember the last time I laughed this much; my cheeks hurt from all the smiling.

As the night winds up and the songs slow down, Theo pulls me into his arms, and we sway to the beat. At some point during the evening, he removed his jacket, waistcoat, and tie and rolled his sleeves up to his elbows. He looks even hotter now that he's more casual, but I don't know how that works because he looked a vision while dressed to the nines. Maybe the champagne bubbles are getting to me.

He holds my hand against his chest, and I can feel how warm he is, his body heat pulsing into me. His other arm is wrapped around my waist, clamping me against him as we slow dance in a little circle. Everyone else seems to disappear as I press my face into his neck, breathing him in.

He smells delicious, all rich and manly with a hint of spicy aftershave left from when he got dressed this morning. I commit it all to memory and catalogue it as one of the best moments of my life.

Blissfully happy, I don't want the night to end.

Unfortunately, at just after midnight, the party draws to a close, and the music stops.

Theo steps back and smiles down at me, reaching out and brushing his finger against my cheek, leaving a burning trail in its wake. "Looks like the party's over, Luciella."

A thrill zips around my body when he uses my full name. People rarely call me it, only really my parents and grandparents. I'm surprised he even remembered; he's been calling me Luce all weekend—not that that's a bad thing though. I like that coming out of his mouth too. Maybe it's just his voice …

We say our goodbyes to the people left around, agreeing to meet some of his family downstairs for breakfast, and then I follow Theo to the lobby and into the lift. My body is all jittery as I wonder what happens now.

Is the night over? Will he kiss me? Do I want him to?
Duh, stupid question, Lucie. Yes!

We stand on opposite sides of the lift, facing each other. He's not even touching me, but I can feel my hormones building at an alarming rate just because his eyes don't leave mine. I'm not sure if he can feel it, too, but the temperature in the lift seems to grow hotter as the air thickens with lust.

When the doors ping and slide open, I break eye contact and step out, holding a hand to my chest in a pathetic attempt to stop my heart from hammering against my ribcage.

Stopping outside my door, I deliberately take a while to retrieve my keycard from my clutch bag. I just need a minute to catch my breath and collect my thoughts.

Theo leans one shoulder on the wall next to my door, casually crossing his ankles as he shoves one hand through his hair, messing it up and making it flop back across his forehead. His jaw is tight, and his eyes are solely focussed on me.

"I had a great night," I say, biting my lip.

He nods, a smile twitching at the corner of his mouth. "Me too."

There's a moment of silence. I can hear my own heart beating.

"Well, good night, Luce." He leans in, dropping a soft kiss to my cheek.

Disappointment grips me, and my hand automatically fists his shirt, not letting him pull back, as a small whimper leaves my lips. His body stills against mine, just a hair's breadth away. We're so close, and I think I feel him tremble, but it could be me instead. When he eventually pulls back, my hand acts of its own accord. I reach out and push his hair from his forehead. I've been dying to do that for the last hour.

His hand catches mine, and he presses my palm flat against his chest, holding it there as his gaze flicks from my eyes to my mouth. Slowly, he leans in, making me lean back against the door as he traps me in a little cage with his body, the heat of him pulsing into me.

I'm so attracted to this man. My lust is a living, breathing thing, clawing at my insides, demanding I move closer, that I pull his mouth to mine to get a taste of him—and this time, remember it.

My body is desperate for an epic skin-deep affair, where I get to screw the life out of the hot guy just for one night. Maybe I could follow that line of muscle at his hips and get down on my knees to see what he tastes like. Thoughts of his hands gripping my hair, his mouth on my body, the kind of frenzied passion I saw on that video from last night … I want that so badly, I ache.

This might be my last chance. Tomorrow, I'll go back to the humdrum of normality—lying awake on my uncomfortable second-hand bed in my best friend's flat, wondering if Lucas is letting that gym bunny sleep on my Egyptian cotton sheets.

My inner voice is screaming at me, reasoning how I need to indulge in some wild rebound sex for the night.

It turns out, my inner voice is a slut—she also sounds suspiciously like Aubrey.

I look up at Theo, our eyes meet, and I gulp. I want him more than I've ever wanted anything. This is probably my only opportunity to sleep with someone as hot as him. We could have one mind-blowing night that I'll get to hold on to for the rest of my life and compare all future guys to— *yeah, you might be hot, but you're not Theo Stone in a posh hotel with a view of a lake hot.*

I hold his gaze, hoping to convey without having to say it that I want him to make a move. Yes, I'm that chicken that can talk the talk but not walk the walk. I need him to start the engine and kiss me first; after that, I can drive the damn car. I just need a little jump-start to boost my confidence. After Lucas, I'm a little lacking.

The muscle in his jaw twitches as he reaches out, brushing his fingers across my cheek before curling his hand around the nape of my neck. I arch my back, moving impossibly closer. I can feel how hard he is already; his erection pushes against my stomach and almost drives me insane with desire. My whole being is taut like a bow. Sparks flicker to life between us.

My hands are on his chest, so I can feel his heart thumping rapidly under my palm. When his head starts dipping towards mine, my insides rejoice, and I hold my breath, just waiting for our mouths to connect. My blood sizzles; the waiting is torture.

At the last possible moment, I see a brief flash of something akin to panic flicker in his eyes, and he seems to have a change of heart. Instead of kissing me, he turns his head slightly, setting his cheek to my temple as he hugs me.

No! Just a hug? This is how it ends?

Disappointment surges through me, and I accidentally let a needy whimper slip from my lips. His incredible smell engulfs me, and I can't help but lean in and tuck my face into the crook of his neck. My nerve endings are like live wires, sparking dangerously.

He huffs out a breathy groan, and his shoulders slump, his lips brushing against my cheek as he speaks, "Shit. I got nervous and wimped out. Did I just fumble the bag?" His voice is thick with arousal as it blows across my ear, causing goose bumps to break out on my skin. His arms tighten on me, crushing my body against his.

Hope prickles at my subconscious. Chuckling, I shake my head. "No, you didn't." I actually like that he's nervous; it gives him a cute edge. I'm nervous too. It's been a while since I've been this close to a man—not counting last night, of course.

"No?" He pulls back, his hopeful eyes searching my face as his teeth sink into his bottom lip.

Shaking my head, I slowly slide my hands up his chest, relishing how his whole body tightens when I tangle one hand into the back of his hair, fisting the soft strands. My heart thumps erratically. "Try again," I encourage.

He blinks and swallows, and just like that, his nerves are gone; instead, his eyes blaze with white-hot heat. It's scorching; I feel like it might burn me up. I've never had anyone look at me like that before. My body softens against his, and I grip his shoulders for support as his eyes say he wants to devour me whole.

I'm not sure I'm even ready for the kind of passion I can see burning there. It's exhilarating and frightening at the same time.

His hands cup my jaw, tilting my head as he moves in so close that I can taste the champagne on his breath. Every inch of him presses against me. I'm trapped between the door and his hard body. I couldn't move an inch even if I wanted to—which I don't.

His thumb traces across my bottom lip, and I see his pupils blow out with desire. "I've been thinking about these lips all damn day. They're so red. Like my favourite cherry Push Pops I used to suck on as a kid." His voice is gravelly and seems to have a direct line to my core.

I'm so uncomfortable; I can barely keep still.

"Bloody hell, Theo, stop teasing me. Either kiss me or leave me alone, so I can go jill off while I imagine you did!" I'm getting antsy now.

"Jesus." His nostrils flare, and his eyes widen in surprise.

I must admit, I'm a little surprised myself. I don't know where that came from.

He chuckles and teasingly traces his nose up the side of mine, shifting on his feet. Where he moves, it causes our chests to rub; my nipples are already hard, so the friction is maddening. My eyes drop closed as a flutter of pleasure grips my core.

Oh man, can you come from not even being touched? Because I think I'm close.

I've been on edge all day, and this is too much.

Suddenly, his lips brush against mine, a featherlight kiss that makes my knees weaken. I whimper and slide my arms around his neck, carelessly dropping my clutch bag on the floor as I hold on to him for dear life. He kisses me again, harder this time, his teeth scraping on my bottom lip. My hand tightens in his hair as the kiss deepens. When his tongue traces along mine, he groans into my mouth, and the kiss swiftly changes into something else entirely. It's no longer sweet and soft; it appears that his passion has spiked, too, and he presses against me desperately, one hand moulding over my hip, his fingers digging into my skin, causing a little pleasurable pain that sends my body into a frenzy. His other hand grips the back of my neck as he kisses me like he can suck out my soul. It's wild, confident, possessive, masterful. I love it so much that another of those small, pleasurable flurries hits me. I've never been so turned on by a kiss. Scratch that. I've never been this turned on, period.

He breaks the kiss and rests his forehead against mine. A low moan rumbles in the back of his throat. It's my new favourite sound.

"You taste like that fucking chocolate cake from dinner. I didn't think the damn thing could taste any better, but I was wrong," he growls, licking my lips.

I'm gasping for breath as he moves, slipping one of his legs between mine, forcing them apart; his thigh presses against my core as his erection pokes into my stomach.

When his mouth claims mine in another scorching kiss, the ache between my legs becomes unbearable. Unable to keep still, I move my hips, rubbing my sex against his thigh, seeking out that delicious friction, moaning into his mouth. Every part of my body is hypersensitive; my brain is slowly dissolving, and my nerve endings zip and crackle. I can't think of anything but chasing the pleasure as it grows and grows so quickly that I can barely keep up.

My orgasm hits me out of nowhere. My body shatters. I tremble all over, and Theo's arm wraps around my waist, holding me upright as I gasp his name and throw my head back, not even feeling it when it thuds against the door.

"Holy shit." His mouth pops open, his eyes dancing with excitement. "Did you just come"—he blinks and looks around—"in the hallway?"

My face flushes as I struggle to come down from my high. My body feels boneless and weak. His arms are probably the only things keeping me upright.

"Don't gloat," I rasp breathlessly, tightening my arms around his neck as a massive smirk slips onto his face.

"Well, I think I'm entitled to a little gloat after that. I didn't even touch you before you went off. That was glorious, Luce." The delight is easy to hear in his tone. He dips his head and kisses the sensitive spot under my ear before pulling back to put his forehead to mine as I catch my breath.

His eyes burn into mine with both passion and need. There's promise in his eyes. That one look says it all … he's not done with me yet.

And just like that, I want him again.

"Would you like to come in?" My voice is breathy and husky. I'm still riding my bliss cloud. I'm not even ashamed. I want more, and this time, I want to take him over the edge with me.

He smiles wickedly. "Is that a trick question?"

"No." I grin and trace my hand around his collar, fingering the button at his Adam's apple as my body heats from the inside out. "We're both adults. Neither of us is too drunk to consent to a one-night stand. I'm attracted to you, as evidenced by the fact that you just made me come without lifting a finger—or a dick—"

He laughs at that, his eyes twinkling with pride.

I continue, "And I think, unless I've misread the signs spectacularly, you're attracted to me too …" I look up at him through my eyelashes.

"I am." He smirks at me and shifts his hips, his erection grinding against my stomach as proof.

My lust ratchets up five more levels.

I blush and shrug one shoulder. "Well then …"

"Well then …" He nods, leaning in, kissing me again.

It's all hot tongues and nipping teeth, and it scrambles my brain. I can't get close enough to him. He pulls back sharply before I'm ready, and a soft whine of protest slips out of me, but he just stoops and picks up my clutch bag and room key I dropped earlier, inserting the keycard into the lock. My eyes drift down, seeing the light turn green, and then we're on the move inside. Arms tangle, mouths meet, the door to my room slams closed behind us, and I think I might die from the anticipation of what's about to happen.

I'm pinned against the wall as our tongues slide against one another.

Suddenly, Theo pulls his head back and puts his forehead to mine, his eyes shining with excitement. "You know, I don't think I'm ever going to recover from watching you come whilst dry-humping my leg in a hotel hallway. I think you just ruined me." He shakes his head, his eyes still awed.

Giggling, face flaming with embarrassed heat, I cover his mouth with my hand. "Stop talking, and let's do this."

He nods in agreement, and we stumble our way over to the bed, my hands already fumbling with the hidden zipper at the side of my dress. Theo steps back and watches as I ease the thin straps off my shoulders, pushing the material down, shimmying it over my breasts and waist, leaving me in my black lace underwear. His eyes are dark and predatory as he watches every inch of flesh be exposed. Usually, I would feel self-conscious. I'm not exactly the skinniest girl in the world. Lucas described me as *cute but chunky*. But the way Theo is watching me—eyes tight, teeth sinking into his bottom lip, palm pressing against the crotch of his trousers as if it's painful—it makes me feel like the most beautiful girl in the world. I can practically taste his lust as his eyes caress my body, skimming over my breasts and stomach. The dress pools at my feet, and I look up at him, watching as he watches me. It's incredibly sexy.

He gulps, his eyes meeting mine again. "You're fucking beautiful." His voice is thick with lust. "Am I allowed to touch you?"

A smile twitches at the corner of my mouth. A consensual king. It turns me on even more. "Yes, please. And thank you."

Chuckling, he retrieves his wallet from his pocket, tossing it onto the bed before he steps forward, and his mouth crashes against mine. His hands go straight to my bum, eagerly palming and gripping it, groaning appreciatively into my mouth as he lifts me off my feet.

I smile against his lips and wrap my legs around his waist. *Oh, so he's a butt man. Good to know.*

While he manoeuvres us onto the bed, his hands don't leave my body. As he presses me down into the mattress, his fingers work deftly at my back, unclasping my bra and sliding it off. The cool bite of the air-conditioning hitting my oversensitive nipples makes me gasp, and he uses it to his advantage to slip his tongue back into my mouth.

Fumbling with excitement, I get to work on his shirt buttons, opening a panel at the front to reveal those abs and muscles I've been lusting after since we were on the beach yesterday. My breath catches, and my mouth goes dry.

Before I can undo the last couple of buttons, he moves, kissing down my neck, across my collarbone, his mouth closing over my nipple. A bolt of pleasure draws a gasp from my lips. I wriggle, and my eyes drop closed.

"You taste so good," he groans. His mouth and hands lavish attention on my body, teeth scraping, lips peppering tiny, open-mouthed kisses over my breasts, stomach, and hips as his fingers curl around my underwear, sliding them down so slowly that I decide I might die before this night is over.

The ache is building again. I need him inside me. I'm about to start begging when I realise he has other ideas. He's heading down south, and I get so excited that I can't keep still. My hands thread into his hair as I look down to watch; my heart is in my throat.

As he kisses and nips at the skin at the insides of my thighs, he smirks up at me. "I shaved this time; you should be good tomorrow."

I snicker, but my laugh is cut off as he drops his head, his tongue tracing along my slit in one long stroke. Pleasure zings up my spine, and my back arches off the mattress as my eyes roll into the back of my head.

"Oh, bloody hell. This is legit my favourite thing ever," I moan breathily.

His arms wrap around my thighs, holding me in position as he draws his head back, eyes meeting mine. "Note to self: Lucie's favourite thing ever is having her vagina licked."

I giggle, but it dies on my lips as he dips his head again, his hot tongue meeting my sensitive flesh. Groaning, I press my hips up against his face as my hands fist into his hair while he works his magic, whipping me into a state of frenzy and euphoria.

It doesn't take long for his talented mouth to push me over the edge. My heartbeat is crashing in my ears as I come again, bowing off the bed and covering my mouth with my hand as I moan his name and squeeze my eyes shut. Slumping back, I suck in a ragged breath. I'm already spent, and I've done nothing so far. I'm two orgasms in, and he's still mostly clothed. I'm seriously lacking here.

Getting up to his knees, he unfastens the last couple of buttons on his shirt that I didn't manage to undo. His gaze lingers on me, jaw tight, eyes blazing, pupils blown with desire as he drinks me in. I sit up and help rid him of his clothes, my fingers tracing across muscles, delighting in the warmth of his skin as they follow that exquisite V down to where it disappears into his trousers.

God, he's mesmerising and delicious.

While he eases his shirt off his shoulders, I get to work on his belt and zipper, eagerly pushing his trousers down over his hips and thighs, taking his boxer shorts with them. My hand traces over his arse, and memories of seeing that cute little butt this morning make my mouth water. When his erection springs free, I whimper and press my thighs together at the sight of it, just imagining what's to happen next.

Unable to stop myself, I reach out and close a hand over it, stroking the hard length from base to tip.

Theo groans and looks down at my hand wrapped around him. "I've been thinking about what those pretty nails would look like while wrapped around my cock ever since I saw them at the wedding."

Heat burns across my cheeks at his admission. I smile, and we both watch, enthralled, as I stroke him. My nails look great against his skin. His forehead creases with a frown, his lips part in pleasure, and then his head drops back on his shoulders as he lets out a long, breathy sigh. While he's distracted, I lean forward and do what I've also been thinking about a lot of the day. I close my mouth over the tip of his cock and taste him.

"Fuck!" His whole body tightens as his attention snaps back to me.

I smile inwardly and push forward, sucking gently, worshipping each little ridge and groove with my tongue, loving how his hands shoot to the back of my head, pulling at the slide and clips I have holding my hair in place. He's gently thrusting into my mouth as he finally works my hair loose, shaking it out around my shoulders.

One of his hands grips the back of my neck, and he pulls his hips back, his dick leaving my mouth with a wet pop. "Nope, that's enough of that. You're gonna make me come."

"Isn't that the point?" Devilishly grinning up at him, I lean in and suck him again, taking as much of his length into my mouth as I can without gagging, using my hand on the rest. I revel in his moan of pleasure, feeling pride spike inside me.

His hand fists into the back of my hair as he gently thrusts into my mouth again, groaning, his protests forgotten as I work my magic. "Wait, Luce." Another groan. "Shit, Lucie." Another thrust and then a gasp. "Luciella, stop." He pulls back again, breaking contact, and his eyes flash with playful reprimand as he shakes his head. "You're bad."

Grinning, he kisses me again passionately; I can taste myself on his tongue as he guides me onto my back. When he planks over the top of me, I can't help but admire his stamina. I'm a ten-second-plank girl at most; my arms would be shaking like jelly by now. He's incredible. Raking my nails up his biceps, I feel his taut muscles, and for some strange reason, I want to lean over and bite them. He seems to have awoken my dormant crazy.

Raising my head, I kiss him again, and the last of his restraint is gone. Things become frantic between us as he reaches for his wallet and pulls out a condom. Ripping it open with his teeth, he slides it over his length and then lowers his body to mine. The skin-on-skin contact is delicious, and I'm so lost in a fog of desire that I can barely remember my own name. My leg wraps around his waist, and my fingers scratch down his back as he enters me so slowly that I think the feel of it might just stop my heart. It's euphoric, and my moan is so loud that he has to cover my mouth with his to muffle it. The feeling of fullness is like heaven, but when he starts to move, I come undone.

The weight of him on top of me, the feel of him moving inside me, it's too much, too good. We've reverted to just basic, carnal desire, all tongues, teeth, hands, tangling breaths, and pleasure. I raise my hips, meeting his thrusts as my fingernails dig into his back, urging him on. When he breathes my name and nips at my earlobe, my passion rises to dangerous levels, and my teeth sink into his shoulder. He grunts, and his thrusts become harder, causing me to moan louder and louder as the pleasure intensifies.

His mouth lavishes attention on my body, hands tracing every inch, as if he wants to memorise it. Pushing up, he sits back on his heels and pulls my legs straight up his body, wrapping an arm around my thighs to hold them in place. The new position makes me feel things I've never felt before. My eyes flutter closed as I try to cope with the building sensations. Each thrust shatters my mind a little more. My pleasure is climbing to impossible heights, small bursts of it exploding behind my eyelids. This is the best sexual experience of my life. I'm racing towards my end. Flurries and ripples of pleasure join and converge, combining into waves, growing stronger until they form a tsunami that crashes over me.

I climax so hard, I see stars, and he follows soon after. The moan of pleasure he makes when he comes sears its way into my brain, lodging there. I hope I can always remember the sound, even when this weekend is merely a distant memory.

I'm exhausted when he moves my legs from his shoulders and flops down next to me, throwing his arm over my stomach as I stare up at the ceiling and try to catch my breath. My brain is swimming in endorphins; I can barely think straight. He wasn't lying when he said how long he could last for. It felt never-ending. The boy has so much stamina that I might not be able to walk straight tomorrow. My muscles ache deliciously, my brain is melted, and my lungs gasp for air like I ran my own half marathon. I've never felt so alive—or close to death.

"I think I died," I mumble.

He chuckles, rolling to his side, peppering soft kisses around the base of my throat. "You're welcome."

His arms tighten on me, pulling me against his body as he kisses my forehead. He's still breathing heavy, sweat glistening on his skin, and I press my nose against his chest, unable to stop smiling.

"Okay, you were right; that sex was better than the chocolate cake. Maybe I have been doing it wrong," I admit.

He bursts out laughing, and when I look up at him, I see he's grinning broadly.

His fingertips lazily trace up and down my spine. "I'd rate that a twelve out of ten."

I laugh so hard that I snort unsexily, but I don't even care when he teases me about it because I'm lying in his arms, blissfully happy and thoroughly sex drunk, if that's even a thing.

seventeen

THEO

"**A**hh, shit, shit!"

I startle and jerk upright, wrenched so fast from an idyllic sleep, where I was cuddling with a beautiful, naked girl, that I'm disorientated. I look around for danger but see nothing. The room looks as it should, no intruder, not even a spider.

What the hell?

At my side, Lucie rolls onto her back and throws her hands over her face, hissing through her teeth as she swears again.

I blink, shocked, having zero clue what's happening. The only explanation I can think of for this outburst is that she woke and realised we were in bed, naked, again and is freaking the heck out.

Is she regretting last night that much? Or did she not realise who I was? Maybe she thought she was snuggling with someone else? That thought makes my stomach burn with jealousy. I don't want her with anyone else.

"Luce, what? What's wrong?"

I reach out and wrap my hands around her wrists, attempting to ease her hands from her face, but she just groans and awkwardly pushes herself up to sitting, using her elbows, hands still clamped tight.

"My eyes. Damn it. I fell asleep with my contact lenses in. Ah, crap on a stick."

I huff out a relieved breath and close my own eyes, my stomach unclenching because this isn't about regret of our night together. *Thank God.* "Ouch. Are you okay?"

She nods and takes her hands from her face, wincing over at me, blinking furiously. It's too cute. "You're not supposed to sleep in these disposable ones; they go all dry and hard, and they irritate like a mothertrucker. I'm gonna go take them out." She swings her legs over the side of the bed and heads for the bathroom, butt naked.

A moan of appreciation leaves my lips as my eyes rake over her. Her arse is spectacular. I saw it a bit last night and had my hands on it, of course, but seeing her walking away from me naked like that? I'm achingly hard in an instant. Seeing that butt in clothes is nothing compared to seeing it in its full naked glory. I want to sink my teeth into the thing.

This is the second morning in a row I've woken naked with her; it's heaven.

I didn't expect this to happen at all … yeah, after meeting her in that lift and seeing how hot she was, I certainly *thought* about it happening, but I didn't think about it *seriously*. I honestly expected this weekend to be a long, painful, awkward weekend of misery that I spent the majority of drunk. I didn't expect Lucie to be so amazing. I certainly didn't expect to start to fall for the emotionally unavailable little Italian intern with the gorgeous smile and the brilliant banter.

Raking a hand through my hair, I glance over at the clock. It's just before nine a.m. We agreed to meet with my parents and grandparents for breakfast at half past nine this morning for one last hurrah before we all split up and make our separate ways home. I don't want to do that now though; I want Lucie all to myself for a while longer. I decide to see how Lucie feels about cancelling and getting room service instead.

After a few minutes, she comes back out. My eyes immediately slide over her. She's delectable in the morning. Her sleepy face and messed up, postcoital hair really get my blood pumping—down south, of course. I am a guy after all. I can't help it; she's gorgeous.

When I told her last night she had ruined me by coming on my thigh in the hallway, I meant it. That was the singular most erotic thing that had ever happened to me, and yet that was only the beginning. After that, she continued rocking my world, shaking the very foundation of my being. I fell asleep last night with a self-satisfied grin on my face, mentally replaying the sounds of her moans, as she cuddled up to me with her face pressed into the crook of my neck. Bliss.

She chews on her lip as she leans one hip against the wall and fiddles with her hands, playfully rolling her eyes. "So … we're naked together again."

I shoot her a smug grin. "You can't resist me; that's what the issue is." *Jeez, I hope that's true. I don't want to just be a one-night stand to her!*

"I knew you'd still be gloating about the hallway incident." She chuckles and walks to the bed, picking up her glasses from the bedside cabinet and slipping them on.

"I might gloat about that for the rest of my life."

She giggles, her cheeks flushing pink. Unable to resist, I reach out and take her hand, pulling her onto the bed with me, easing her down and moving so I'm half-hovering over her. I want her. Last night didn't rid me of my desire for her; if anything, it's made it stronger. Propping myself up on one elbow, I stroke my hand down her side, gripping her hip, revelling in the feel of her skin under my palm. Her arms come up, wrapping around my neck; as her eyes meet mine, I can see the excitement dancing there. I take that as a great sign that we're on the same page.

"How are your eyes?" The whites of them look a little pink and irritated.

She shrugs one shoulder, one of her hands slowly sliding up my neck and weaving into the back of my hair. "They're okay. I'm totally blaming you for it. You short-circuited my brain last night, so I forgot all about my contacts." She grins up at me flirtatiously as I press my body harder against hers.

"My bad. How can I make it up to you?" My lips brush against hers as I speak, and I feel her excited tremor.

"I can think of a couple of things you could do," she purrs, moving one of her legs and hitching it over my hip as she arches her body into mine. It's a clear invitation.

Last night wasn't merely a one-night stand after all; she's extending it to encompass the morning too. *Hallelujah*.

"Just a couple?"

My insides rejoice, and I press my lips to hers, kissing her passionately. She moans in the back of her throat and kisses me back immediately, her arms tightening on me as my hand slides down her body to cup her bum.

"This arse," I groan, peppering small kisses across her jawline.

"What's wrong with it?" She gasps as I squeeze and knead it.

"Nothing. It's bloody perfect, Luce. Best arse I've ever had the pleasure of setting my eyes on," I breathe the words against her skin as I kiss around the base of her throat.

She giggles, but her laugh turns into a moan as I move my hips slightly, and my erection rubs across the wet heat of her sex. My whole body tenses when I feel how turned on she is by me. I want to go down and do her *most favourite thing ever* again. But first …

I pull back a fraction and look at her, and her flushed, excited face is almost my undoing. "Should I cancel breakfast with my parents, or do you want this to be real quick?" *Please say cancel.*

She gulps and looks up at me. "I feel bad, cancelling on your parents."

"But?" I prompt hopefully.

She grins. "But we can always meet them for coffee or something later."

My lips crash against hers as I practically growl in victory. She kisses me back hungrily, but I force myself to pull away before it gets too heavy.

"Let me text my dad and tell him we're not coming."

She whimpers as I move away from her, and my body immediately misses the contact of her. Pushing myself up off the bed, I go in search of my trousers from last night. I abandoned them somewhere with my phone in my pocket. After finding them, I sit on the edge of the bed and open my Messages app.

Just as I find my dad's message thread, Lucie's arms wrap around me from behind, her hand splaying across my chest, fingers scissoring around my nipple. The heat of her body against my back is maddening, and I try to type out my letdown message as quickly as possible. The trouble is, I can't concentrate and keep hitting the wrong letters. It's taking a ridiculously long time to write out a simple lie.

Lucie trails open-mouthed kisses around the back of my neck as she palms my chest and stomach, fingernails scratching through the hair below my navel, heading even lower. When one of those pretty manicured hands closes around my painfully hard shaft, I forget what I'm doing and simply look down at it in awe. I can barely breathe. I didn't realise I had a thing for nails until I saw hers yesterday.

My skin is prickling with excitement, my balls clenching in anticipation. When she teasingly bites the column of my neck, it turns me on so much that my brain instantly switches to savage mode.

"You keep biting me, and you're gonna get fucked hard," I growl.

Her breath hitches, and I feel her smile against my neck. "Promises, promises."

STAND-IN SATURDAY

Her teeth gently sink into the skin of my shoulder just as I hit Send.

Without warning, I drop my phone, twist, and wrap my arms around her, tackling her to the bed. She squeals in delight, and I crash my lips against hers, intending to make good on my threat.

We decide to forgo our planned paddle boarding session and instead take a nice leisurely float on the loch in a rowboat. I thought it might be something romantic, an excellent way to end the weekend. The hotel hires them out directly from the beach out front. I spotted them on Friday while I was searching for stones to skip with Carys.

I can't stop grinning, which makes my cheeks hurt a bit. I'm deliriously happy. I'm having a blast with her, and the sex … forget twelve out of ten—she gets all the damn points. We've already had sex once this morning, and then while I was singing to myself in the shower as we waited for our room service to be delivered, in she walked behind me. Let's just say, hand jobs and watching her ride my fingers are my new go-to shower activities.

We only have a few hours before we need to leave to go to the airport, so I intend to pull out all the stops to ensure that she falls for me too. I don't want this to end up being another one-sided thing. I've had enough of that for the last year or so. I like her, but I'm not sure if she likes me for anything other than physical pleasure. She hasn't mentioned where we stand, and I don't want to ruin anything by asking, so I'm just rolling with it for now and trying not to think about her getting back with her ex next week when she makes him jealous at her dad's party.

I hold her hand and help her into the rowboat, waiting until she's seated before the guy from the hire place and I ease the boat into the water. She's grinning as she grips the sides, laughing when the boat rocks from side to side as I clamber in, too, and sit on the seat, facing her. Gripping the oars, I row us out. Lucie sighs in contentment and leans back, stretching out her legs so they go between mine, crossing her ankles. Her hair is piled up in a messy bun high on top of her head. She's wearing a flowery, fitted pink crop top that exposes an inch of luscious belly and a pair of frayed jean shorts that cut off mid-thigh. Her legs are long and take up all my attention. I'm pretty sure the girl is trying to kill me.

We chat back and forth about our lives, our jobs, movies, books—everything really. It's so easy to talk to her that it's sort of scary. She even has a go at rowing for a bit because she said she's never tried before, and then we just sit in the middle of the loch and float. No one else is around; they're all likely packing, seeing as it's going-home day, and pretty much the whole hotel was taken up with wedding guests. We have to go soon, too, but we have another half an hour at least before we even need to think about going ashore to pack.

It's peaceful, tranquil, and perfect. As we sip on bottled water and Lucie plays music through her phone, I realise it couldn't be any more romantic even if I'd tried.

It's quiet but a nice quiet. Companionable and easy. Birds chirp, water laps on the sides of the boat, the girl sitting opposite me is exquisite. This is pretty much one of the best days of my life.

Lucie tips her head back onto her shoulders, basking in the sun, legs stretched out in front of her, her top showing yet hiding all her perfect curves. My eyes rake over her, my artist's brain cataloguing the shadows and lines, her serene expression, the freckles peeking out from under her sunglasses, the dip at her collarbone, how the sun kisses her skin. I'm itching to draw her again, just like this.

"I wish I'd brought my sketchpad." I frown at my own lack of forethought.

She smiles over at me. "Yeah, the view is amazing." She shields her eyes with her hand and looks out over at the mountains peaking in the distance.

"It is," I agree, my voice gravelly with lust again, my gaze fixed on her.

She turns back to look at me, and a smile tugs at the corner of her mouth.

Leaning over the side, she dips her hand into the water before pulling it out, only to lazily draw her wet fingers across the base of her throat. The move makes my balls tighten. I'm not sure she meant it to be sexy—she's likely hot, and she wanted to cool down—but intentional or not, I'm now at full mast. Beads of water run between her breasts, and I watch avidly, imagining following the wet trail with my tongue.

She dips her hand again. "Ever done it on a boat?" she asks casually, tracing her palm across the smooth surface of the loch.

I blink, my mouth popping open. *No way. She isn't saying ...* "Seriously? You want to do it now?"

She turns back to face me, her eyebrows shooting up. "Theo, I'm not saying I want to have sex with you on the boat."

"Oh." Disappointment hits me harder than I'm ready for. I clearly read the situation wrong. My pervert hopes were raised and then dashed in less than ten seconds.

She leans in closer; her smile is a smirk. "I'm also *not*, not saying it."

Laughing, I catch on immediately. Nodding eagerly, I reach for the buttons on my shorts at the same time she reaches for hers.

Best. Damn. Weekend. Ever.

"I've decided I'm buying a boat," I announce.

Lucie laughs and watches as I hop out of the rowboat, pulling it further up onto the sand so her shoes won't get wet when she disembarks.

As she jumps off the boat and onto the beach, she winces and shifts on her feet. "Oh my God, I'm not sure I can walk; you know, you might have to carry me. I'm not used to all this sex. My poor cooch has taken a battering in the last twelve hours."

I burst out laughing and step closer, tracing my fingers across her cheek, dipping my head to kiss the tip of her nose. "In that case, allow me, *signorina*."

While on the boat, when I wasn't buried balls deep inside her, Lucie taught me a few basic Italian words and phrases. So far, I know how to order two ice creams and ask if she wants to have sex. No joke, that's what she taught me. *Vuoi fare sesso?* It's my new favourite saying, especially when she was speaking it with her sexy Italian accent caressing all the vowels.

I turn and squat in front of her in invitation for a piggyback, holding my arms ready to catch her.

"I'm too heavy," she protests.

"You weren't too heavy when you sat on my face earlier …"

She snort-laughs and grips my shoulders. "You're so filthy sometimes; you make me blush."

I take that as a compliment and grin wider. "Are you getting on or what?"

"If you die, just remember, you asked for this." Her grip tightens on my shoulders, and she jumps onto my back, wrapping her arms around my neck as I loop my arms around her thighs.

I'm unable to temper my goofy grin as I carry her up the beach and to the hotel. We're laughing and joking around the whole time, the flirty banter bouncing back and forth. Her arms are loosely wrapped around my neck, and her cheek occasionally brushes against mine as I walk. It's so nice that I'm almost tempted to suggest we don't go home today, that I pay for another couple of nights here and she could call in sick at work. I don't want my time with her to end.

As I step into the hotel, Lucie and I are both snickering like little kids because she just blew a loud raspberry on the side of my neck. The first thing I see are my parents, Amy and Jared, and Anne and Peggy, all sitting in the lobby, drinking coffee and talking. Silence falls over them as they look over at me with Lucie wrapped around my back like a koala. Amy beams, and so does my mother. Jared raises one eyebrow at me. I know him well enough to understand his question without him having to verbalise it; maybe it's a twin thing. We didn't get cool telepathy, but I can tell what he's thinking most of the time from his expressions.

This one is … *You hit that?*

I nod a resounding yes and smirk proudly.

He understands and gives a small incline to his head in congratulations, his lips pressed together to disguise his smile.

"Uh, hey, guys," I greet, walking over, carefully squatting and setting Lucie in a spare seat next to my mum. I'm trying for casual, but I just got laid on a boat, so really, I'm grinning from ear to ear. I might as well be wearing a sign, announcing it. "Lucie got something in her shoe."

They all see through it, of course, probably because when I look back to Lucie, she's beet red and chewing on her lip. Mum clasps her hands together in her lap and looks at us like we're the cutest thing since Jared and Amy.

Peggy leans forward in her chair, pursing her lips. "Ah, that explains it then. Silly me, I thought maybe it was some weird foreplay thing," she teases, knowingly winking at Lucie.

"Mum!" Anne gasps, nudging Peggy's arm as everyone laughs.

"Um, no, just a pebble, Peggy," Lucie lies, shuffling awkwardly on her seat. Gripping my wrist to get my attention, she looks up at me. "Shall we get a drink before we go pack? We have time, right?"

After checking my watch, I nod. "We do, provided you're not gonna take longer than half an hour to throw your stuff in your bag."

"It won't take long at all; I already did most of it earlier."

I nod down at her. "Great. I'll go order. What do you want? *Vuoi fare sesso, bella*?" I jokingly try out my newly learned sex-request phrase and grin smugly at her.

Jared chokes on his drink, dribbling Coke down his chin and coughing as his eyes go wide. Amy frowns and worriedly pats him on the back as she hands him a napkin.

Realisation dawns on me, and I turn to my brother and wince apologetically. "I forgot you speak Italian."

Lucie lets out a small gasp, and then she chuckles and shakes her head. "Just a cappuccino, Theo, thanks."

We spend just long enough downstairs with my family to drink a cup of coffee, and then we say our goodbyes. Lucie is hugged a lot. My mum tells her she's welcome at the house anytime, and then she gives me a *you'd better keep hold of this one* look that I choose to ignore. I'm doing my damned best, but it's not my call. This is all Lucie's decision if this goes any further. Peggy "accidentally" gropes my bum as I hug her goodbye. I watch as Lucie exchanges numbers with Amy. It's so sweet how well they get on. Amy vows to let Lucie know all about her honeymoon to Bali when she gets home in two weeks.

Once we've hugged everyone twice (cue another bum grope from Peggy), we excuse ourselves to go upstairs to pack. We are the only ones getting this flight. Other people are flying out today, too, but they're flying into a different airport, seeing as it's closer to their homes. Only Lucie and I are flying back to London this afternoon. I must admit, I'm a little glad because it means I get her to myself some more.

After packing up our stuff and dropping off my hired wedding attire and my fancy-dress costume with the concierge (Jared prearranged to have most stuff couriered home again along with the wedding gifts), we check out of the hotel, handing back our room keys, and then we cram ourselves into the ridiculously small hire car and head for the airport.

Our flight isn't boarding for a while, so once we've cleared customs and untrustworthy-looking Lucie has had her second pat-down of the trip, we head for the food court.

I nod towards the bar. "Need some Dutch courage again? I might have something stronger this time, see if I can dull my pain receptors before you crush my hand again on the flight." I send her a teasing wink.

She smiles gratefully and nods in agreement.

We have two drinks before they call our flight. Again, Lucie opts for the window seat and sits there, a little pale and nervous, one hand pressed to her stomach.

I lean over and drop a kiss on the top of her head, taking her hand and lacing our fingers together. "We'll soon be home, Luce. Don't worry. I got you." I'm not expecting the level of disappointment that hits me as I say it. I don't want to go home.

She nods and leans closer to me, setting her head on my shoulder, her hand gripping mine for dear life.

As the plane ferries us back to London, I'm acutely conscious that we haven't spoken about what this all means and what happens now. I'm hopeful it means she wants to see me again. She's ruined me for other girls. I need to see this through.

I can't help but wonder, *Is she my version of Amy?*

Maybe fate threw me a bone that day I got stuck in the lift with her.

Our chemistry is electric. It's like hanging out with a best friend that you fancy the shit out of. I've never had that with any of the other girls I've dated. Something deep down is telling me that this might be something special and that I need to nurture it and try everything to hold on to it.

This weekend has left a scar on me, and I'm not only talking about the *fingernails scratching at my back* or *teeth sinking into my shoulder* kind. I mean, it's left a scar on my heart. I want this all to happen again and again. I want to be the first thing she sees in the morning and the last thing at night. I want more of her than I think she's willing or able to give because she's still hung up on a guy she caught cheating on her.

Is this just a weekend-long affair in her eyes?

I have a horrible, dejected feeling in my stomach that this is purely a physical thing for her, an itch she needed to scratch and I was in the right place at the right time. I don't think she feels the same about me. Her stipulation of our bargain was for me to accompany her to her dad's party and let her use me to make Lucas jealous, but to what end? So he realises he made a monumental mistake and they give it another go? She deserves better than that. The thing is, I'm not sure she believes that.

How much I like her scares me a little. I want to see her again after this, to keep getting to know her, to build on this weekend and see where it can go. But I don't want to come on too strong and ruin it or rush her. She's delicate, still hurting for her ex, and she likely isn't ready to trust another man after he broke her heart so carelessly. I need to tread carefully.

We went into this weekend with boundaries and a clear agenda to get what we wanted. For me though, that agenda has changed. I want her. I want more.

Have I done enough this weekend to claw her attention from her ex? Who knows? Maybe this weekend is the start of something for her too.

God, I hope so.

I spend most of the flight sketching her, my spare hand wrapped around her thigh as she absentmindedly trails her fingers up and down my wrist and reads her book. It's luxurious.

Once we land and disembark, we head through customs. I walk her to the taxi rank and feel my heart sinking with every step because I don't want to say goodbye.

Stopping next to the kerb, I reach out and touch her hip, hooking my finger into her pocket and giving it a playful tug. "Thank you for coming with me this weekend. I had a really great time with you." There's so much truth in that sentence. I had a blast, something I never thought I would say about the wedding I had been dreading for the last year.

She smiles up at me and pushes some stray hair back into her messy bun before shouldering her massive handbag. "I did too."

Okay, Theo, just man up and ask! "So"—I take a deep breath—"when am I seeing you again?" I mentally cross my fingers and look at her hopefully.

Her forehead creases with a frown. "Um, next Saturday, at my dad's party," she says sarcastically. "You'd better not be punking out of our agreement now that I've fulfilled my part! I have a signed contract; don't make me sue you for everything you own." She purses her lips and jokingly slaps my chest.

I catch her hand and hold it against my chest, pulling her closer to me. "Of course I'm not punking out. I just thought … maybe we could meet up before then. Hang out?" *Or make out.*

Understanding crosses her face. "Oh! I'm not sure I'll have the time this week. It's gonna be manic with work because I took Thursday and Friday off last week." She smiles apologetically, her hand giving mine a gentle squeeze. "Plus, didn't you say Cambridge was, like, an hour away on the train?" She scrunches her nose and shrugs. "There's no point in you travelling all the way to London just to see me."

There's every point in the world, Luce.

"Okay. It was just a thought." I force a smile, trying to cover my disappointment. No, it's not disappointment. I'll admit I'm the tiniest bit devastated by her knock-back. I thought maybe I'd done enough, but obviously, she's not ready to move on yet.

A taxi pulls up next to us, the driver rolling down his window and expectantly looking at us. I nod at him and grip Lucie's suitcase, stowing it in the boot for her.

Stubbing my toe against the pavement, I clear my throat. "So, you'll let me know about the party? You said posh, so I'm thinking … suit and tie?"

If so, I'll have to raid Jared's wardrobe again while he's away. Luckily, I have a key to their apartment.

Lucie nods and turns her nose up. "It will be a bit posh, yeah. Mostly my dad's business contacts and stuff. I'll book you a hotel somewhere near my flat, so we can share a taxi on the way back. You won't want to get a train home that late, so you might as well stay in London for the night. I'll text you the details once I've booked it."

Ouch. I'm not even staying with her. "Sounds good."

She smiles widely and wraps her arms around me, hugging me tightly, pressing her face into my neck. My heart thumps in my chest as I hug her back, tracing one hand up to cup the back of her head, my other arm clamped around her waist, holding her against me. Her smell makes the hair on the nape of my neck stand on end. It's delicious. I drop a kiss onto her temple, letting my lips linger there, savouring every last millisecond.

"I'll see you next Saturday then, Luce."

"Thanks for an epic weekend. I had a great time, and your family is lovely. I hope me being there helped it not hurt as much, watching Amy marry your brother."

I grunt and nod, not knowing what to say to that. She isn't privy to my epiphany about it not being Amy I wanted. "See you soon."

When she pulls from my arms, I reach over and open the car door for her, leaning on it as I watch her slide in and settle her handbag next to her on the seat.

As I'm about to close the door, she says, "Oh, and, Theo? Thanks for the orgasms." She sends me a flirty wink and a cheeky smile.

I burst out laughing. "You're most welcome."

Watching her wave goodbye from the window of the taxi as she speeds off is painful. How have I allowed myself to catch feels for another unavailable girl? I truly must be a masochist.

eighteen

LUCIE

By the time I let myself back into the flat, it's after six thirty, and I'm exhausted, but at the same time, I can't keep the smile off my face. This weekend was incredible, a relaxation and bit of time away that I hadn't even realised I needed so badly. My stomach rumbles as I smell remnants of Aubrey's dinner. I skipped lunch because of pre-flight nerves.

"Is that you?" my best friend calls from the living room. "Come in and tell me *everything*!"

I smile and dump my suitcase by the door as I head in, seeing her sitting on the sofa, nose stuck in her Kindle, probably reading some submission or other. "Hey. I'm going to make a cup of tea and a sandwich. You want one?"

"Tea, yes. Sandwich, no. There's some leftover chicken chow mein in the fridge if you want that instead."

My eyes widen. "Hells yes. You're the best!"

I head into the kitchen, flicking on the kettle and finding a takeaway container in the fridge. After dumping it into a bowl, I nuke it in the microwave while I make two cups of tea. By the time I take it all back to the living room and plop down onto the sofa next to my best friend, she's turned in her seat, legs tucked up under her bum, expectantly looking at me. We haven't spoken since Thursday morning, so she knows just the bare minimum about my weekend from the texts we exchanged. She's going to lose her mind when I tell her about the life-altering sex.

I shove in a bite of food, chewing quickly because my stomach is aching with hunger now. "I had a great time. Theo is adorable and hilarious. We day-drank and did some water sports together. The place was stunning, and the wedding was beautiful. It was everything you'd want your dream wedding to be. His family is lovely." I skirt around the issue, knowing what she's waiting for. I'm dragging out the suspense to torture her.

"Annnnnnnd?" Her eyes are wide with a silent question: *did you follow my advice and jump his bones?*

I give a little nod.

She squeals and spills some of her tea down herself as she pumps the air with one fist. "Tell me. I want to hear *all* of it!"

And so I tell her all of it—from meeting him at the airport right through to us saying goodbye at the cab stand a little while ago. I don't leave anything out, and she sits there, riveted, her eyes not leaving mine the whole time, apart from when she steals my phone and watches the TikTok videos Theo tagged me in. She hasn't seen them because they're on his accounts, not mine.

"Wait … he wanted to see you again? Oh my God, Lucie, he asked you out, and you said no?!" Her voice is so screechy, it makes me wince.

I scoff and roll my eyes. "He wasn't asking me out. He was suggesting we hang out. There's a difference."

"He likes you!" She blinks and disbelievingly shakes her head. "Bloody hell, I didn't realise my best friend was so damn clueless!"

"He doesn't!" *Trust me, he's into someone else.* I want to say it, tell her about Theo being crazy about his new sister-in-law, but I can't because I don't want her to dislike him. It's not his fault he likes her; hell, even I like Amy. You can't help who you fall for in life, and he wasn't an arsehole about it. In fact, he was gallant and supportive, and it made me hold him in even higher regard because of how he handled the situation.

He doesn't *like me*, like me. I was merely a distraction to him and a chance to get his leg over, and although it was great at the time and I'll never regret my weekend or the incredible sex, I'm not into casual hook-ups in real life. We had that one fantastic weekend, but neither of us is in a position to take it any further. It would simply be friends with benefits, and I'm not into that. I have to focus on my career, get myself back together, and maybe make Lucas beg for forgiveness.

Maybe in another life, un-broken Lucie meets un-infatuated Theo, and more than just one amazing weekend happens. But this is not that life.

It's just after nine o'clock the following night when I text Theo with the details of the hotel I've booked for him. It's just around the corner from my flat, so we can share a taxi back after the party. I'm already in my pyjamas (aka vest top and a massive pair of granny knickers; it's damn hot, and I miss the air conditioning of my Scottish hotel room), and I'm in the process of making a cup of tea to take to bed with me while I read when my phone rings.

I startle and look down at my screen: *FaceTime video call from Theo.* My heart gives an unexpected squeeze. As I answer it and his handsome face fills my screen, I beam a smile.

"Hey!"

He grins. "Hi. Now a good time?"

"Course. You okay? You'd better not be calling to cancel on me." My stomach clenches as I wait for his answer.

I'm not prepared for this party if he's not coming; he's like a piece of battle armour I'm going to wear. My courage wrapped up in a hunky six-foot-two package. Plus, I also want to see him again. It's only been twenty-seven hours since we said goodbye at the airport, and I already miss his jokes and his smile.

"Not calling to cancel. Just calling to say hi." He drops down onto his bed, sitting up against the headboard.

He's not wearing a shirt; I can see the skin and toned muscles across the tops of his shoulders. It makes my mouth water.

"Are you naked?" Stupidly, I try to angle my head, so I can peek down to get a look at the good stuff.

He chuckles. "No. Are you?" He moves his phone away and upwards, so I get a full-body shot, and I see he's wearing a pair of soft-looking grey tracksuit bottoms. Nothing else. The V line and that small spattering of hair make me squirm on my feet.

"No." I shake my head and pan my screen, too, but just the top half, so he doesn't see my massive granny knickers I sleep in when the weather is stifling.

Aubrey struts into the kitchen behind me, heading to the fridge. "Ooh, if you're making tea, can I have one, too, please, babe? One of those sleep teas that tastes like feet." She glances over her shoulder, and her eyes widen. "Are you FaceTiming?" Her lips press together to suppress her squeal of delight as she walks over and places her hands on my shoulders, beaming at Theo. "Hey! We haven't officially met. I'm the BFF. I'm sure you've heard all about me." She sends him a wave, her eyes twinkling with excitement.

Theo laughs and nods, shooting her his perfect, toothy smile. "I did. Hi, Aubrey. It's nice to meet you."

A little thrill goes through me that he remembered her name. I like that he listens to me. Lucas never used to listen to me unless it had to do with work. He'd ignore things I told him and things I arranged or if it was someone's birthday, and then he'd turn it around on me, blame me for not telling him in the first place. Theo listens to everything I say. I love it.

"I heard all about you too," Aubrey replies smugly.

"Nothing good," I playfully chime in, rolling my eyes, making our drinks.

Aubrey chuckles wickedly. "I still can't believe you made her dress up as Wonder Woman."

"Ah, Aubrey, don't bring that up. She'll start cursing me in Italian again." Theo winces, and we all burst into laughter.

Aubrey picks up her mug. "I'm gonna go to bed, let you two catch up. G'night."

"Good night," Theo and I both say at the same time. When she's gone, I take my tea and head to my room. "FYI, Aubrey likes you. She wants to date you if you're interested?"

Theo's eyebrows knit together in a frown. "I'm not interested. I've got my eye on someone already."

My stomach squeezes for some unknown reason. Must be the sushi I ate at lunch. "Ah, but she's married now." I send him a knowing smile.

"I wasn't talking about Amy, Luce."

He's met someone else? Ugh. The knowledge stings.

We end up speaking for over an hour. I don't even get to read my book. By the time we hang up, my battery is almost dead on my phone, and my eyes are heavy.

I sleep well that night, dreaming about Theo's smile and the way his breath blew across the top of my head as I snuggled in his arms. It's the nicest dream I've had in years.

STAND-IN SATURDAY

My week passes incredibly quickly. Work is indeed busy, as I thought it would be. Some days, I barely have time to break for lunch. The best part about my week by far? Theo FaceTimes me twice more, and we end up chatting and laughing well into the night on both occasions. It's nice, and when I hang up, it leaves me with a happy feeling simmering inside.

When Saturday comes around, I have a strange mix of excitement and trepidation in my stomach. Part of me doesn't want to go to the party and see the man who broke my heart; I don't want to watch him parading around with his pert, skinny, young gym bunny while eating my parents' food and drinking their wine. The other part of me does want to go. I desperately want to see Theo again. And if I must see Lucas, I want him to see me clinging to someone else. I want it to hurt him; even just the tiniest bit would suffice. He deserves it.

Several times over the week, I've thought about cancelling and making up some excuse, pretend I'm ill with the flu and I can't get out of bed, but each time, I think about how much it will mean to my dad to have me there. I'm his only child, and this party is a big deal for him. He's been working hard his whole life, built up his business with his best friend from scratch, brick by brick, into the massive corporation it is today. He deserves to celebrate his achievements and retire. He and my mother plan on cruising around the world for the next couple of months, soaking up the sun and spending time together. This has always been their life plan.

So, I don't cancel. Instead, I spend Saturday with Aubrey in the salon, having my hair styled into a cute up-do with a few loose curls framing my face. I have my nails done and get waxed, plucked, and buffed, primping myself until I look in the mirror and an almost stranger looks back at me.

The dress I chose for tonight is an off-the-shoulder red bodycon dress that falls just below the knee. It moulds around my shape, showing off everything, and I must admit, it makes my bum and cleavage look killer. Lucas will both love and hate that I'm wearing this dress. He's only seen me in it once. I purchased it a year or so ago for a work dinner I was attending with him. When I walked out of our bedroom in it, he did a double take and then refused to let me leave the apartment, wearing it, because it was too provocative. He ordered me to change, citing I looked like a cheap escort and that I'd embarrass him if I walked in, wearing this. But before I could take it off, he frantically fucked me up against the wall. I want to remind him of that night. How he couldn't resist me, how he gripped my hair and wrapped his hand around my throat and was almost manic as he told me I was never to wear anything this tight in front of other men, how no one got to look at me but him, how I was his and always would be.

If ever there was a dress to get Lucas's attention, this is it.

I head to the bottom of my wardrobe and look at my shoes. I've picked out two pairs for tonight, both gold and strappy, but one of them has a sexy three-inch stiletto heel, and the other is a more conservative one-inch. I prefer higher shoes, always have. I'm a bit of a shoe snob. My dream is to one day own a pair of red bottoms, ridiculously tall, sexy ones I can barely walk in. I bend, my hand hovering over both pairs.

The reason for my indecision? Lucas hates it when I wear heels. I'm five foot six, barefoot, so add in the heels, and that takes me to five-nine—only one inch shorter than my ex-fiancé. He loathed it and always said he preferred it when I looked smaller and daintier. Obviously, it was an ego thing, and he didn't like me almost being his height. But for eight years, I only wore flats or a tiny heel to please him. Since we split, not only have I stocked my wardrobe with belly tops, but also some tall heels that make me feel good about myself. Confidence comes anyplace you find it, and mine is found in a pair of killer heels.

I look back at myself in the mirror, my mind whirling. As the doorbell rings and I hear Aubrey shout that she'll get it, I reach down and grab the stilettos. Sod it. Theo is so tall that even in these heels, I'll barely come up past his chin. He always makes me feel small and dainty anyway. Screw Lucas. The whole point of tonight is, I'm supposed to be showing him that I've moved on and make him die with jealousy.

I sit on the bed and put them on, fastening the straps around my ankles, taking deep breaths to try and calm my nerves. I can hear Theo in the hallway, talking to Aubrey, and the sound of his voice makes me smile. I've missed him all week. Talking to him on FaceTime hasn't taken the edge off. I can't wait to see him again.

Deciding to forgo a handbag so I don't have to carry it all night, I shove my bank card into the back of my phone case and find my lipstick before heading out of the room. Theo has his back to me.

Aubrey sees me though, and her eyes go wide. "Damn, girl, if you were on a red carpet, you'd even give Blake Lively a run for her money."

I chuckle, but my eyes are firmly on Theo's back. As he turns, my breath catches. He's in a black suit and a crisp white shirt, which he's left unbuttoned at the throat so a tiny sliver of tanned chest peeks out from the top. It fits him to perfection, and I feel a little internal swoon threaten to break free. I gulp as my desire for him makes my palms sweaty.

Damn. Panty-melt central. Clean-up on aisle two!

Theo's eyebrows shoot up as he sees me. He raises his hands and laces his fingers together behind his head, blowing out a big breath, his eyes going wide. "Fuck," he growls.

I can honestly say that in all the years Lucas and I were together, there was never a moment in our relationship when I looked at Lucas and thought about pinning him down to the floor and ravaging him until we both passed out. I fancied him; don't get me wrong. He's a good-looking man, and he has a commanding presence about him that not only makes him a great businessman, but also gives him that attractive, masterful edge (just ask his personal trainer).

But Theo …

I sigh dreamily and step closer to him. "Jeez, you look so handsome."

Unable to control myself, I reach out and touch the lapel of his jacket, smoothing down his shirt as an excuse to feel the hardness of his chest against my fingertips. He smells intoxicating and edible. I want to lean in and press my face into the side of his neck, inhale so deeply that my lungs burst. My head is fuzzy with desire.

"You should model. I could arrange a photoshoot for you; we could put you on some book covers. They'd be instant bestsellers."

They'd sell a million copies if he were on the cover. I'd snap one up without reading the blurb just so I could have it on my bedside cabinet and it be the last thing I saw before I went to sleep.

Theo doesn't smile at my suggestion. In fact, he doesn't even look like he heard me as he drags his eyes down my body—from the top of my head to the tips of my shoes and back again. When his eyes meet mine, his pupils are blown.

"Lucie …" He huffs out another breath, and I chew on my lip, waiting to see if he suggests I change, tells me I look like a classless escort. "You look …"

I wince and wait.

"Beautiful." His voice is almost a whisper as he steps closer to me, reaching out to curl his fingers around my hip. "So. Fucking. Beautiful." He breaks up each word for emphasis, shaking his head as his other hand moves up to cup my neck. He pulls me against his hard body.

Beautiful? My insides clench, and embarrassingly, I feel tears prickle at my eyes because of his compliment. It's so in contrast to the last time I wore this dress that my heart gives a pitiful whimper.

My hands come up, resting on his hard chest as I feel slightly wobbly. His thumb tracing across my jawline makes goose bumps break out on my skin and my nipples pebble. When he makes a low moan in the back of his throat, I clench my thighs to relieve the ache that throbs in my core in response.

Why am I so attracted to this man? It's unfair!

Aubrey clearing her throat drags me out of the fog of desire I'm lost in. I blink as if coming out of a daze and swallow awkwardly, stepping back as heat sears across my cheeks.

"You want me to take a picture of you two?" she offers.

I nod dumbly as I look back at my best friend, seeing her massive grin. Her eyes twinkle with excitement as she pulls out her phone. Stepping back to Theo's side, I feel a little thrill as his arm loops around my waist. I look up to see he's looking at me at the same time; we smile at each other, and heat blooms in my belly.

When Aubrey's got the photo she wants, she clasps her hands together and eases past us. "Well, you two have fun together. I won't wait up." She disappears into the living room after sending me a wink and a mouthed, *Oh my God*, behind Theo's back.

I look back at Theo and smile shyly. "Are you all set? How's your hotel?"

He texted me earlier to say he was all checked in and asked if he needed to bring wine or anything to the party.

"Hotel is fine. It's only five minutes away."

"You really do look so handsome, Theo. God, you're gonna make Lucas shit a brick when we walk in together." I grin, imagining the jealous expression on his face.

Theo's eyes tighten as he smiles weakly and looks down at his feet while he stuffs his hands into his pockets. "Okay, so what's the plan for tonight? What do you want me to do?"

I don't really have a plan. Operation Make Lucas Sick As a Pig is basically me just winging it in a gorgeous dress with a hot guy at my side. I think about it and then shrug one shoulder. "Well, I want to make Lucas eat his heart out.

I want him to miss me so much that he falls at my feet and tells me what an idiot he is and how he can't live without me."

Theo looks incredible. He is definitely the one to make Lucas jealous and to show people I've moved on and moved up—even though my heart still hurts.

"I want you to look at me like you adore me, like you can't keep your hands off me and you want to rip my clothes off," I finish.

I turn and bend, fiddling with my shoe strap that I didn't fasten properly in my haste to see him. When I stand and glance back, I see Theo's eyes are on my bum, his jaw is tight, and his bottom lip is rolled into his mouth. His gaze travels the length of my body so slowly that it makes me squirm on my feet. He's looking at me like he wants to eat me, and he's doing that eye-fucking thing again. The heat of his gaze seems to set my insides on fire as I remember how mind-numbingly good being with him is.

I grin and nod. *Oh yeah, that'll do it.* I point to his face. "Yes! Just like that. Have you been practising? That's perfect. Save it for when we get there though, okay?" I pat his chest, not wanting him to use that bad boy up too quickly.

He lets out a strangled laugh, and his eyes drop to his feet as he rubs at his forehead with his fingers. "Look at you like I want to rip your clothes off? I think I can manage that. Let's do this then."

nineteen

THEO

I'm going to die before this night is over.
  That dress ... fuck!

My brain has melted. I can barely form a coherent sentence. The sexy red material hugs every inch of her, showing off her curves, the dip of her waist, her pert bum. *Dear God, that bum!* I gulp, swallowing down my inappropriate desire for her as I reach up and rake my hand through my hair, just for something to keep my hands busy with so I don't reach out and grab it.

She looks a vision tonight. Hot, beautiful, sexy, classy. She makes my mouth water. I have the hottest date ever. The trouble is ... this dress, the perfectly styled hair, the utterly breathtaking gorgeousness ... it isn't for me tonight. It's for Lucas. This is all for him. She told me she wanted to look so smoking hot that he died from jealousy; well, I have a feeling she's going to get her wish.

And I hate that thought.

"The Uber's here," Lucie says, looking down at her phone.

I nod, and we shout our goodbyes to Aubrey and head downstairs to meet the car.

"Would you mind putting these in your pocket? I didn't want to bring a bag with me tonight." Lucie looks over at me hopefully as she holds out a phone and lipstick tube.

"Sure." I stuff her possessions in my pocket, loving that she asked. That's the type of thing a boyfriend usually does. I know I shouldn't take pleasure from it, but I do.

Unable to resist touching her as we walk down the steps and out into the warm evening air, I set my hand on the small of her back. As soon as I do, my hormones spike again. The tiniest, barest touch, and she sets me on fire. I'm not sure what her trick is. She's like an aphrodisiac.

Once we're settled in the back seat, I shove my hand into my pocket and bring out Jared's black tie I brought with me. I wasn't sure of the dress code tonight, how posh she actually meant, so I figured I'd give her the choice. "I brought this. I didn't know how dressed up you wanted me."

Shaking her head, she puts her hand over mine and pushes it back down towards my pocket again, giving me a weak smile. "You look perfect. No tie."

I nod and put it away, noticing how tense she is. Her posture is stiff, and she presses a hand over her tummy, as if nauseous.

Reaching out, I close my hand over hers, squeezing tightly, hating the small, grateful smile she gives me as her fingers link through mine.

"Okay, Luce? You look nervous."

I lean over and kiss her temple, breathing her in, loving how her eyes flutter closed, and she leans into the kiss, making a small, unconscious whimper as her hand tightens on mine. She doesn't need to answer the question. I can feel the tension coming off her in waves. I need to make her feel better, and then an idea hits me. I sit back and shove my hand in my inside pocket, bringing out my battered pack of playing cards. I was fooling around with them at the hotel, killing time while I waited to come and meet with her. I didn't even realise I'd accidentally put them in my pocket until I was halfway to her flat tonight.

"I'll take your mind off it."

As I open the box and begin to shuffle the cards, Lucie lets out a soft laugh. She's watching my hands, so I show off a little, cutting and shuffling the deck with the precision that comes from years of practice. I move them around with my fingers and flick them between my hands like they do on TV, trying to impress her. Her eyes glitter with an excitement that makes my chest ache.

"Amy mentioned that you do magic. I wasn't sure whether to believe her or not."

I nod, keeping my eyes on her as I fan the cards out in one hand, holding them out to her. "I love it. I started when I was five after Aunt Theresa bought me a magic set in a box for Christmas." I nod towards the pack. "Pick a card and look at it, but don't let me see."

She turns in her seat and grins as she reaches out and picks one, stealthily looking at it behind her hand, her teeth biting into her bottom lip. I instruct her to put it back on the top of the pile. I make a grand show of shuffling them, and then I place my hand over the top of the cards and give them a dramatic shake. When I fan the cards back out again, one is upside down—her card.

It's only a simple trick, sleight of hand. I flipped it while distracting her with hand flourishes and showing her there was nothing up my sleeve. But she falls for it.

Lucie gasps, her eyes widening with delight as she grips my forearm. "Oh my God. That's amazing. Can you show me how to do it?"

I tilt my head. "I could, but then I'd have to kill you."

She pouts, her eyes pleading with me, and I know I'm done for. I'm already whipped; this isn't a good sign for me.

I playfully roll my eyes and blow out a breath. "Fine. But if I get thrown out of The Magic Circle for revealing secrets, you're in for it."

For the rest of the car journey, I show her how it's done. She hangs on my every word, squealing with glee, beaming a megawatt smile as I slowly do it over and over, talking her through it. She has a couple of tries but is positively terrible.

But by the time the Uber stops at our destination, I've done what I intended—distracted her and made her feel better. I've distracted myself, too, which is good. I don't want to admit it, but I'm nervous too. I'm meeting Lucie's parents tonight; I want to make a good impression. If I have my way, I'll be dating their daughter soon, so I need them to like me.

When I climb out of the car behind Lucie and look up at the substantial semi-detached three-story house, my eyes widen, and I let out an appreciative whistle. "Damn, this is your parents' house?"

Lucie nods mutely, pressing her hand over her tummy again. Her anxiousness is obviously back.

"This is where you grew up?" I glance up the exclusive tree-lined street, cataloguing the expensive cars parked out front of the row of beautiful white Georgian houses.

We're in Chelsea, one of the most expensive postcodes in London. I can't picture a young Lucie learning to ride a bike on a street like this; she's too down to earth. I didn't even realise she came from money.

"Oh, heck no." She vigorously shakes her head. "This is the product of my dad working pretty much seven days a week for the last twenty years to build his company. When my parents moved here from Italy, all they had was a lofty idea for a business but no money to their name. My dad and his best friend built their empire up from nothing. Most of my childhood was spent just above the poverty line. My parents only moved to this house about six years ago. I've never lived here; I moved out a couple of years before they bought it. Beautiful, isn't it?"

I nod, still digesting. "I don't even want to ask what a house on this street sells for." Probably anywhere between five and ten million would be my guess. I gulp, now even more intimidated with the thought of meeting her parents. I'm so out of my depth here, it's ridiculous. I reach into my pocket and pull out my tie again. "Maybe I should put this on."

Lucie steps closer to me, reaching out to grip the lapels of my jacket; the flirty look she sends me makes the skin on my neck prickle. "No. I told you, you look perfect. Smart casual with a side of hot as fuck."

I burst out laughing at her choice of description. My arm darts out, wrapping around her waist, and I tug her against me. "You think I'm hot as fuck?"

She grins teasingly. "Do you want me to come on your leg again to prove it?"

Ah, hell. "Yes." I nod eagerly, my fingers digging into her back so she can't pull away.

All week, I've been replaying my weekend with her, and she has to go and mention that right as I'm about to step into an expensive-looking house and meet her parents. Now, I'm battling an erection. Damn girl.

She giggles, and pink climbs over her cheeks, making her look adorable. "Come on. Stop with the flirting, and let's go inside."

"You started it."

"And I'm finishing it too." She grips the sleeve of my jacket and gives me an encouraging pull towards the path that leads to the front door.

My mouth is dry as dirt as we climb the front steps. My palms are sweating, so I wipe them on my trouser legs, trying to calm down. As we approach the door, I can hear the party already in full swing inside; people are talking and laughing, and the smell of food permeates the air. Lucie's finger hovers over the doorbell, but she doesn't press it. Instead, she looks back at me, her forehead creased with a frown, her eyes tight with worry.

"Um … my parents don't know why Lucas and I split, so please don't mention the cheating. Oh, and I didn't tell them we went to Scotland together last weekend, so don't mention that either. Also, although I want you to look at me like you want to rip my clothes off, my parents can be a teeny bit old-fashioned, so don't be grabbing a handful of arse or sticking your tongue down my throat in there, okay? Keep it subtle. The guests at the party will mostly be older business associates and their partners; it's going to be a tad snooty." She winces apologetically. "We only have to stay a couple of hours. We'll show our faces, do the rounds and say hi to a few people, and make Lucas regret the day he ever met his personal trainer, and then we can leave."

I nod, clenching my teeth at the mention of Lucas's name. Every time she says it, the ball of jealousy in my chest expands. I didn't realise it was possible to hate someone you'd never met. "Why don't your parents know about the cheating?"

Lucie sighs and fiddles with her necklace. "His dad and mine are best friends and business partners, and Lucas works for the company too. We decided not to drag them into our mess, and so we told them the split was amicable so as not to cause friction for anyone."

I tilt my head to the side and raise one eyebrow. "Is that the royal *we*? Or did *Lucas* decide that was for the best? Seems to me like he came out smelling of roses, and you got the raw end of the deal there, Luce."

She blinks, her mouth opening for a reply but then closing again. She knows I'm right. He is the one in the wrong, but he gets to keep his reputation intact while she lost her home and job, and no one even knows the real reason. He's even more of an arsehole than I thought.

Smiling sympathetically, I lean in and press a kiss to her forehead, wrapping my arms around her and hugging. She whimpers and hugs me back tightly, clinging to me like I'm a life raft and she's stuck out at sea. Her fingers dig into my back as she presses against me.

Turning my head, I run my nose along the side of her jaw, breathing her in. Her perfume, mixed with the vanilla smell of her shampoo, makes my senses prickle with desire.

She feels so right in my arms, as if she's meant to be there. I don't want to let go.

Disappointment that she's not mine hits me like a kick to the balls. I'm gutted that she's still intending on using me tonight to make her ex jealous. I know that's the agreement we made in the lift, but all week, we've been talking and messaging back and forth. I hoped maybe I was gaining ground, making her think of me as something other than a friend she had a hot weekend with once. We get on great, and it's glaringly obvious that this sexual tension between us hasn't gone anywhere during the week apart. I want her to want me here tonight, at her side, because she wants to spend time with me, not because she wants to use me as a point score against her cheating ex. I still don't know if this farce is intended to hurt Lucas or win him back. I'm in limbo at the moment, waiting to see which way this goes.

With her in my arms though, I know I need to put up more of a fight. I can't just roll over and let Lucas waltz in and steal her back from under my nose.

I gulp and pull back a fraction, sliding my hands up her body until I cup her neck. Tilting her head so she has to look at me, I stroke her jawline with my thumbs.

Her eyes appear slightly dazed as they meet mine. Her luscious ruby-red lips look so inviting that my brain almost malfunctions with the desperate need to kiss her.

I want her. I'm crazy about her. All week, I've missed her so much that it's like I have a gaping hole inside me. I've spent each day just looking forward to the next time I speak to her. FaceTiming with her every other day has been the high point of my week; seeing her smile lights me up. But it's only served to prove to me that I want more.

She needs to know I'm into her. She needs to know she has options. I need to man up and spell it out and see what happens. This might be my last opportunity. If she gets back with her ex tonight, it might actually kill me.

"Luce …" I begin.

She blinks up at me, but before I can attempt to formulate my jumbled thoughts into words, the front door swings open, and we both look over to see an older version of Lucie standing there, her eyes bouncing between the two of us, her mouth pressing into a thin, disapproving line.

twenty

LUCIE

My mother does not look pleased. I can tell by the way she doesn't blink and the way her head tilts a fraction to the left. She smiles, but it's the type of smile she gives to people who try to tell her that pasta is not a food group. Never tell my mother that pasta isn't a food group—if you want proof of this, ask my old cookery teacher at school.

Although she might have a smile on her face, in her head, she has already killed you twice over and is mentally swiping through suitable locations to bury your body. That polite smile is currently directed at Theo. I have the insane urge to dive in front of him and shield him with my body. Theo does not deserve the animosity I see building in her eyes.

I step away from his warm embrace, missing the contact immediately, and his hands drop down to his sides. I blink and swallow. Being close to Theo like that hazes me out a bit; it's like he weaves a spell over me, dazzles me so much sometimes that it's as if I were in a bubble where it was just him and me and none of our problems could permeate through. Everyone else disappears. It's nice. I kind of wish it would last forever.

"Mamma, hi," I greet. "The doorbell must be broken. We rang twice." I shrug innocently.

Without speaking, she leans out of the door and presses the bell. Chimes ring deafeningly loud in the hallway behind her. She doesn't even flinch.

"Ah, you fixed it. Great job." I grin and step over the threshold, ignoring Theo as he lets out a little chuckle behind me. I wrap my arms around her because if there's one thing my mother cannot resist, it's hugs from her only child. "I missed you. I haven't seen you for ages!"

It's not been ages; it's been three days. She popped into my work on Wednesday to take me for a surprise lunch (basically so she could tell me again how important it is for me to attend tonight).

I pull back, and her hands cup my face as she leans up and kisses the tip of my nose.

"Ah, Luciella, I'm so pleased you could come. This is going to mean so much to Papà. He will be thrilled to see you."

I pat her elbows and nod. "Of course. I wouldn't have missed it. You look beautiful, Mamma."

And she does. She's wearing a flowy black gown that kisses the floor. My mother has always been glamorous, but tonight, she looks stunning. Her dark hair is pulled up, her ears and neck glitter with jewels, and her lips are painted the same colour as mine. It's the Gordio signature shade for nights out—the one Theo said made my mouth look like his favourite childhood lollipops.

"Thank you, darling. So do you. *Magnifica*." She looks me up and down, her eyes glittering with affection as she gives a chef's-kiss hand gesture that makes me laugh.

I step back and motion to Theo, who is standing tall at my side, obviously blissfully unaware that the smile Mamma is giving him is not a warm welcome, but more of an *if I see you touch my daughter again, you'll lose the ability to wipe your own arse* silent warning. "I'd like to introduce you to my date, Theo Stone. Theo, this is my mother, Stella Gordio."

Her eyes tighten again as she turns her attention to him, holding out her hand for a polite shake.

"Mrs Gordio, it's lovely to meet you. You have a beautiful home." Theo gestures around the hallway in example, shooting her a charming smile.

He looks so boyishly cute that I don't know how she can retain her hard composure, but she does.

She nods. "Thank you, Mr Stone."

"Call me Theo." He grins and waves a hand.

Mamma doesn't answer or return the gesture of telling him to call her by her first name. Instead, she turns back to me and switches to speaking in Italian, so Theo won't understand. "How long has this been going on?" She inclines her head at him, but her accusing eyes don't leave mine.

I switch to Italian too. "Not very long. Please be civil. He's a genuinely lovely man. Besides, I wasn't aware that I didn't have a plus-one invitation for tonight."

"But Lucas will be here."

"Yes, you told me he would be."

She holds my gaze for longer than necessary before giving a barely perceptible nod and pulling back, clasping her hands together. Her expression is that of a polite host now, and she switches back to English. "Well, come on in and enjoy the party. Are you hungry? We have lots of food laid out." She turns to me. "I've ordered a big cake for Papà as a surprise. When they do the speeches, the catering staff is going to bring it out. Chocolate cake with vanilla buttercream and fresh raspberries inside. He is going to love it."

"He will." I grin and nod, loving the idea.

My parents live in this huge house, have several cars, and can jet off on month-long holidays at the drop of a hat, but at their core, they are still such simple folk. My father will be delighted when he's presented with his favourite cake.

"Well, come on. We can't stand in the hallway all night. Let's go join the party," Mamma says.

We follow her up the hallway, two pairs of stiletto shoes clacking on the marble tiles. As we walk, I reach out and slip my hand into Theo's, holding on tightly, trying to soak up some of his confidence and the general air of ease he always has about him. With each step further into my parents' house, my anxiety grows. My heartbeat pounds in my ears, and I feel a swirl of panic brewing inside. The thought of seeing Lucas and his new girlfriend is making my stomach roll. I don't really know what to expect to happen tonight … or what I want to happen. I clearly haven't thought this through properly. My brain is a bit muffled, like it's stuffed with cotton wool.

Theo brings my hand up to his mouth, planting a gentle kiss on my knuckles, and my heart stutters in my chest as I look over at him. He sends me a cheeky wink and gives my hand a squeeze. And just like that, my panic subsides.

As we all step into the formal living room, Mamma turns and smiles. "I'm going to go find your father and tell him you're here. You go say hello to everyone." She waves to the room as she saunters off through the crowd.

My eyes widen as I take in the array of people standing around, drinking flutes of champagne the catering staff is handing out from silver trays. Everyone is dressed in posh evening wear—suits and formal dresses. My eyes scan the women, and I groan. They're all in muted colours—blacks, navy blues, dark purples, greys.

My eyes drop to the floor as I brush some non-existent lint from my thigh, now wishing I'd worn something more inconspicuous. I'm going to stick out like a sore thumb in this red hooker dress. *What was I thinking?*

At my side, Theo steps closer to me, his free hand brushing against my hip as he dips his head to talk to me. "Are you okay? What did I miss in the hallway?"

"I'm fine. It was nothing."

He frowns, and I long to reach up and smooth the lines away with my fingertips.

Going up on my tiptoes, I press a kiss on the edge of his jaw. "Honestly, Theo, it was nothing. She thought I was coming alone; that's all."

He nods, his arm snaking around my waist, hand resting on the small of my back as he pulls me closer to him. "Okay. So, give me the skinny on these people. Any good gossip I should know about as we're going around and saying hi?"

"Nope. They're all pretty boring."

Over his shoulder, I see my dad heading through the crowd, patting people on the back, nodding greetings, but his eyes are firmly latched on me. I smile widely and pull away from Theo, readying for the bear hug I know I'll get. I'll freely admit, I am a bit of a daddy's girl.

"Hey, Papà!"

My father grins, too, crinkles forming around his eyes as he holds out his arms and engulfs me into his embrace. "*Ciao, bambina.*" He pulls back and plants a kiss on each of my cheeks. "Now that you're here, the real party can begin."

I chuckle and beam at him. My dad is my hero. He's a brilliant husband and father. All his life, he has worked hard, sacrificed so much to give my mother and me a wonderfully full life. Though he is as soft as a teddy bear with my mother and me (he really does love his girls), woe betide anyone who upsets them. I wouldn't want to get on the wrong side of him.

"Papà, this is Theo Stone." I wave at my fake date for the night. "And this is my father, Tomas Gordio." I wave back at my dad, biting the inside of my cheek as I watch the exchange between them. "Theo is an incredible illustrator who does freelance work at my company. We met at my office."

Theo sticks out his hand. "It's nice to meet you, sir. Thank you for allowing me to come to your retirement party. Lucie's told me all about you."

My dad glances down at the outstretched hand and then looks up at me questioningly.

Holding my breath, I nod in encouragement and shoot him the begging eyes.

Papà sighs resignedly and puts his hand in Theo's, giving it a shake. "Nice to meet you too. So, a book illustrator? Do you have many works published?"

I breathe a sigh of relief as Theo and my dad engage in some polite chit-chat about his job, where Theo lives in Cambridge, and then they start talking about golf when Theo asks what my father plans to do with all of his free time now that he's retiring. My father is nice to Theo, but as someone who knows him well, I can see he isn't willing to give him a chance. He's businesslike and standoffish, and his shoulders are stiff. This is merely polite conversation. I know why, and I can't even blame him. Lucas and I were together for so long that everyone thought we would finally join our families—even I believed it. My father watched Lucas grow from a babe in his arms to the man who runs the sales division at his company. Of course, he is going to hold out hope of us reuniting and not be overly keen on seeing me with someone else even if it is all for show.

After about ten minutes of talking, my father is called off to greet another guest, and Theo and I wander the room, conversing easily with my parents' friends who have known me since I was in pigtails and training bras. Theo is a natural people person, and his stranger chat is on point. He's engaging, witty, charismatic, and funny, fitting in with the snooty business-type people with an ease and grace I wish I had.

When we finally make it across the room and stop at the buffet table, we're just starting on our second glasses of champagne.

Theo's shoulder bumps mine, and he smiles over at me as we pick up bone china plates and look over at the visual feast. My mother went all out with the caterers.

STAND-IN SATURDAY

"Is it acceptable to start on the dessert already, or do I have to stuff in a few prawn vol-au-vents first?" Theo eyes the array of macarons, cake pops, and selection of classy layered desserts artfully arranged in posh shot-sized glasses laid out at the back of the long table.

Grinning, I pick up a chocolate-dipped strawberry, holding it up to his mouth. His beautiful amber eyes twinkle as he leans in, his gaze locked on mine as he takes the whole thing into his mouth, biting off at the stalk, lips closing around my fingers in the process as he gives a little suck.

The move sends a bolt of something straight to my core, and I watch his mouth, mesmerised as he chews. "Blimey, Theo, was that supposed to turn me on? Because if so, you succeeded." I'm breathless now as my body temperature hikes up a couple of degrees.

He grins smugly, shrugging one shoulder, and reaches over to pick up a handful of strawberries and some cake pops. "I can't help it if you have a food fetish."

More like a Theo fetish. A giggle escapes my lips, and I look down at my plate, feeling my face heat up. *Damn it, he turns me so girlie sometimes; it's ludicrous.*

As we stand and stuff our faces with desserts (neither of us even goes near the real food), I look around the room. My gaze lands on Marie and Fred Maitland, Lucas's parents, who are across the room, talking to another couple I don't know. I raise my hand, sending them a wave. Marie inclines her head in acknowledgement but doesn't smile. Instead, she elbows Fred and leans in to say something to him. Fred's head swivels in my direction, and his eyebrows pinch with reproach. My stomach clenches. I've always had a good relationship with them. Even after the split, they've been nothing but loving and supportive towards me, but now, their expressions and hard eyes seem hostile. I don't know why.

"Who are they?" Theo asks, slipping his arm around my shoulders. "You've gone all stiff, so I'm assuming we don't like them."

I chuckle and bump my hip with his, looking up at him and rolling my eyes. He's too funny sometimes. "Mr and Mrs Maitland. They're Lucas's parents. And we do like them."

As a waitress walks past, I pick up a glass of orange juice from her tray and smile gratefully. Just as I'm about to take a sip, I look back over to Marie again and see *him*. Lucas. He's just stepping to his mother's side. She leans in and whispers something to him, and the smile falls from his face as he looks over at me. Our eyes meet, and I gulp. The air suddenly feels stifling. This is the first time I've seen him since the day I walked out. I can't move. I feel trapped, like a deer in headlights. Although I knew I'd see him, I still wasn't quite prepared.

twenty-one

LUCIE

Lucas looks good, as always. Smart and professional in his three-piece charcoal-grey suit, black tie, and matching pocket handkerchief. I picked out that suit. I picked out all his suits. His dark blond hair is styled neatly but is a tad longer than normal, curling around his ears and the nape of his neck, in a way he hates. Maybe gym-bunny girl isn't as good as me at booking his appointments and reminding him to go. His distinctive pale icy-blue eyes bore into mine from across the room, and I feel a cold trickle of something run down my spine. He doesn't smile, but he does tilt his chin up in a silent greeting.

I nod a silent hello, too, and my hand tightens on my glass. Eight years of my life I spent with this man. I gave him everything of myself, gave up things I'd dreamed of for him. He is such a massive part of me. But … the thing that surprises me is … seeing him doesn't hurt as much as I thought it would. During the span of the last three months, I mentally built this moment up, repeatedly thought about seeing him again. I imagined what it would feel like to look at him and know he wasn't mine anymore, how much it would hurt. I wondered if it would feel as bad as when I walked in early from my spin class and caught him naked with that girl. That day he ripped my heart out, I always thought it would feel like that again, seeing him for the first time … but it's a bit of an anticlimax.

I feel … okay.

My eyes flick behind him, searching out my replacement, but I can't see her yet.

When I look back to Lucas, I notice his jaw is tight, and his eyes drag over me in my dress. The disapproval is so easy to see on his face; he might as well be holding a neon sign, announcing it.

He remembers.

And he still hates it.

Good.

His back is ramrod straight, his nostrils flare, his eyebrows pull together, and when his eyes meet mine again, they're hard and judgemental. I almost want to flinch away immediately, but I force myself to raise my glass and take a sip of my juice before I turn my back on Lucas and look up at Theo.

Theo grins and reaches out, brushing a curl of my hair behind my ear, his fingers trailing across my cheek. I let out the breath I didn't realise I had been holding and try to ground myself by staring at the little freckle he has under one of his eyes.

"Lucas is here." My voice is barely above a whisper, but he hears me.

His mouth snaps shut, and he nods slowly, pushing his plate onto the table, chocolate-dipped strawberries no longer important. My affection for him ratchets up another notch at how quickly he went from jokey Theo to supportive Theo. I love it.

"Okay. What time is he at?"

"He's at, like, your one o'clock?" I guess.

I reach out and fiddle with one of his shirt buttons as his hand traces across the bare skin at my shoulder blades, and his eyes flick over in Lucas's direction.

"Grey suit, blond hair, eyes blazing like fire, ready to burn me alive?" Theo asks, dipping his head and nuzzling his mouth against my ear.

His hot breath blowing down my neck is almost too much, and I shift on my feet and press closer to him, needing reassurance. I'm immensely glad I have him with me. He's playing his side of the bargain to perfection; anyone looking on would think that he really does adore me, exactly like I asked of him.

"That sounds about right."

Lucas always did have a hard hundred-yard stare.

"Looks like you're getting your wish. He's jealous as hell."

Theo's nose runs up the side of my cheek, and my breath leaves me in a dreamy sigh. I don't know how he does it. One touch, and I'm like putty in his hands, even with my cheating ex standing thirty feet away.

"Forget him, Luce. Come dance with me?"

I need to do something because I don't want to keep standing here. I can practically feel Lucas's stare boring into the back of my head. It makes me want to squirm, but I keep my chin up and focus my attention solely on Theo. As soon as I nod in agreement, his fingers slide down my shoulders and over my arms, tickling their way down until he gets to my hands. Interlacing our fingers, he smiles and nods over his shoulder towards where a few people are dancing to the music that plays quietly in the background.

My smile returns as I let him lead me along to the makeshift dance floor, where he pulls me into his arms and we sway to the beat. It's nice. As we dance, Theo whispers silly jokes in my ear, twirling me, flirting with me until the tension in my back eases, and I melt into his embrace and start to have a good time again. A couple of songs in, Lucas is long forgotten.

It's then I decide that being stuck in that lift with Theo is probably the best thing that could have happened to me. I can't imagine being here on my own tonight. I'd be knocking back the shots by now—or crying in a taxi on my way home already.

One of my hands is loose in Theo's while my other grips his shoulder as I rest my temple against his cheek, breathing him in. I close my eyes and pretend we're back at the wedding, dancing there together instead of here, where I know people are watching and judging me.

Theo's hand traces up from the small of my back until it cups the back of my neck, his fingers toying with my necklace as his forearm clamps me to him. "This dress is driving me wild, Luce. I have the most beautiful date ever tonight."

My confidence spikes at his compliment, and I grin against his shoulder. "Really? Does she mind you dancing with me?"

He laughs, his chest rumbling against mine, and my tummy gives a little flutter. When he pulls back, our eyes meet, and I get trapped there. His smile is dazzling. When his mouth starts heading towards mine, I smile and lean in, too, eager for it. When our lips connect, he tastes of strawberries and chocolate mousse. A tiny moan slips from my lips, and my hand tightens on his shoulder, using him for support as my knees weaken. It's only a soft, chaste kiss, but it feels like more. It's intimate and sensual, just perfect. He pulls back and rests his forehead against mine as we continue to dance. I can't stop smiling.

"Excuse me."

That voice … I'd know it anywhere.

I wrench my face away from Theo's and turn my head sharply, seeing Lucas standing next to us. His eyes are wild, his jaw is clenching with anger, and his hands are in tight fists. Up close, I can see the darker flecks of blue around the pupils of his pale blue eyes. Theo was right; they're blazing with fire. It's like staring down the barrels of a gun. I'm not sure I've ever seen him so mad, and I've seen him mad! My chest constricts.

"Mind if I cut in?" Lucas asks.

My hand instinctively tightens in Theo's. I don't want to dance with him.

Theo nonchalantly smiles over at Lucas. "Actually, I do. Her dance card is filled for the night. Sorry, buddy." He sends him a playful wink, which just makes Lucas madder.

His top lip twitches with a barely contained snarl as he turns his attention back to me. "Lucie, I'd like to talk to you." It's a command, not a request.

The hair on my nape prickles. His jealousy is palpable; it hangs in the air so thickly that I can almost taste it. Surprisingly, it doesn't bring me the joy or closure I was hoping for.

"I'm busy, Lucas." My voice is clogged with emotion and cracks on his name. Theo's hand strokes my back gently, as if offering me support. "Go talk with your sofa-shag girl instead."

"I'm not with Meredith. We were never a thing."

Meredith. I didn't know her name until now. It's not what I expected a fiancé-stealing ho to be named.

"You looked like a thing last time I saw you." I challengingly raise one eyebrow and then turn my attention back to Theo, ending the conversation. Or so I hope.

"Lucie—" Lucas's hand shoots out, wrapping around my upper arm, roughly yanking me away from Theo, his fingers digging into my skin with bruising force.

Theo instantly reaches out, too, grabbing Lucas's hand and shoving it off me. "Wind your neck in, shithead. She said no." His voice is practically a growl as he steps closer to Lucas, eyeing him harshly.

The height difference is so apparent that Lucas has to tilt his head as they lock eyes. I bet he hates it.

My mouth pops open in shock, and I grip the back of Theo's jacket, giving him a slight pull. "Don't, Theo. Please don't."

Starting a fight in the middle of my father's party is the last thing I want tonight. Theo obliges and steps back to my side, but his posture doesn't loosen. He is seething mad. It's weird how, even at a time like this, I can find that a little hot. I like that he's stepping up to my ex and defending me.

I wave my hand at Lucas in a shoo gesture. "Lucas, please just go back to your date."

His rage-filled eyes flick to me. "I don't have a date. I came here alone tonight. I was hoping you and I would be able to talk things through."

My breath catches. *He didn't bring a date?*

He came here alone, and now, I look like the bad one, bringing someone with me. This is the reason for my mother's shocked and disappointed face at the door when she saw me with Theo. She knew Lucas was going to corner me tonight. They likely all knew. This was probably all cooked up and planned over a Maitland-Gordio game night. Operation Get Lucas and Lucie Back Together Again. No wonder Marie and Fred were looking at me so disparagingly earlier. They think I'm parading Theo around just to hurt their son.

And they're correct.

That is the exact reason I brought him here with me. This is literally what I signed that lift contract for. This moment. This hard, blazing look in Lucas's eyes, where I can see that he regrets what he did, that he misses me, that he might even want me back.

I don't know how to feel. I don't know what I want. My brain is all over the place, firing too many thoughts for me to be able to process them properly. This is all too much; it's like sensory overload. I'm a little light-headed.

Before I can recover, Lucas's mother stalks over, her arms folded across her chest, a wide-eyed Fred trailing along behind her.

Marie leans in, her glare accusing, her voice low so the people around us can't hear her words. "Lucie, how could you do this? You knew Lucas was going to be here tonight. This is not fair on him."

Not fair? Not fair is walking in exhausted from your exercise class, only to find your so-called loving fiancé banging another girl, doggy style, on your two-week-old dream sofa. They didn't even have the decency to put down a throw to protect the velvet. *That's* what's not fair. But I can't say that because they don't know. No one knows.

I look to Lucas, pleading with him to step in here. He has the opportunity to be the bigger man. If he cares about me, wants to talk things out like he said, he should step in and put a stop to this. Defend me. Even if he doesn't tell them the reason for the break-up, he has the power to step in now and disperse all this anger towards me. I've done nothing wrong here. I'm the victim in all this.

He eyes me, a twitch of a smile at the corner of his lips, as if he's enjoying having the upper hand and seeing me squirm. And when his mother sympathetically looks over at him, instead of jumping to my aid, he lets his shoulders slump defeatedly, and his gaze drops to the floor; he's hamming it up, playing the *little wounded boy* routine to make me look even worse.

Marie continues, her voice hitching with a little sob, and my heart clenches. We've always been close; I hate that she's upset over this too. "How could you bring someone tonight when you knew it would hurt Lucas? This is so selfish, Lucie. I would never have expected this of you."

Tears prickle at the backs of my eyes. My mouth opens and closes, but no sound comes out.

When Theo's hand closes over mine and he squeezes, it makes my heart ache. He raises his chin and is the only one who steps in to help me. "Excuse me, Mrs Maitland, but I think you're forgetting that your son is a grown adult. I'm sure if he had wanted to talk to Lucie in the last three months, he could have picked up a phone and called her. But he didn't. None of this is Lucie's fault. How exactly does moving on with her life make her selfish? You'd prefer her to sit around and wait for Lucas to decide he wants her back? Be real. Life doesn't work that way." His tone is sharp and scathing. He turns his attention to Lucas. "And you. Don't you ever grab her like that again, or I will fuck you up. Got it?"

I get another rush of affection for him. He is such a great guy.

People close to us stare, stunned, but the rest of the party continues, oblivious.

Theo turns to me and motions his head towards the open patio doors at the back of the house. "Shall we get some air, Luce?"

I cling to his hand, nodding dumbly, my heart beating so hard that I can hear it pulsing in my ears. He confidently strides through the room, guiding me along behind him. It's still light outside as we step into the fresh air and walk slightly around the corner, so we're out of view of the other guests.

When Theo turns to me, his eyes are shining with sympathy. "You okay?"

Am I? I'm not really sure. My vision swims with tears, but I fight against letting them fall as I half-nod, half-shake my head, shrugging one shoulder noncommittally. "Yeah. No. I don't know. Thank you for helping me. You're amazing, you know that? I really appreciate you stepping in and defending me when he didn't."

Without my permission, a tear slides down my cheek, and Theo reaches out, softly wiping it away before wrapping his arms around me and pulling me against his hard body. His smell fills my lungs, and I press my face into the side of his neck, soaking up his comfort like a sponge. The hug is luxurious and takes out the sting of what just happened. I don't know how long we stand like that, but it's not long enough. I want to live right here, in his arms, protected from the world.

Sighing deeply, his breath blowing across my shoulder, he pulls back and smiles down at me. "I don't like seeing

STAND-IN SATURDAY

you upset. He's not worth you being upset over, Luce." His hands cup my jaw, and he wipes more tears away as they glide down my cheeks. "He's an absolute bellend. And a dumb shit for letting you slip through his fingers. He doesn't deserve your tears, Luce. I hate that you're still in love with him."

His forehead creases with a frown. There's something blazing in his eyes, a passion that is half-mad, half-sad. I can't work it out.

"You ... you have options. You know that, right?" He gulps, gently pushing my hair away from my face. "You could move on if you wanted to, Luce. You could forget him. You could move forward and be happy with a man who would appreciate how amazing you were, someone who would know how lucky he was if he got to call you his."

He dips his head and kisses my forehead, his lips lingering there. It's so sweet that my eyes drop closed, and I grip his waist, not letting him move away.

"I-I like you, Lucie. I'm crazy about you actually." He says the words against my forehead, and my eyes fly open as I wonder if I heard him right.

He's crazy about me? Me?!

Theo pulls back a fraction, the tip of his nose brushing mine. "I missed you so much this week. It's the silly things I missed most. Like how you snort when you laugh really hard, or how your nose wrinkles when you're trying to decide something, or how you twiddle your hair around your finger when you're reading your book, or how witty you are. You make me laugh like no girl I've ever met."

His eyes burn into mine. I can't look away; I can barely breathe.

"I think you're perfect, Luciella Gordio."

His thumb strokes across my cheek, leaving a burning trail in its wake. A tiny whimper slips from my mouth at his sweet words. No one has ever said that to me before.

He licks his lips and continues, "Every part of you is perfect. From your big green eyes to your sassy, sugar-obsessed mouth, right down to your bum that drives me wild. I like everything about you. I think us meeting in that lift meant something. And I know you're still hurting over that dickhead and that you brought me here to make him jealous, but ... Luce, I don't just want to be a stand-in for Lucas. I want to be your leading man. I want to be the one who causes you to smile down at your phone when my name pops up on your screen. I want to be the one who kisses you good night, the one who makes you happy, the one you can't live without."

What is happening? My shock makes my skin break out in goose bumps. This is the last thing I expected to come out of Theo's mouth. He likes Amy. He's smitten with his brother's new wife; he told me so himself.

"But ... you like Amy," I whisper, my mind reeling, his words on repeat.

"You're perfect. Every part of you is perfect."

My heart squeezes in my chest.

"No." He firmly shakes his head. "I just thought I did. In the beginning, I'll admit that, yes, I wanted to date her. I thought I was in love with her. Seeing her with my brother made me jealous as hell. I like Amy, she's epic, and I thought I was jealous of them because I wanted her for myself. But last weekend, at the wedding with you, I realised I wasn't even upset that they were getting married. When I watched her walk down the aisle to marry Jared, I realised it wasn't actually *her* I was jealous of. It was their relationship. Their easy, fun, and loving relationship. They're soul mates, and I realised *that's* what I was jealous of. That my twin has found it and I haven't.

"I know now that it was never Amy I wanted. I just wanted someone epic *like* Amy. Someone I can be myself with and who accepts and likes everything about me. Someone who makes me so happy that I smile, even when I'm just thinking about them. Someone I can't get enough of. I think that might be you, Luce. Since I met you, you've kinda consumed me. You're amazing and smart and funny and brave and beautiful. You've dazzled me, and I'm hooked. I'm crazy about you, and I wish you weren't still hung up on a guy who didn't treat you right. I wish there were none of this baggage and that you were available. But I need you to know that you have options. If you wanted to give it a go with me, I'm here for all of it."

I blink, so shocked that I can barely process his words. *Where did this all come from?* My brain isn't working right. I can't take it in.

He wants to be with me?

I've never even considered dating Theo. We were merely strangers who became acquaintances and then friends, all while fulfilling a role for each other. And, yes, that turned into mind-blowing sex, but that's all it was supposed to be, just two adults seeking pleasure in each other for a few days. It wasn't supposed to be anything more. We weren't supposed to catch feelings.

I don't know what to say. All I wanted from tonight was for Lucas to get jealous and to feel a small iota of the pain that I felt when I walked in on him with that girl, that I've still felt every day since. And maybe, though I've never admitted this to anyone, I secretly wanted him to fall at my feet and beg me for another chance so passionately that I'd have no choice but to take him back. Because I loved him so much when we were together that I almost don't even know who I am without him now.

But here is a wonderful, hot, adorable guy standing in front of me, telling me he's crazy about me and that I have options.

What do I do with that? My brain is reeling.

This thing with Theo was never supposed to happen. I thought he liked Amy, so I didn't even allow myself to daydream how it would be, being with him properly, after last weekend ended. Now that I know he likes me, my head is spinning like a top, and I don't even know what I want.

He's terrific, but I'm still in love with Lucas … aren't I? Eight years I was with him. Yes, he hurt me and ripped my heart out, but you can't just turn feelings like that off—though I wish I could. I'm so confused that I can barely think straight.

Theo is watching me, waiting for me to speak. I don't even think he's breathing. Swallowing awkwardly, I try to formulate words, but they're just *gone*.

Thankfully, high-pitched tings cut through the air, the sounds of someone tapping a knife on the side of a glass, and seconds later, my mother sticks her head out of the patio door, and her eyes land on me.

"Oh, there you are! Come, Luciella. Papà is about to make a speech." She expectantly holds out her hand to me.

Oh, thank goodness. Precious few minutes' reprieve where I can work out what I want to say!

I nod at her dumbly, and Theo steps back, letting his arms drop from my waist as he forces a polite smile and turns to my mother.

Still in a daze, I walk away from him, my heart in my throat.

The speeches are relatively short. I stand at the front, next to Mamma, who beams with pride as my father thanks everyone for coming and talks about his grand plans for a lazy future. After, a few people step up and say lovely things about my dad and funny stories about what it was like to work with him over the years. I don't dare look at Theo or Lucas. I clap and toast and sip champagne along with everyone, trying to pretend like I don't feel as if I'd been put through a wringer.

After the cake is carried out and my dad has made a big show of blowing out the candles and grinning like a loon, it's over, and instead of going back to Theo, who is chatting with one of my father's managing directors I introduced him to earlier, I point over my shoulder and mouth the word, *Bathroom*, at him.

He nods in understanding, and I slink away through the crowd, trying to clear my mind. My thoughts flick from Theo to Lucas and back again. I'm still none the wiser.

As I wander up the deserted hallway towards the bathroom, I'm so lost in my own head that I don't hear Lucas approach until his hand closes around my wrist.

"We need to talk," he states, and he pulls me into one of the spare bedrooms, closing the door behind him.

Twenty-two

LUCIE

"Lucie, we need to work this out. I hate being without you. I miss you so much. I'm sorry. I'm *so* sorry. I love you, sweetheart."

I'm standing in the middle of the room, my mouth agape, staring at him, trying to take it all in. Lucas never apologises for anything, and right now, he's almost grovelling. My insides clench, and I wring my hands, unable to look away from his pleading, hurt expression.

This is everything I've wanted from him for the last three months—him to say he's sorry and that he doesn't want to be without me. This is what I wished for when I cried myself to sleep for weeks after we split.

He steps forward, reaching out and taking my hands in his. I let him because I'm too shocked to protest.

"I was stupid. I should never have cheated. I don't know what I was thinking. It must have been a moment of insanity or maybe the strain of work. You know I was stressed over that Apollo account all that week; maybe the pressure got to me, and I had a psychotic break or something. That's the only explanation I can come up with. It was only a one-time thing, just a mistake. I'm not with that girl. I haven't even seen her since that night." He shakes his head, his expression imploring as his thumbs stroke the backs of my hands.

"Did you stop going to the gym then, or did you have to find another? Bet that was a shock to the system, having to fill out your own membership paperwork for once. Is that why you want me back?" I don't know where the dig comes from. My brain still isn't engaged, so it must have just been bitterness dripping from my tongue automatically.

Lucas can't do anything for himself. I took care of everything for him. I single-handedly ran his office and did most of his job for him. A little bit of menial paperwork to fill out is below his pay grade.

Lucas's eye twitches at the disrespect, but he lets it slide. I'm never normally this bold with him. Usually, I let him steamroll me into things.

"I want you back because I love you," he replies. "Lucie, give me a chance to make it up to you. I'm sorry I hurt you. I wish I hadn't done it. I miss you. You're the one for me; you always have been. Please come home, sweetheart. It's awful, being without you."

He pulls me towards him, raising my arms and guiding them around his neck, and then his hands gently stroke my face, my neck, my shoulders. My eyes flutter closed, and my heart aches in my chest. Dipping his head, he plants soft, persuasive kisses at the corner of my mouth, peppering them across my cheek as his arms wrap around me, his embrace cloaking me in such familiarity that it's almost like sinking into a warm bath after a long and weary day.

I gulp, and emotion swells inside me. All my adult life, all I've ever wanted is to be loved by this man, and here he is, showering me with affection, telling me his life is awful without me.

With his arms still around me, he walks me backwards until I'm pressed against the wall. He crowds in, every part of his body touching mine, smothering me with affection until he's all I can think about.

His aftershave fills my senses. I recognise it immediately—Creed Aventus. He's always worn it; it's so Lucas that I could pick him out of a line-up with my eyes closed. This is the same expensive aftershave he would spray on me before we went out to meet his friends, so everyone would know I was taken. I used to love the smell. I used to revel in the knowledge that Lucas was so low-key obsessed and possessive of me that he felt the need to mark me with his scent, so he could keep me to himself.

But now ...

A shiver tickles down my spine, and my eyes pop open. A cold sensation spreads across my insides, but I don't know why.

He pulls back, his hands cupping my face as he stares down at me. "I love you, and you love me." It's not a question; it's said with the confidence he's always had.

As he leans in, his nose traces up the side of mine, and his breath blows across my mouth, making my lips part as I suck in a ragged breath. My head is fuzzy, my mind all over the place. I don't even know what I'm doing right now. I'm kind of lost.

As his mouth slowly heads towards mine, my eyes flick down to his lips, and my heart thumps wildly against my ribcage. When his lips finally close over mine, I whimper, and my arms tighten around his neck as I automatically kiss him back.

The kiss is nice. The way his mouth moves against mine is achingly familiar ... but I realise it's not giving me the feels I get when Theo's lips are on mine. Kissing Lucas used to be as natural as breathing, but ... it feels wrong now. His kisses don't make my heart sing or my body vibrate with excitement. As Lucas's hands wrap around my hips and he trails kisses down my neck, there are no tummy butterflies or sighs in happiness, no burning need to press so close to him that we meld into one ... like there is with Theo.

I squeeze my eyes shut. Now that my mind is on Theo, I can't get it off.

I think about his beautiful smile and his laugh that makes my skin prickle with pleasure. I think about the little line he gets between his eyebrows when he's sketching, his love for his niece and nephew, how his hugs feel, how he's always subtly making sure I'm okay, supporting me and propping me up, and the hilarious things he comes out with. Being with Theo is something like I've never experienced with a guy before. He makes me feel so at ease in my own skin that I can fully let my guard down for once and let him glimpse the real me, the girl I had to temper down and all but push into a lockbox because I didn't suit Lucas's version of ideal. With Theo, I don't feel the need to hide myself or change for him. He just likes me the way I am. I've never had that.

As Lucas's mouth finds mine again and he kisses me urgently, nipping at my bottom lip, attempting to deepen the kiss, I realise … it's not him I want. It's Theo.

And just like that, my mind snaps back to the present.

I clamp my mouth shut and turn my head, moving my hands to Lucas's shoulders, pushing him away from me. "Stop it." My voice is a breathless whisper.

He doesn't take the hint. He crowds back into me, his thumb tracing across my bottom lip, his eyes boring into mine. "So, you got stuck in a lift with that prick, huh? I saw it on Twitter—that's how you met. And you went to Scotland with him last weekend?" His eyes narrow in accusation as he pins me with his hard stare.

I frown, confused by his change in direction and by his question itself. *How did he know I went to Scotland?*

I'm about to ask, but he cuts me off.

He sighs, a knowing smile twitching at the corner of his lips. "Do you think I don't know what you're doing, Lucie?" His voice is calculated and controlled. "Bringing in some guy to try and make me jealous. Going away with him. Parading around in this dress that you know I hate. Are you that desperate to get my attention?" His fingers close around my upper arms, and he pulls me tight against his body, inclining his head to growl directly into my ear, "Well, you've got it, sweetheart. Is that what you wanted when you put on this whore dress and high-heeled shoes? You wanted me to take one look at you and fuck you against the wall again like a dirty little slut?"

Before I can react to his words, he spins me around, pushing me face-first against the wall so fast that the air whooshes out of my lungs in one big burst. Instantly, he presses in against my back, pinning me there with his body. Against my backside, I can feel how hard he is already as his hands slowly slide down my body, spanning over my hips.

A cold shiver tickles down my spine.

No. This doesn't feel right. Something's wrong, my brain is screaming at me, but I don't move.

My chest is tight. I can't draw in a breath. A memory or sensation prickles in the back of my mind. This sensation, this *fright*, I've felt this before …

I shake my head, my words caught in my throat.

"No?" he whispers. His breath blowing across my ear makes me shudder.

"No."

Suddenly, he spins me back around to face him. I lose my balance in my high shoes, and a small pain tears across my ankle. I slam back against the wall, letting out a whimper. Lucas instantly cages me in, his arms on either side of me as he leans in, trapping me there. His hard ice-blue eyes are inches from mine. They're cold and unflinching. He's furious about the dress. A few months ago, I would have cringed away under the heat of his gaze, but now, I force myself to look him full-on in the eyes.

"I can wear what I want. We're not together." I raise my chin confidently; unfortunately, my voice comes out as a pitiful croak, so it loses all its authority.

Lucas's mouth crashes against mine so hard that my head bumps the wall and my lips mash against my teeth. It's an angry kiss. I can almost taste his fury. I can also taste blood … and that's familiar too.

This is wrong. I don't want this.

Forcing my arms up between our bodies, I shove him a couple of feet away from me and forcefully shake my head. "Stop it! You don't get to just decide we're back together. You cheated on me. You can't just kiss me and make everything okay again!"

"Lucie, sweetheart, let me make it up to you. I already said I'm sorry. What else do you want me to do?" His voice is suddenly soft and loving. His bottom lip juts out in a pout as his eyes meet mine.

His sudden one-eighty turn has me instantly on edge. I should be used to this, his mood swings and him twisting and turning like this to keep me off guard, but I'm not.

We're both breathing heavily as we stare at each other in silence. My mind is still whirling, but it finally settles on something that's niggling away at me.

"How did you know I was in Scotland?" I cock my head and look at him quizzically.

"What?"

"Scotland. How did you know I was there last weekend with Theo?" I didn't tell anyone. The only ones who knew were Aubrey and Theo's family.

His jaw tightens. "I saw it on Instagram. You, dressed like a hooker, acting ridiculous with *him*." He practically growls the word *him* as he jerks his thumb over his shoulder towards the door. "The location was tagged as some hotel in Scotland."

I frown. Something is clawing at me, a thought in the back of my mind, just out of reach. "But … but how did you see that? I didn't repost it. You can't see it on my account. I was just tagged."

I know this is true because Aubrey couldn't see it when she was looking for the videos when I got home and told her about them. She hadn't known about them until that moment, and when she checked, it turned out, you couldn't see them from her account because Theo had only added my username in the description of the posts, not added an official tag. In the end, she had to resort to watching them on my phone, clicking on my notifications so she could see it.

Lucas shrugs and rakes a hand through his hair. "I don't know. I just saw it." His tone is defensive, and his eyes dart away from me.

My back straightens as I realise the only way he could have seen it. "Are you signed into my Instagram account?"

He doesn't deny it.

My heart clenches as the truth clangs in my stomach like a lead balloon. "You are." More truth hits me, and my brain is now reeling. "And my Twitter too. You just said you knew Theo and I were stuck in the lift and that you saw it on Twitter." I gulp noisily. "But I didn't like or comment on Theo's tweet, so no one else could have seen it, apart from his followers. The only way it's linked to me is that notification. So, you must be signed in there too?"

His Adam's apple bobs as he swallows. His jaw tightens, and he folds his arms over his chest and shrugs. "Maybe I am. You were always on my phone; maybe it's still signed in from you going on there. How should I know?"

But that's a lie. I was never on his phone. He was the one who liked access to my phone, but he always hid his phone away from me with passcodes that I wasn't allowed to know.

That means that he deliberately signed into my social accounts to keep tabs on me. It wasn't an accident.

The conniving little bastard!

I blink, and it's like everything hits me at once.

Small hints that Aubrey dropped for years, which I ignored because they didn't fit the narrative I had. When she brought up shady things Lucas said or did, I would defend him and make excuses—even to myself. Although some of the things she used to bring up sounded bad, I'd explain them away because *of course* stuff seemed bad if you took it out of context.

You can't just pick and choose what you want to remember and skim over the rest.

But unfortunately, it looks like I did precisely that. I chose not to see what was right in front of me.

But now, I know.

What Lucas and I had was not right.

My whole life had changed when we got together. It was wonderful at first. He showered me with affection, built me up, and pampered my heart until I fell so hard and so fast that I would have done anything for him—and I did. It started with me turning down my university placement. I barely gave it a second thought because choosing between him or my dream, he won every time. After that, I stopped seeing my friends because he didn't like them. I lost contact with everyone, except Aubrey—and that was only because the stubborn wench refused to be ghosted. Lucas managed to slyly cut me off from everyone and everything I knew, isolated me until I thought all I needed was him, all the while making me love him so much that I didn't even care or question it. He controlled every aspect of my life—our money, where we went, where I worked, who I saw, what I wore—and I let him.

Over the first couple of years of our relationship, he built me up, only to systematically tear me down after that until I was so dependent on him, so in tune with his will, that I thought it was what I wanted too. He conditioned me with little digs, passive-aggressive comments about my appearance, my achievements, flaws in my personality, following them up with loving kisses and smiles and *I'm only kidding, sweetheart* or *Can't you take a joke* comments, so I didn't even notice he was oppressing me. Slowly, he broke my confidence and my spirit, moulded me until I was his idea of perfect. But even that wasn't enough. Even after I pandered to his every whim and hung on his every word, he still went and cheated.

The realisation feels like I've been struck in the heart. I press my hand to my forehead and suck in a deep breath. Everything I thought I knew about him—about us—has shifted. I can see it clearly now, all the ways he hurt me, manipulated me, ground me down. He never raised a hand to me, never physically hurt me, apart from some rough kisses or sex if we were fighting, but emotionally, he's scarred me.

I always thought Lucas was my Mr Right. Instead, he was my Mr Oh-So Wrong, and I never knew until now.

"This"—I wave a hand between us—"this isn't healthy. This isn't right, Lucas. You're a manipulative arsehole, you know that? You controlled every aspect of my life. You lorded over me like my keeper and had me dancing around, trying to please you, so afraid of not being what you wanted that I forgot all about what *I* wanted. You crushed me, Lucas. Crushed my spirit, and I never even realised."

He makes a disbelieving scoffing sound in his throat. "Don't be obtuse! Jesus, you've always been so dramatic. I thought you'd grown out of your immature phase." He rolls his eyes and steps closer to me, reaching out to grip my upper arm again, pulling me against his body. "So, I might be signed into your social media. So what? It's not like I meant any harm. I was just checking what you were up to, making sure you were safe so I could step in and take care of you if you needed my help. I was looking out for you, like I always do. I love you, Lucie. Always have. You and I are meant to be. I need you, and you need me. We're nothing without each other."

I gulp, and ... I almost believe him. When he gives me the puppy-dog eyes and his hand strokes my waist, I almost bloody fall for it again.

But he's wrong. I *am* something. I am *worth* something. Over the last three months, I've slowly taken my life back, put the broken pieces of myself back together again, summoned inner strength I didn't know I still had, and I've kept calm and carried on.

The old Lucie that Lucas had long since squashed and suppressed has started to resurface in the months we've been apart. Steadily creeping back is the old fun-loving, daring Lucie who, at fourteen, made a deathbed promise to her nonna to always live her life to the fullest and to never be afraid to jump because *what if I can fly*, but I never found out because I was too scared to take the leap.

I forcefully shake my head. "You're so wrong, Lucas. I'm not *nothing* without you. I'm *me* without you. And you know what? That's good enough." Saying the words out loud is empowering. *This* is the closure I should have been seeking, not to hurt him with jealousy, but this—me standing up for myself and knowing that he has no power over me anymore. This is everything.

And the fact that his whole body stiffens and his eye twitches? Well, that's just the icing on the cake.

I confidently raise my chin. Now that the weight of Lucas's domination is off my shoulders, my mind flicks to Theo. Adorable, lovely, magic-performing Theo, who likes me just the way I am—belly tops, sass, snorty laugh, no make-up, big bum, and messy hair. He likes all of it. He thinks I'm perfect—every part of me.

What am I even doing here? Why am I wasting time arguing with Lucas when I could be dancing with Theo right now? He told me he likes me, and I left him hanging. What is wrong with me?

"You should get some help, talk to a professional, fix this problem you have with control before you ruin your next relationship with your toxic traits. Goodbye, Lucas."

I awkwardly step around him and head for the door, wincing because my ankle twinges, but I don't give him the satisfaction of seeing me limp. As I reach for the door handle, he calls my name.

I turn, seeing his arms arrogantly crossed over his chest.

"I hold all the cards here, sweetheart. I could ruin you. One word from me, and you'll never PA for any decent firm in London. Didn't you ever wonder why, even with your experience, you couldn't get another PA job?" One side of his mouth kicks up into a wicked smirk.

My back straightens at his words.

He shrugs. "So far, I've only thrown out a few scattered kernels of a lie whenever anyone has come to me for a reference, but if you walk out of that door now, I'll pull in every favour I'm owed, and I'll spread the word to every company in London that you're an incompetent, untrustworthy, useless assistant who fucks up even the simplest of tasks. They won't touch you with a bargepole."

The penny drops. This is why I had trouble finding a job when I first started applying to places. So many of them, I was confident I had aced the interview and impressed them with my ideas and achievements from the last eight years. I walked out of so many job interviews, certain I had it in the bag—I even had a few winks and the telling *I'll speak to you in a couple of days* phrase with my goodbye handshakes—but then a week or so later, a letter would arrive, telling me I'd been unsuccessful but wishing me luck in the future.

"You messed up my references? Why would you do that?"

"Because I wanted you to come back to work for me. I thought you'd see sense when you couldn't find anyone to hire you, and you'd come grovelling back. You and I are meant to be, and we both know it," he replies. His voice is calm and reasonable, as if that were a perfectly legitimate reason for messing with someone's life.

But the thing is, I'm not even angry. I never wanted to PA in the first place. *He* was the one who set it up for me to work for him, likely because he wanted to keep me close, I now realise. Not being able to find another secretarial job pushed me to re-evaluate what I wanted, to take a chance (and a significant pay cut) and put myself forward for the intern programme at the publisher when Aubrey came home and told me about it. I'm working towards my dream job right now, and it seems I have Lucas to thank for it.

Lucas cocks his head to the side and takes a step towards me. The glint in his eye tells me he thinks he's won. "Here's what's going to happen now. You're going to go tell that arsehole that you're sorry but you don't ever want to see him again. Then, we're going to go to our parents and announce the good news—that we're back together. You know they'll be thrilled. Then, we'll leave. The first thing you'll do when we get home is throw this fucking dress in the bin. I never want to see you in anything this tight again."

But his words have no power over me anymore. I'm done. Mentally, I've finally severed all ties.

I press my lips together and wait until he's finished, and then I coolly shake my head. "No, Lucas. The era of you telling me what to do has ended. So, here's what's *actually* going to happen now. You're going to eat a bag of dicks."

His mouth pops open comically, his eyebrows shoot up into his hairline, and his eyes widen with shock at my words. I burst into a fit of giggles and catalogue his expression, taking a mental picture purely for my own future replaying pleasure.

Extending my free hand, I flip him the bird. "This conversation is over. You are officially cancelled," I say confidently and then wrench the door open and stride through it without looking back. I've never been prouder of myself.

Twenty-three

LUCIE

In eight years, I don't think I ever fully breathed.

As I walk down the hallway, heading back to the hubbub of the party, I feel like a weight has been lifted off my chest. I never realised how toxic our relationship was. I thought I was so happy with Lucas, but looking back at it now with a fresh perspective, maybe I never was.

I spot Theo. He has his back to me and is chatting and laughing with a group of five people I vaguely recognise from previous parties. My heart leaps at the sound of his laugh, and I chew on my lip as my tummy fizzes with excitement.

This man likes everything about me.

Grinning like a moron, I head straight over to him, ignoring the small, uncomfortable twinge in my ankle each time I take a step. When I get to him, I slip my hand into his and squeeze.

He turns and smiles down at me. "Hey, there you are. I was beginning to think you'd ditched me or that you'd eaten a bad prawn …" He teasingly raises one eyebrow, and I burst out laughing.

Not bothering to answer, I step into the heat of his body and wrap my hand around the back of his head, pulling his mouth down to mine.

He grunts in surprise but immediately kisses me back. His soft lips feel so good against mine that I melt against him, my insides turning to goo. One of his arms slips around my waist, holding me steady when I wobble on my tiptoes, and the other comes up to cup my jaw. His smell, his taste, the feel of him against me—all of it combined is a heady mix that intoxicates me. I feel drunk on him; it's beautiful. The little moan he makes in the back of his throat sets my body on fire, and his lips part against mine. As the kiss deepens, every nerve ending in my body seems to zing, and I smile against his lips.

This is how it's supposed to feel when you're kissed by a man.

He smiles, too, and pulls back a fraction, his arms tightening on me. "Oh, so you missed me, too, huh?" he whispers, his lips brushing against mine as he speaks.

I smile and nod. "I did." There's too much truth in that sentence.

He grins and lightly kisses me again. "Where were you?" he breathes, his fingers tickling across the skin at the back of my neck.

I brush my nose up the side of his and sigh. "Fighting with Lucas."

His body stiffens, and he pulls back to look at me, his expression hardening. "Do I need to kick his arse?"

I chuckle at the venom I could hear in his words. "I already did."

A smile twitches at the corner of his mouth. "You did? That's my girl."

His words hit me hard. *"That's my girl."*
God, it sounds incredible.

I glow with pleasure as I chew on my lip to try and suppress my loony grin. Before I can say anything back, a hand closes around my shoulder, and I'm yanked from Theo's embrace with so much force that my ankle instantly barks with agony. I stumble, barely managing to regain my balance before I completely fall. I yelp and wince, grabbing on to the wooden sideboard for support, lifting my foot from the floor as the pain burns brighter.

Lucas's eyes are hard and ferocious as he glares, pointing an accusing finger at me. "Stop whoring yourself out, Lucie. For fuck's sake, you're embarrassing yourself … and me! We're leaving. We'll deal with this when we get home!"

At his words, people stop what they're doing and turn towards us. Their eyes are curious and shocked at his outburst. This is a side of Lucas no one gets to see but me when we're alone. He's usually the consummate professional, unflappable in public.

With my face flaming, my stomach dips, and my eyes widen, but as Lucas reaches out to seize my arm, Theo moves faster. Grabbing a handful of Lucas's shirt and tie, he yanks him away from me while his free hand curls into a fist and slams into my ex-fiancé's face. It connects with a dull, muted thud, and Lucas groans in pain as he staggers back, slamming into the wall, narrowly avoiding taking out a waiter who jumps out of the way at the last second.

I gasp.

Lucas recovers quickly, launching himself at Theo, and they crash back into the cupcake station, sending colourful cakes and sprinkles everywhere. They're scuffling on the floor, fighting for the upper hand. Theo definitely gets it, but Lucas manages to land a couple of hits too.

People stare, open-mouthed, at the scene unfolding in the middle of my father's retirement party. My heart is in my throat, and I flinch when I see Lucas's fist connect with Theo's cheek.

Oh, please don't let him get hurt!

"Theo, stop, please."

I don't bother appealing to Lucas's better judgement. When he's in a rage, there's no pulling him back; you have to let it simply fizzle out. I push myself towards them, intending to break it up, wincing and limping with every step, but my father gets there first.

Wrapping his arms around Theo's chest, my dad pulls him back up to his feet and drags him away from Lucas as Fred makes a dive for his son, doing the same.

Theo is furious as he growls at Lucas, "I fucking warned you not to grab her again, didn't I? You don't put your hands on her like that! Are you insane?"

They're both thrashing, trying to break free of their restrained holds so they can finish what they started. Lucas screams profanities, his face going beet red, as he kicks out his leg, trying to strike Theo. He looks a mess. His hair is everywhere, his shirt untucked, waistcoat buttons ripped open. His lip is split, and there are blood drops on his white shirt. Meanwhile, Theo is barely breathing heavy.

"That's enough!" Papà roars. Hissing a string of Italian profanities, he lets go of Theo and manoeuvres himself between the fighting pair, putting two hands on Theo's chest and shoving him back a couple of steps. "This stops now!" My father's eyes are blazing as he jabs an angry finger in Theo's chest. "You get out! You're no longer welcome here. How dare you walk into my house and show this level of disrespect!"

I hobble to Theo's side and desperately shake my head. "Papà, you don't understand—"

"I understand perfectly!" Papà snaps harshly. His eyes flick back to Theo, who has gone very still, his face a mask of stony resignation. "You're uncouth riffraff, coming in here and starting fights! We don't want your kind here!"

Anger sparks in my stomach. None of this is Theo's fault, and once again, Lucas gets away with murder.

Papà sneers at Theo as he continues, "You stay away from my Luciella. She's spoken for and to be married!"

And now, I'm mad. Eye-twitch kind of mad.

I raise my chin and clumsily step forward, throwing my hands up in exasperation. "I'm not spoken for anymore, Papà! Lucas and I broke up, remember? What is it with you men and not taking no for an answer?" I cry angrily. "And Theo was only defending me! Lucas grabbed me first. None of this is Theo's fault."

"It's okay, Luce. You don't have to," Theo says, his hand touching the small of my back, obviously trying to calm me down.

It doesn't help.

My blood is boiling in my veins. I hate the way they're all looking at him. He's the loveliest, kindest man. He doesn't deserve anyone to ever look at him with such revulsion and disgust.

Fred frowns over at me. "Well, you did insist on bringing someone here just to rub it in Lucas's face tonight. What did you expect to happen? How much can someone watch their fiancée kissing someone else before they snap? How long has this been going on anyway? Was he the reason you and Lucas split?"

And now, I'm cut-a-bitch mad.

My teeth gnash together as he speaks. I almost can't breathe around my anger. "Ask your son why we broke up, Fred! He's the one who fucked someone else, not me!" My voice is shrill and neurotic; I'm so angry.

There's a collective gasp from the crowd, and fifty or so sets of accusing eyes now swing in Lucas's direction.

My father recoils, his mouth popping open. "What?"

I nod, my eyes prickling with indignant tears. "Three months ago, I walked in on him screwing someone else in our living room. That's why we broke up. And that's why I left and didn't look back. It had nothing to do with Theo. I didn't even know him back then."

Marie whimpers, "Oh, Lucas, no."

My father gulps and turns back to look at my ex-fiancé. "Is this true?"

Lucas's eyebrows pull together, and he scowls at me hatefully, obviously livid that I let the cat out of the bag and rescinded our agreement to keep his cheating on the down-low. "Yes, but it was only—"

Before Lucas can finish his sentence, my father pulls back his arm and punches him full in the face. Lucas staggers backwards into Fred, who grunts and shoves him away from him.

My father's shoulders slump, and he looks over at his best friend as he massages his knuckles on his punching hand. "I'm sorry, Fred. I had to."

Fred shakes his head, glaring at his son, who is now wiping blood from his nose onto the back of his hand, looking a little dazed. "Don't be. I kind of want to do it myself."

Marie steps forward and puts her hand on my shoulder. "I'm so sorry, Lucie. You should have told us. Why didn't you say, darling?"

I shrug and look down at my feet, grimacing and trying to adjust my stance so it's less painful. "I didn't want to make things difficult for anyone. Fred and Papà are best friends, and I didn't want any animosity to ruin that. Plus, Lucas still works for the company."

Fred's eyes tighten. "Not for long. He can find somewhere else to work."

I recoil and shake my head. "That's not necessary. I don't care as long as he's nowhere near me."

"It is necessary. His work has gone downhill since you left. He's been missing obvious things, leaving projects uncompleted, missing deadlines. And last month, he made a huge blunder with the autumn budget figures that almost cost the company a hundred thousand pounds! Fortunately, someone spotted it just before it went out the door."

Oh my God. That's because that's all the stuff I used to do for him! Above and beyond my role as his assistant, but I did it regardless.

Fred continues, "Your father and I spoke about it, and we decided to give him a break. We let things slide because we assumed he was heartbroken over losing you. But now that I know he brought it on himself, he can suffer the consequences. If he weren't my son, he'd have been fired weeks ago." He turns to Lucas. "I suggest you turn in your notice and start looking for other employment Monday morning."

"You can't do that!" Lucas rages.

Fred straightens his shoulders. "As joint owner of the company, I can do whatever I damn well please! Turn in your notice and find somewhere else to work."

Lucas shoves away from the wall, his head swivelling in my direction as he lurches forward, eyes narrowed into slits, jaw so tight that the muscle twitches at his temple. I stiffen, readying for any attack, either verbal or physical.

But Theo moves, too, stepping in front of me. "This is a teachable moment for you, Lucas. The lesson you should take from this is, don't ever fucking touch her again—or else." Theo's voice is calm, but his anger simmers just underneath. His warning is clear as crystal.

They glare at each other for a few seconds, the air thick with their clashing wrath, before Lucas turns and strides away, roughly shouldering ogling spectators out of the way as he storms out, slamming the front door behind him.

My mum steps to my side, her arms wrapping around me and leaning in to kiss my cheeks. "Why didn't you tell me what had happened? Luciella, all this time, I've been matchmaking, trying to get you two back together. I feel awful!"

I pat her arm and reach out to wipe the tear that's fallen down her face. "It's okay, Mamma."

From the corner of my eye, I see my dad step to Theo's side, and I turn to watch the exchange, my heart in my throat.

"I'm sorry I jumped to conclusions. I did not see what had started it. I just assumed …"

Theo shakes his head. "It's fine. Don't worry about it. So … I take it, this uncouth riffraff is okay to stay, or do you still want me to leave?"

Papà chuckles awkwardly and shakes his head. "Let's start over. Hi, I'm Tomas." He holds out his hand.

Theo grins the boyish smile that makes my heart ache as he places his hand in my dad's. "Theo."

"Nice to meet you, Theo. You have a decent right hook on you, by the way."

"Ditto."

Papà grins sheepishly and massages his hand again. "Well, I wasn't always this respectable, you know. When I was in my early twenties, I used to hang out in some pretty shady bars back in Italy. I always enjoyed a good scrap, usually over a woman. Speaking of which"—he leans in and raises one eyebrow—"you want to date my daughter? I will warn you; I'll be vetting her suitors more closely from now on."

Theo laughs and turns back to look at me. I hold my breath, waiting to see if this whole clusterfuck situation has changed his mind. Maybe I'm too much work. Maybe this messed up family drama is too much for him.

"Yeah, I want to date your daughter. But it's her choice where we go from here."

A sigh of relief leaves my lips, and my insides rejoice. My dad smiles knowingly and pats Theo on the back, gently pushing him in my direction, winking at me, and then waving his hand to my mother to call her away.

Theo smiles weakly, his eyes shining with concern. "Are you okay, Luce? That was intense."

I nod and hobble towards him, grimacing. "Yeah."

Instantly, he reaches for me, his forehead creasing with a frown. "Are you hurt?"

I shrug one shoulder and bob-shake my head noncommittally. "I just twisted my ankle. I'm okay."

Without answering, he bends, wrapping his arms around me, and picks me up bridal-style, as if I weigh nothing at all. I squeal and throw my arms around his neck, grinning delightedly.

Talk about swoon!

"Not gonna protest about being too heavy for me to carry?" he teases.

"No, I remember your argument from last time."

"Not too heavy when you sat on my face …"

Giggling, I press my nose against the side of his neck and breathe him in. I'm not sure I'll ever get enough of his smell.

"Let's go take a look at your ankle. Get you some ice."

The waitress who was scurrying around in the background, trying to pick up the scattered cupcakes, stands and looks over at us. "I can get you some ice. Come with me."

Still carrying me, Theo effortlessly follows her through the room and hallway and into my parents' grand, sleek kitchen. Gently setting me on one of the dining chairs, he kneels at my side and eases my leg up, carefully resting my foot on another chair he positions in front of me. We both look down at my ankle. It's swelling rapidly.

Reaching for the buckle on my shoe strap, he hisses through his teeth, wincing apologetically as he delicately unfastens it and slides my shoe off. It hurts so much that I grit my teeth and squeeze my eyes shut, so I don't cry.

When the waitress comes back and hands Theo a tea towel with ice wrapped inside, he props it up against the egg-shaped swelling and grimaces.

He sits back on his heels and looks over at me, one arm resting across my thighs, his thumb stroking the material of my dress. The concern I see in his eyes makes my insides dance.

The skin on the side of his jaw is red and sore-looking, so I reach out and softly touch it. *My poor baby. What a damn hero he is.* "I'm not sure why, but you look hotter with a bruise."

He chuckles. "It's the bad-boy thing; chicks dig it."

I smile and nod in agreement. Leaning forward, I plant a little kiss on the bruise, wishing I could take the pain away. His body stills.

"I should never have got you involved in this, Theo. I was so stupid for bringing you here, just to score points. I'm sorry."

He shrugs. "I'm not. I had a great time tonight, if you take away the last, like, fifteen minutes or so. The food is delicious, the drink is free, and the company isn't too shabby ..."

I chuckle and stroke his face again, relishing in the feel of his skin under my fingers. When I look at him, my feelings hit me full force. I like him—*a lot*. He's so lovely. Now that Lucas is out of the picture, I can finally move on. See where this goes with Theo, start with a clear, fresh head and see what happens. I'm acutely aware that I've only known him two weeks, so this might not go anywhere ... but I have hope. Deep down, I now know that even if it doesn't work out with him, I'll be okay. I've survived worse. I've started over once; I can do so again. I believe in myself now. Lucas underestimated me—hell, I even underestimated myself, but I vow, no more. From this moment on, I'm going to stand up for myself and go for what I want.

And right now, what I want is Theo. My fingers trace over his cheek. Judging by the way he makes my whole body come alive, I have a suspicion that I won't need to worry about starting over. I think he's right about what he said earlier—being stuck in that lift with him meant something. Only time will tell, and I can't wait to find out.

His eyes meet mine, and there's a hopeful glint to them that nearly knocks me sideways. "So, earlier ... you kissed me."

"I did." I nod and pull him closer, my breath coming out in excited pants.

His arm slips across my body, hand curling around my thigh. "What does that mean?"

"It means, this is the start of a beautiful friendship."

He groans. "Friendship? No, Luce. No more friend-zoning me, please. Come on, take a chance and go on a date with me." He brushes his nose up the side of mine, setting butterflies the size of fruit bats loose in my stomach.

"Another fake date?" I tease.

"No," he says gruffly. "No more fake dates. A real one."

I purse my lips and pretend to consider it. "I'll tell you what. Why don't we Rock, Paper, Scissors for it? You win, and I'll go on a date with you. I win, and we just stay friends."

A frown lines his forehead, and his lips press into a thin line. "If that's what you want. Let's leave it to fate then. See if the karma gods really are on our side."

Biting back my smile, I bring my hands up, one fist on my palm, and I look at him expectantly.

He nods and mirrors me.

I hold my breath, and my excitement fizzles in my tummy as we thump our hands on our fists.

One …

Two …

On three, we throw our shapes.

Theo's shoulders slump as I reach out and wrap my paper hand around his rock fist, squeezing gently.

"Friends it is then," he says, frowning down at my lap as he sighs dejectedly.

Chewing on my lip, I reach out and grip his shoulders, pulling him closer to me. "It's a good thing I don't believe in karma, huh?"

His eyes widen, and he raises one eyebrow in silent question, his body stiffening.

"I'd love to go on a real date with you, Theo Stone," I whisper, not trusting my voice to work.

Immediately, he lights up, beaming a smile over at me that's so dazzling I'm momentarily stunned, and then he leans in, pressing his lips against mine, arms wrapping around my body, kissing me with so much care and passion that it makes my heart ache.

Now, I feel at home. Right here, in this moment with him. I never want it to end.

I grin against his lips, happier than I have been in years.

epilogue

LUCIE

I wake to my pillow moving under my head. Only it isn't my pillow. I'm lying on Theo's arm, and he's trying to discreetly slide it out from under my neck without disturbing me.

I groan sleepily and wrap my hands around his forearm, pulling it back across my torso and pressing my face into the crook of his elbow as I snuggle back against his body that's spooning me from behind.

"I gotta get my arm back," Theo whispers in my ear, tracing his nose across my cheek.

I smile and tighten my hold on it, interlacing our fingers. "Nope, this is my arm now."

He chuckles softly, and it rumbles into my back when he half-leans over me, pressing me down into the soft mattress. As he kisses the back of my neck, I shiver as a wave of lust washes over me.

"You know what today is?" he asks, his fingers slipping beneath my pyjama top, his knuckles brushing against the skin on my waist.

"I do."

I grin into my pillow, my body tingling with pleasure because he remembers. I didn't expect him to—he is a guy after all. I didn't mention it and didn't plan on making a big deal out of it, but today is our six-month meetaversary. Six months ago, I got stuck in a lift with a handsome stranger who ate my doughnuts and signed a contract for an exchange of fake-date services. Six heavenly months of his time. It's gone by in the blink of an eye.

Theo smiles against my shoulder and massages my back with his free hand. "Yep. Today is the day I have to go help Jared paint the nursery. So, I gotta go."

My mouth pops open. He hasn't remembered after all. I don't know why, but I'm a little disappointed now. I hadn't thought he would, but then I got my hopes up for a couple of seconds. I hide my disappointment by planting a kiss on his forearm.

"Of course. What time is your train?" I glance at the alarm clock. It's only just after seven a.m.

He begins kissing the back of my neck and nipping at my shoulders. I can feel the hardness of him against my bum, and it makes an ache of longing build between my legs as my brain fogs with lust. I want him. Six months on, and he can still whip me into a frenzy with one kiss; it's insane really.

"Soon. I gotta go get showered."

He moves to pull away, but I shake my head. He's started something now. There's no way I'm going all day, being a horny, unsatisfied beast. Moving my arm behind me, I close my hand over his erection and squeeze him through his pyjama trousers. The feel of him in my hand makes desire pool between my legs, and I close my eyes, breathless with anticipation.

He groans into the back of my neck. "I don't have time. I gotta go."

My hand doesn't listen as I rub gently.

"Luce ..." His voice is a whispered plea as he shifts his hips, rubbing his erection against my hand. Suddenly, he moves, making me roll further onto my tummy as he presses more of his weight onto my back. It's divine. "I literally have fifteen minutes to shower and get dressed before I need to leave."

"And five of those minutes can be spent with me. Skip the shower."

You can't beat a morning quickie; they always guarantee I start my day on a high note.

He chuckles, his breath blowing over my hypersensitive skin. A shiver of excitement trickles down my spine, and my teeth sink into my bottom lip. "Just five minutes? You plan on being fast."

I nod. "Stop wasting time, Mr Stone. Are you going to make me come before you leave, or do I have to do it myself once you're gone?"

"I love it when you get all demanding and sassy," he growls. "Okay, let's play a super-fast game of gold medal, silver medal." Translation: who comes first?

His teeth nip at my earlobe as he tugs at my pyjama bottoms, pushing them down over my hips and thighs. He groans as his hand brushes across my sex and feels how excited I am already. Fisting his erection, he lines up and sinks into me from behind. My breath whooshes out of me as my eyes roll into the back of my head.

What follows is a hard, frantic quickie, which leaves me breathless and grinning in a state of bliss. Of course, I win the gold. Theo always makes sure.

"I gotta go now, Luce. Sorry to smash and dash."

I burst out laughing at his phrase.

He kisses across my back, tongue trailing down my spine, his hand kneading my rump. He groans against my skin. "Jeez, will I ever get tired of this arse?"

I hope not! I squeal as his teeth playfully nip it before he pushes himself up off the bed.

Flopping onto my back, I twist my head and smile, contentedly watching him as he pulls on jeans and then looks in his wardrobe for a T-shirt. His back still makes me all kinds of giddy. A naked Theo back is one of my favourite things ever.

"Want to take me for dinner tonight?" I ask.

We might not really be celebrating, as it's not a proper anniversary, but we could at least not have to cook.

A frown lines his forehead as he apologetically looks over his shoulder at me. "I'm not sure I'll be back in time. Depending on how long it takes to paint the nursery and assemble all the furniture, I might be back late. Or if we don't get done today, I might stay over with Jared and Amy, so we can finish tomorrow." He tugs on a *Drop Dead Fred* T-shirt.

I pout, hating that idea. "You might not come home?"

He shrugs. "I don't know, Luce. I don't want to stay there, but we'll have to see how it goes today. I'll call you in the afternoon and let you know how we're getting on. But I likely won't be back in time for dinner, so don't wait for me before you eat."

I pout because he's going to be gone so long. But I can't really be annoyed. When Theo moved to London to be with me two months ago and we rented this flat, Jared spent several days here, helping us decorate and move furniture. So, the least Theo can do is go there and help them decorate their nursery, readying for the new baby Stone who will make its appearance in just over three months' time. Everybody is excited about meeting him or her—none more so than Theo. As a "professional uncle," as Amy describes him, kids definitely call to Theo's inner child. I try not to let myself get too broody, thinking about it.

"Don't let Amy do any of the hard work today," I warn.

He shakes his head. "She won't; don't worry."

Amy and I get on great. She's like the sister I never had. In fact, I get on brilliantly with all his family. Even though Theo moved here to London for me, we still go to Cambridge a couple of times a month to visit with all his friends and family for day trips or nights out and sometimes for weekend-long visits. Plus, they come here too. It made sense for Theo to move instead of me. He can do his illustrations from home (mostly from the bed, I've since found out), so this is the only way we could make it work without me commuting. Though, I must admit, if he had been dead set against the idea, I would have moved to Cambridge to be with him. What's a short train ride when you get to come home to the love of your life every night? It would have been worth every second. But thankfully, he was totally open to the idea of moving. Add another line to the Reasons Why Theo Is the Best Boyfriend in the World list!

After pulling on a hoodie (it's damn cold in February), he heads to the bathroom, brushing his teeth and fixing his sex hair, and then disappears into the kitchen.

I settle back into the bed and reach for my Kindle; I have another half an hour before I need to get up and get ready for work. I can hear the kettle boiling and Theo making a huge amount of ruckus in the kitchen. Minutes later, he comes back to the bedroom and sets a cup of tea down on my bedside cabinet.

Cue a mental swoon.

Theo climbs on the bed, planking over me. It's so hot that I immediately want him again. I can never get enough of his body. I'd feel sorry for him if he didn't love it so much.

"I love you. I'll see you later," he says, leaning down and placing a soft kiss on my lips.

My insides dance with happiness. Every time he says those three little words, it's like they have a direct line to my heart. They still thrill me every single time.

"I love you too." And I do, more than anything.

"Have a good day. Oh, by the way, I just made you lunch. It's in the fridge."

My heart stutters at his thoughtfulness. "You did? What did you make?"

"Coronation chicken sandwich. That's the last of it from yesterday." He winks at me and plants a tender kiss on the corner of my mouth.

Oh my God. My mind is instantly consumed by thoughts of the sandwich. I might even eat the thing for breakfast.

Theo is an amazing cook. His mum taught him a lot when he lived at home, and his coronation chicken is to die for. He makes it from scratch at least once a week because he knows I love it. Right now, I don't even care that our kitchen will be a mess when I walk in there. Theo is not a tidy partner to live with. Even simply adding his premade filling to bread just now, he will have somehow used every plate, bowl, knife, and chopping board we own. But it's a small price to pay for him.

"You are too good to me, you know that? Honestly, how did I get so lucky?" I trace my finger around his collar.

Six wonderful months I've been with him, and every day, he makes me feel so treasured that I could cry. I love him so much, I could burst.

He kisses me again, and I taste toothpaste and coronation chicken. It's so hot that I groan as he pulls away.

It looks like I'm still going to be a horny, unsatisfied beast all day after all.

"I'll call you. Love you, Luce," he says over his shoulder.

"Bye, baby." A content sigh leaves my lips as I sink back into my pillows and grin up at the ceiling.

Aubrey leans against the tea room counter, stirring her mug as she eyes me. "Let's go for lunch today. Come on, let's grab a big bowl of cheesy chips and a cream cake. Everyone knows calories don't count on hump days."

I wince apologetically and shake my head. "I can't. I brought lunch in with me." As I think about it, I debate on eating it when I get back to my desk. It's only just after nine in the morning, but if I did, it would mean I'd get to go for chips too.

No, don't be greedy, Lucie. Jeez, you have no willpower!

Aubrey pouts and drops her teabag into the bin. "You suck. Let's go for coffee then instead. I can get a cake from there."

"I don't think I can. I have meetings all afternoon today, so I need to prep for those. I think I'm going to have a working lunch and eat at my desk."

I pick up my mug, emblazoned with the phrase *Boys who draw books are better*. Theo gave it to me as my Christmas present. It is a joke, a dig at my *Boys in books are better* work mug he'd seen on a visit to the office one time. On Christmas morning, I found it hilarious and loved it immediately, but then I loved it even more when I found the gold bracelet with a small diamond heart hanging on it, wrapped up inside the mug.

"Ugh, fine. Looks like it's lunch alone for Aubrey." Aubrey rolls her eyes and picks up her mug, too, and we both walk out into the Hummingbird Ink office.

"Don't work too hard," I joke.

"Never."

We split off, going our separate directions. I head over to my desk and sit down, taking a sip of my tea and letting out a happy sigh as I press the power button on my computer.

That's right. I have my dream job.

In the last six months, I've worked my arse off, which didn't go unnoticed by David, my manager up in the children's imprint. So, when a job came up for junior editor in the romance imprint, David didn't hesitate in pushing me to apply. My CV, accompanied by his glowing recommendation, netted me the job, and for the last month, I've been living it up as junior editor. I love my job, and life couldn't be better. All day long, I get to swoon over fictional heroes, and then I get to go home to my very own real-life one.

Letting out a happy sigh, I give my mouse a shake, waking up my screen, ready to start my day.

My morning is so busy that it flies by. By the time I put the phone down from an agent friend of mine I've been talking to about a submission for a debut author, my stomach is growling with hunger. Glancing at the time on my computer screen, I see it's almost twelve already. My stomach rejoices.

Reaching under my desk, I shove my hand into my bag and bring out a lump wrapped in tin foil. My mouth is already watering. When I peel back the foil and see a chunky sandwich with yellow saucy chicken oozing out of the sides, the bread cut thick, just how I like it, I grin down at it excitedly. When I take a bite, I groan in pleasure; it's like an orgasm on the tongue. I never tried it before I got together with Theo, and now, I can't get enough.

Chewing, I pop the sandwich down on its foil package and turn my attention to my phone, about to message Theo to see how he's getting on, when Aubrey, who is in the process of walking past my desk, trips and bangs into my chair, throwing whatever she was carrying in her closed fist all over my desk.

I gasp and reach out to steady her. "What a klutz. Drunk much?" I chuckle. "Are you okay?"

She stands and nods, looking down at my desk and grimacing. "Yeah, but your lunch isn't."

I groan as I look down at it to see that my beautiful lunch is now covered in curls of pencil shavings and little flakes of lead. "No!" I pout and reach out, brushing the worst of it off. "Would you judge me if I still ate it?" It's an honest question; I'm not averse to the idea.

Aubrey half-gasps, half-laughs. "Yes! Don't be gross."

I'm still debating on the pros and cons of risking lead poisoning when she takes it from my hands and throws it in the bin. I stare down at my sandwich in the bottom of my rubbish bin in a state of mourning.

Aubrey brushes crumbs from her hands. "I'll buy you lunch to make up for it. Come on, let's go now." She looks down at her watch.

"Ugh, fine." *It's not like I have a choice.* "Why were you carrying pencil shavings anyway? Why not sharpen it over the bin in the first place, like a normal person?"

"Where's the fun in that?" She grins.

Plucking my bag from the floor and shoving my phone back inside, I follow Aubrey out of the office and around the corner to the lifts.

As luck would have it, my manager, Judy, is just stepping out of it. "Oh, are you two heading out? Great timing. Here." She holds the lift doors open and grins at us.

Quickening my step, I smile gratefully and step in. "Thanks, Judy. See you in a bit. You want anything? Aubrey's buying." I playfully elbow my best friend as she steps in next to me.

"No, I'm fine, thank you. You have a nice time though." Judy winks at me, her eyes bright.

There's someone else in the lift already, standing in the corner, reading a newspaper. I can't see them properly, only their legs. I reach out to press the ground floor button but see it's already illuminated.

"Oh, bugger. I forgot my phone." Aubrey sticks her hand out, catching the doors as they're about to close and stepping over the threshold. "I'll meet you at the café. Grab us a good seat." She shrugs and sends me a little wave as the doors slide closed, separating us.

STAND-IN SATURDAY

Groaning at the turn of events, I stick my hand in my bag again, intending to message Theo, when the lift suddenly judders, and the lights flicker as it grinds to a halt.

My eyes widen in disbelief. "Oh, you have got to be kidding me. Again?" I reach out, jabbing the Help button. I should have learned my lesson from last time and taken the stairs. My non-existent thigh gap would approve.

"Let me take a look. Here, hold this," Newspaper Guy says. He places a lightweight, rectangular green-and-white box in my hands and reaches to press the Help button too.

Flustered, I step to the side and roll my eyes. *Oh, because, you never know, maybe I was pushing the button wrong ... men!*

Taking a deep breath, I look down at the package in my hand. It's a box of three Krispy Kreme doughnuts. On top of it, there's a bright pink Post-It note. In black Sharpie, it says: *Open me, Lucie.*

What the ...

I frown, confused, and pop the lid on the box.

Inside are three biscotti doughnuts—my favourite—and each one has a word iced onto the top.

MARRY. ME. LUCIE?

My breath catches, and tears spring to my eyes as I turn back to Newspaper Guy. Theo is on one knee, a black leather ring box in his hand as he grins up at me, his eyes sparkling. My spare hand shoots up, and I cover my mouth, chewing on my lip as I smile so widely that my face aches. I've never seen anything more beautiful.

"Hi, baby," I mumble through my hand.

"Hey." He chuckles and reaches up, taking the doughnuts from me and setting them on the floor before he pops the lid on the box, exposing a beautiful diamond ring nestled among the cream silk folds.

My heart clenches.

"Six months ago today, I met my best friend and the other half of my soul. Getting stuck in this lift with you is the best thing that's ever happened to me, Lucie. I love you so much. I never imagined I could be this happy or be this in love with someone, but that's because I didn't know what love was until I met you. You're my everything, Luce. Your smile lights my world up. I want to be with you for eternity, plus a day. Because even eternity isn't long enough to spend with you."

Oh my God. A tear slides down my face at his sweet words. My heart is fit to bursting.

"So, what do you say, will you marry me?"

I take a deep breath, allowing his words to sink into my memory before I reply, "Yes, please. And thank you." I nod eagerly, my insides glowing with pleasure.

Theo laughs, his smile widening as he leaps up, wrapping me in his arms and crashing his mouth against mine. The kiss is so passionate and heartfelt that it almost knocks me sideways.

He pulls back slightly, his eyes sparkling with joy as he plucks the ring from the box and looks at me expectantly. A squeal of delight escapes my lips as I hold out my left hand and watch as he slides his promise onto my finger.

"You're mine now," he says, bringing my hand to his lips and softly kissing the ring.

"I was yours six months ago. You had me in this lift when you mentioned day drinking."

We both laugh, and he wraps me in his arms again, pulling me against his body as he kisses me so sensuously that my brain almost malfunctions, trying to process it.

"So, you didn't really go to Cambridge today to help Jared?" I ask as we catch our breaths and he presses his forehead against mine.

"Nope. That was merely a ruse to throw you off the scent."

I grin and tighten my arms around his neck. "I didn't think you knew what today was."

"Course I did. Not likely to forget meeting you, am I? It's imprinted on my brain."

Swoon!

STAND-IN SATURDAY

"And we're not really stuck in this lift again, are we? Because you don't look like you're about to start panicking, like last time."

He laughs and shakes his head. "No. I had to bribe a few people to make this happen." He reaches over and presses the intercom button. "We're all done in here. Thanks."

"Roger that!" comes the security guard's tinny voice through the speaker.

As the lift starts up again, I smile and cling to him as I look down at my hand and marvel over his ring on my finger. I feel complete.

When the lift comes to a stop and the doors slide open in the lobby, cheering and clapping and shouts of, "Congratulations," ring in my ears.

I flinch as party poppers explode, and I gasp when I see everyone from my office along with a lot of the people from the children's imprint is here. Aubrey is at the front, grinning a big, toothy smile as she jumps up and down and waves a homemade *Congratulations, Lucie and Theo* banner.

A rush of love for my best friend hits me full in the face. If I didn't already know I had the best friend in the world, I would know it now.

I pull her into a hug. "You were in on this?"

"Of course!"

It finally sinks in. "This is why you ruined my sandwich!"

She smugly winks at me. "I had to get you in the lift somehow, didn't I? You weren't supposed to say no to lunch. Theo was adamant you'd have already eaten your sandwich before ten a.m., so you'd need to eat again."

"The cheek!" My mouth drops open in mock outrage as I slap Theo's chest with the back of my hand.

He knows me so well. I almost bloody did eat it several times over.

Suddenly, a thought occurs to me. I turn to Theo and grip a fistful of his T-shirt, pressing closer to him as I look up at his handsome, grinning face. "Oh my God, imagine if

I'd said I didn't want to marry you. This crowd jumping out would have been so awkward."

He shakes his head. "I knew you'd say yes. We both know we're endgame, Luce. I wasn't worried."

His confidence in us thrills me.

He continues, "I've actually been ready to ask for a while, but I wanted to wait until your parents came back from Italy, so I could get your dad's permission."

My teeth sink into my bottom lip at his thoughtful gesture. That would have meant a lot to my dad. There wouldn't have been any problems getting his blessing though; my father adores Theo. They even go golfing together whenever my parents do make it back from jet-setting around the world.

"That's so cute," I coo. Another rush of love hits me so hard, I can barely cope with it.

"Here you go, lovebirds."

I break away from Theo's eyes and see that Donna, the receptionist, has wheeled over two small suitcases and set them in front of us.

I frown in confusion. "What are those for?"

Theo's hand traces up my back, pulling me close to him. "For us. We've got a flight to Scotland in a couple of hours, and I rented us a wooden lodge for the week. It's right on the edge of Loch Lomond."

No way! I gasp, delighted, and look from my suitcase to his face, my smile falling when I realise it's not possible. "That sounds incredible, but I can't." The disappointment makes my stomach clench. "Baby, I can't just sack off work. I have meetings all day."

Judy steps forward. She's holding three expended party poppers. "It's a good thing Theo has already cleared it with your manager then, huh?"

My heart melts, and I let out a little whimper as I look up at my fiancé's grinning face. "You did?"

He wraps his arms around me. "I did. I thought it would be nice to go back to the loch, where I first got to know you.

STAND-IN SATURDAY

I figured we could celebrate our engagement in style. You know, wooden lodge, secluded setting with no one to bother us, roaring fires, maybe even a faux bearskin rug." He suggestively raises one eyebrow. "And we're definitely hiring out another boat. It might be a little cold this time of year, but I'm sure I can think of something we could do to keep you warm."

Excitement simmers in my stomach at the mere thought of a romantic getaway with him. I sigh and look at him in awe. "Theo, do I really get to keep you?" My eyes fill with happy tears. *Honestly, how did I get this lucky?*

He nods, brushing his nose up the side of mine. "For eternity, plus a day."

THE END

Not had enough of Theo and Lucie?

Well, good news … the third and final book in the *Love for Days* series is about Aubrey, Lucie's hopelessly romantic best friend. As with the other two books in the series, there will be plenty of hijinks, hilarity, some off-the-charts chemistry, and of course, some Theo and Lucie!

KIRSTY MOSELEY

FANGIRL FRIDAY
BOOK 3 IN THE LOVE FOR DAYS SERIES

HAVE YOU EVER MET THE FUTURE FATHER OF YOUR CHILDREN BUT THEN ACCIDENTALLY FRIEND-ZONED HIM?

As senior editor at Hummingbird Ink, Aubrey Rowe lives and breathes romance. She can tell instantly what will sell, how to make the characters leap off the page and get readers to swoon, and what words to avoid—like *moist*. Ew ... *shudder*. But in real life, Aubrey is a bit of a disaster. It's been so long since she could update a relationship status to It's Complicated that even her vibrator tells her it's got a headache when she reaches for it.

Cue Colton Miller. Musical god with a smile like the devil and a voice like an angel. When Aubrey watches him perform a gig at her local pub one Friday night, she fangirls so hard that she falls at his feet ... literally. The trouble is, she also accidentally friend-zones him. In fact, she pushes him so far into buddy-land that he somehow ends up moving into her spare room and becoming her new flatmate.

Aubrey doesn't mind living with her secret crush. After all, she gets to listen to him sing all night and see him walk around half-naked, like he owns the place. But the longer this goes on, the more desperate she is to let him know that she wants *more*. So, she does the only thing a fangirling, semi-sensible woman on the wrong side of twenty-five can do—she sets up a fake Facebook profile to continue her stalking before finally telling him how she feels.

Her plan is foolproof. Absolutely nothing can go wrong ... right?

STAND-IN SATURDAY

Grab your copy at http://mybook.to/FanGirlFriday.

Stay up to date with all things Kirsty by subscribing to her newsletter. Never miss a sale or new release again. Plus, there's an exclusive giveaway in every one! Subscribe at www.subscribepage.com/sisbackmatter.

OTHER BOOKS BY KIRSTY MOSELEY

SINGLE TITLES

The Boy Who Sneaks in My Bedroom Window
Poles Apart
Reasons Not to Fall in Love (Novella)

BEST FRIEND SERIES

Always You
Free Falling

GUARDED HEARTS SERIES

Guarding the Broken (Nothing Left to Lose, Part 1)
Blurring the Lines (Nothing Left to Lose, Part 2)
Enjoying the Chase
One Wild Night

FIGHTING SERIES

Fighting to Be Free
Worth Fighting For

LOVE FOR DAYS SERIES

Man Crush Monday
Stand-In Saturday
Fangirl Friday

CONNECT WITH KIRSTY MOSELEY

Be notified when Kirsty has a new release:
www.subscribepage.com/newreleasekirstymoseley

Website: www.kirstymoseley.com

Facebook: www.facebook.com/authorkirstymoseley

Twitter: https://twitter.com/KirstyEMoseley

acknowledgements

As always, the first thanks goes to my husband. Lee, thank you for seeing things in me that I don't see and for always being my biggest supporter. You're the best husband and friend in the world.

To my mum for being the kind of strong I wish I were. I love you more than you love pie and mash or jelly tots.

To Kim Sutton, Ann Walker, and Charlotte Coles. Thank you for all your hard work and amazing feedback with this book. Your comments and love for Theo and Lucie made me glow inside. (And sorry, everyone else, but Ann called dibs on Theo, so … *shrugs*)

To Terrie, my PA. Thank you for taking care of everything, so I can just sit back and write. You're my favourite Texan.

To Ker Dukey, my sister from another mister. Shut up. You know I love your face. I don't need to gush about it here …

To Tash at Outlined With Love Designs. You once again nailed the cover! You are fabulously talented, and here's to book three …

STAND-IN SATURDAY

To Jovana at Unforeseen Editing. Thank you so much for helping make this story leap off the page. You are brilliant, and I can't wait to work with you again.

To Gabriella Bortolaso. Thank you so much for helping me with the Italian translations. You're amazing, and also, your accent is the cutest thing I've ever heard!

To Victoria L James. Thank you for pulling me out of the blurb black hole. You rock!

To all the bloggers. I can't thank you enough for all the support you guys always give me. You're incredible, and it really does mean the world.

To my Kirsty's Korner reader group on Facebook. Your enthusiasm and excitement for new books always makes me more excited. I love the group and every one of you. I feel so lucky to have all of your support.

To my dog, Lolly. You never get a mention, but honestly, you deserve one. You've been with me for every word of this book and sat patiently under my desk while I work. World's best dog.

And lastly, to you guys reading this. I have loved every second of writing this book, and I hope you've enjoyed coming along for the ride on the Theo fun bus! This series has been a breath of fresh air for me and has ignited my passion for writing again. Thank you for sticking around and for your support! Hopefully, I'll see you again at the end of book three …

Mwah. X

Printed in Great Britain
by Amazon